THE LAST HOUSEPARTY

THE LAST HOUSEPARTY

PETER DICKINSON

PANTHEON BOOKS
NEW YORK

The Library of Congress Cataloged the First Printing of this Title as Follows:

Dickinson, Peter, 1927–
The last houseparty.
I. Title.

PR6054.I35L3   1982   823'.914   82-47892

ISBN 0-394-51795-4

ISBN 0-394-71601-9 (Pbk.)   AACR2

Manufactured in the United States of America

First American Paperback Edition

About the Author

Peter Dickinson, the son of English parents, was born in Zam-
bia. He returned to England at age seven and attended Eton and
Cambridge. After serving for seventeen years as assistant editor of
Punch, he turned to writing books at age forty. Since that time he
has written eleven detective stories and thirteen children's books.
Several of both kinds have won prestigious prizes, including the
Crime Writers Association Golden Dagger and the Carnegie
Medal for children's books. He currently lives in London and
Hampshire.

1

One cannot say for certain that there was something in the Snailwood genes to cause the men of that family to become partially stuck in their childhoods. In any case the tendency was not strongly marked, and was further obscured by the difficulty of discerning where the games of childhood end and the pursuits of adult life begin among people whose wealth and station have meant that they have never had to do anything serious by way of earning a living, or serving their country in peace or war. Even the practicalities of procreation seem to have presented difficulties, estate and title only once having passed directly from father to son. The estate had been engendered by an almost accidental speculation in the South Sea Bubble, and the title had been bestowed on the first earl because, though without any real interest in politics, he happened to own three or four rotten boroughs necessary to the survival of one of Newcastle's administrations.

On the other hand, frivolities often turn out to have their practical side. The two most obvious examples of this came with the third and fifth earls, the former having built Snailwood Castle in all its romantic extravagance, and the latter having played with trains. The castle in our own time justified its existence to the extent that visitors paid to see it, and the narrow-gauge railway round the park swelled their numbers to the point where, taking in also those who came mainly to look at the gardens, the whole enterprise almost broke even.

The castle was perfectly habitable, indeed many rooms not open to the public were still used, but from the beginning it had somehow possessed the feel of being primarily a toy. This was most marked on first sight, as it was meant to be. The third earl had employed a family of boatmen to bring all his important visitors up the Thames from Marlow, and despite the exorbitant charge for the launch trip this is still much the best way to begin.

At any season and in any weather the first sight of those crenellated turrets rising irregularly above the beeches and chestnuts of the parkland sward and the more varied specimen trees of the gardens proper produces in almost any visitor the genuine romantic thrill the third earl had demanded – and this though most visitors are instantly aware that they are seeing not "the true rust of the Barons' Wars", in Horace Walpole's phrase, but a fake specifically built to evoke that thrill. They are quite conscious of being got at, but the trick is so effectively performed that it would be over-fastidious, even mean-minded, to object. Still, a house designed with that as its primary purpose – rather than keeping the rain out – is definitely a toy.

The guide taking the first party of visitors round on a Wednesday afternoon in April 1980, made the point rather less directly. She gathered her group beneath the portrait of the third earl and told them that he had inherited the title at the age of eleven, his uncle the second earl having been killed by a bullet while watching a duel in the Bois de Boulogne during the brief lull that followed the Peace of Amiens. She did not draw any moral from this incident, though it could well be thought to exemplify another Snailwood tendency: to stand (though not to do much else) in what will turn out to have been in the eyes of history the wrong place. Instead she told them how a few years later the young earl had been trying to duplicate some of Sir Humphry Davy's experiments with flammable gases and had burnt the previous house to the ground. Forced by his own folly into positive action he had determined to build something that would do honour to his hero, Lord Byron – not, of course, the rounded, sardonic, mature and genuinely heroic Byron of *Don Juan* and the Greek liberation, but the young, glum, intense *poseur* presented in *Childe Harold*.

The party of visitors stirred, not impolitely restless – it was too early in the visit for that, and the guide, though she kept her tone on the dry side, spoke with clarity and knowledge – but because this era of the Snailwood story was not to them its main interest. Also that lift of the heart which visitors experience on seeing the towers of Snailwood, and which they retain and probably enhance on a tour of its marvellous gardens, tends to lose its power the moment they step into the deliberate gloom of the vaulted entrance hall. Most still gazed at the portrait of the third earl – school of Thomas Lawrence but with more than a dash of Haydon – wearing the black dressing gown he had ordered on hearing the news from Missolonghi. The dressing gown itself hung in a glass case to the left of the portrait, strangely more imbued with personality than either its painted representation or that of its wearer. The guide pointed to the book the earl was holding and recited the lines displayed:

> *The castled crag of Drachenfels*
> *Frowns o'er the wide and winding Rhine*
> *Whose breast of waters broadly swells*
> *Between the banks which bear the vine . . .*

and so on. The artist had done his damndest to endow with a craggy look the steep but rounded slope of hill on which Snail-wood Castle frowned in the background. The guide explained that for a while the earl had actually insisted on the castle being called Drachenfels, though no one knew whether this was because the coincidence of names had originally persuaded him to build in this style, or whether he had chanced on it after making his grand decision. At any rate he had been unable to impose his will on the customs and insularity of his neighbours, and long before his death in 1868 he had accepted that he was George Daniel Pollixer Digges Hillaby Snailwood, Lord Snailwood, of Snailwood in the County of Buckingham. Even the word "castle" became less and less frequently used.

By the time the guide had moved on to the portraits of his great-nephew the fourth earl, and of *his* second cousin once removed, the fifth earl – the one who had installed the railway line – though she gave only brief accounts of them the attention of the party had dissolved still further. Three children were fingering the joints of an unlikely-looking suit of armour, while a young couple in matching anoraks and T-shirts were peering inquisitively into a mahogany and glass booth which jutted from between fluted pilasters on the wall opposite the portraits. Suddenly these two found themselves in the front row of the audience as the guide switched attention to the booth, explaining that yes, indeed, it was

7

a coin-operated phone-box, installed in the early nineteen-thirties by the sixth earl as a defence against the extravagant use of his telephone by the innumerable guests of his second wife, the Countess Zena.

Magically at the name of Zena the mild ennui of the party lifted. This was what they had come for. Perhaps the guide had actually spoken of the telephone booth in order to produce this effect before leading them into the Great Hall, which she now did, and there Zena was.

A few years before, guides on leading one into the Great Hall would often begin with the story of the third earl in old age endlessly pacing its length each evening, as if to prove to himself that he still had what he had asked his architect for, the largest private room in Buckinghamshire, and muttering as he did so, "I was a fool when I built this." But even in so apparently static a subject as the history of a so-called "Stately Home" tastes change, and Snailwood had at last been fortunate in this respect. Because of the fire in 1820 it had never possessed any crowd-compelling ancient treasures, so since it had been opened in the mid fifties it had really been the gardens most visitors had come to see, with a tour of the house something to take in if the afternoon turned nasty. Now, though the gardens remained the chief attraction, the revival of interest in the thirties meant that it had been worth re-furnishing the Great Hall as far as possible exactly as it had been when Zena had plummeted into these near-stagnant waters with such a notorious splash, and had for a start insisted on making this monstrous room – through which the family had previously tended to scurry, even in summer-time when its Boreal draughts were lulled, in search of smaller and cosier quarters – the place where the life of Snailwood was chiefly lived, the hearth round which she gathered for her week-ends that amalgam of guests whose nucleus came to be known as the Snailwood Gang, but whose occasional members included names as disparate as Frank Buchman and Noël Coward, Dennis Wheatley and Herr Ribbentrop, Herbert Morrison and Constant Lambert. It was still apparent to these latter-day sight-seers that all Zena's drive and confidence had been unable to convert the Great Hall into a comfortable living-room.

"You'd hardly know they were the same woman," said somebody.

"No," said the guide, still gently shepherding the hinder end of the group towards the two portraits to the left of the fireplace. "But as a matter of fact they're both very good likenesses. She should have been an actress, really. She was very changeable."

"You knew her?" said a voice with mixed surprise and doubt, as if speaking to a stranger who claimed to have encountered a hippogriff.

"Oh yes," said the guide. "I lived here. I was only a child, of course."

They gazed at her as if she too had now become an exhibit – a square, confident, shortish woman with a smooth, pale face which looked a little too young for her tidily permed white hair. There was nothing in her appearance to tell them what her position in Countess Zena's household might have been – relative, dependant, child of servants – and her voice gave no clue either, educated and brisk, but lacking any residual arrogance of status. She did not seem to object to being looked at in this manner, but perhaps she would have given a similar impression in almost any circumstances, being one of those people who without obtrusively radiating self-confidence still seem to be so at one with themselves that one feels the outer world cannot ever really jar their inward balance. As soon as her party had gathered beneath the portraits she started her formal talk, beginning with the room itself and the rich armorial stained glass which filled the top half of the six high lancet windows and gave the Great Hall its peculiar atmosphere of dark rich shadows above and plain daylight below. She compressed the first century of its existence into a couple of minutes in order to tell in closer detail of the notorious nineteen-thirties, to reel off a score of famous names who had sat on these chairs and sofas, and to end with an unassailably non-committal account of the accusations, made both before and after the war, that certain members of the Snailwood Gang had been more than mere sympathisers with the ideals of Nazi Germany. This particular group of tourists contained no hotheads, still anxious to argue and accuse. They were more interested in gossip, and the Countess Zena.

9

"She looks a lot younger than the earl, doesn't she?" said a woman, almost as soon as the guide had finished.

"She was his second wife, of course," explained the guide. "In fact the difference was a few more years than you can see because the earl was painted by Birley before he had met her. She wanted a pair for the Birley, but she insisted on it being done by John, because she said that Birley was an embalmer, not a painter – that's a typically Zena remark, by the way. She was pleased with the John, but then she wanted something to show that that image wasn't the only one, so she commissioned the Rex Whistler. I don't imagine she told him to make it different – she wouldn't have to. She'd just see to it that the difference was there for him to paint."

She moved a little away, leaving them to look at the three portraits, while she herself unobtrusively studied their reactions, perhaps attempting to gauge some first faint gust of change in public taste which might soon need to be catered for. It is curious in any case how such things go, how what had originally been the most obviously effective of the portraits was now well on the way to becoming the least successful, while the less pretentious wore rather better. The Birley on the far side of the fireplace had never made much claim to being a masterwork. It was a craftsman's piece – the earl at his front door, wearing gaiters and with a gun over his arm, nearer sixty than fifty, his narrow but florid countenance not exactly vacuous, but at the same time not one on which the eye would rest for long out of interest in the character there expressed. The weapon and the background architecture gave a strong impression of the Englishman whose home was his castle. The portrait – as seems often to have happened with pictures of our aristocracy during periods when it was the normal thing to have oneself painted and as one knew nothing about art one went to the fellow who'd made quite a decent stab at old Jouncer – was now in the process of becoming quaint, and attractive at least for that.

If the Birley was coming up in the market, the John was definitely slipping, despite its announcement, the moment one set eyes on it, that here was a great artist re-creating for posterity the transient beauty of a famous woman. Though indoors, Zena had her arms full of roses and was wearing one of her huge hats. The effect was far from calm. She was striding. The gauzes of her dress swirled with her speed. John, as if determined to show that he was not taken in by the sentimentality of the subject – a pretty woman on her way to arrange flowers – had modelled the face and the bare arms with streaks of a pale but chemical green and denoted the shadows in the carroty hair with a darker green. The brim of the hat, worn almost vertical on the side of the head, was a mauve halo round the beaky profile. This was Zena as hawk-goddess, the roses seeming to struggle helplessly in her grip, her captive prey. The effect was still theatrical, but the mode of theatre had changed. Tosca had become the witch in Disney's *Snow White*.

Time had done less to one's appreciation of the Rex Whistler, which remained what it had always been, a very decorative little piece, its charm enhanced by the slight chill the artist's favourite palette gave to all his work. Zena, in pale blue slacks and a yellow Aertex shirt, sat bareheaded on the stone lion at the eastern end of the Snailwood terraces, very much to one side of the picture so that her body became part of a frame for the fanciful traffic on the Thames below. She was looking over her shoulder at the viewer, as though startled by his sudden appearance in the solitariness she had been sharing with her stone protector. Her dark eyes were misty, the predatory profile of the John turned to show a classic oval. You would not, as the visitor had said, have known it was the same woman.

"There's no earls any longer?" asked a young man who had been peering at Birley's brushwork on the gleaming leather gaiters.

"The sixth earl was the last of the line," said the guide.

"I thought the last two were killed in the war," said another man, in a tone pitched to demonstrate that he too knew a little history.

"That's right," said the woman who was with him. "Don't you remember reading me about one of them getting in trouble with . . ."

She stopped as the man shook his head in warning. A remarkable blush suffused her face. Perhaps to cover the woman's confusion the guide moved briskly to the piano and touched a silver-framed photograph.

"The Earl's two sisters each had a son," she said. "One of them would have inherited the estate, but not the title."

The photograph was of two young men – or boys, only it was so hard to tell with the Snailwoods. One was wearing a cricket cap and blazer, the other a top hat and frock coat with butterfly collar and white bow tie. They were, in the phrase characteristic of captions to photographs in the society magazines of the period, sharing a joke.

"Now," said the guide, "if you'd care to look around for a few minutes, I'll be happy to answer any questions you may have."

The group fragmented, some continuing to study the portraits of Zena, a wife squeaking to a husband to come and look at the wireless, just like Aunt Moo used to have, the three children settling rather noisily to count the scarlet tulips in the enormous bronze urn beneath the gallery, and a few serious thirties *aficionados* moving over to study the line of framed photographs of guests, assembled in the courtyard to have their picture taken as an essential element in the ritual of a Zena "do", or week-end party. The guide moved to a window and studied the sky. One problem of providing guided tours to a house whose main attraction is its garden is that in certain weathers your visitors are likely to flock indoors for a spell, all at the same time. This was just such a day, warm and soft when the sun was out, but with the wind carrying from the west a series of isolated hummocky clouds, hard-edged and silver above but almost purple where they dragged their trains of rain along the valley.

A visitor came and stood beside the guide and she turned as if expecting a question, probably the quite frequent one of why the final photograph in the line showed one of the sitters in Arab fancy dress. But in fact the man – elderly, slow-moving, heavy without particular fatness, merely looked out at the view. There were five other windows he could have chosen for the purpose.

"Changeable," he remarked.

"What?" she said. "Oh, yes. Very."

*   *   *

He did not speak to her again until the tour was effectively over. The next fierce shower had come so the party had stayed in the shelter of the cloisters to gaze between fretted arches across a wide rectangle now pelted with hailstones at the remarkable north face of the courtyard. It was as though the architect had used this range to fit in all the elements of Germanic mediaevalism for which he had been unable to find a niche elsewhere – to the left the buttresses and lancet windows of what seemed to be a section of cathedral, though the guide explained the building merely housed the old coach houses and stables, entered from outside; to the right (and really very successfully) the packed, tumbled, haphazard frontage of a street in some old university town, crammed into this great keep for safety; and at the centre the clock tower. The guide recounted the intricate movements of the painted figures who had appeared each time the clock struck, at the quarters a personification of one of the seasons dancing with her attendant figures until Father Time emerged to scythe them down, and at noon, at a higher level, a crusader and a Saracen fighting blow for blow until on the last stroke the Saracen's head flew from his shoulders.

"Did it really come right off?" asked one of the children.

"It came right off and hung there," said the guide. "It was on a spring, but you couldn't see that from down here. It was like a conjuring trick."

A flush of enthusiasm tinged her voice. It was obvious that as well as having seen the Countess Zena in the flesh, she had watched the clock strike noon.

"Pity they can't get it going again," said the children's mother.

"I'm afraid it would cost the earth," said the guide. "Well, that's the end of the tour. If you go this way round the cloisters you'll find the souvenir shop on the right of the gateway. If you want to buy plants, turn left outside the gateway, go past the garages and follow the signs to the Nursery. I think it will stop raining in a minute. Don't miss the gardens – they're really the best part. And thank you all very much for listening."

Without apparent rudeness she managed to move rapidly out of reach of further questions, and was almost at the corner of the cloisters when a voice behind her called. "Excuse me, madam. One moment."

She turned, stiff, polite rejection ready on her lips. It was the man who had spoken to her about the weather, trotting purposefully forward and feeling in his waistcoat pocket as he came.

"I don't want to be a nuisance," he said. "I could write, but . . ."

Reaching her he held out a card. She took it a little unwillingly and kept it at arm's length to read, "Lauterpracht and Mason. Clock Specialists."

"Is there a chance of me looking over the clock some time?" asked the man. "Internally, I mean to say?"

She handed the card back.

"If you're saying you want to repair it," she said, "I'm afraid it's no go. We've had estimates and they're absolutely prohibitive."

"I know that," he said. "You had one from my partner, Sid Lauterpracht, years back."

"Ah yes, I remember the name. So you'll understand, Mr . . . you're Mr Mason, I take it . . ."

"Right. Sid died in 'fifty-nine, and I took over, but now I've retired. Come to live in Marlow. But, you follow, I still love clocks, and I need something to get my teeth into. I've looked out Sid's report on your clock, and he considered it could be done. The cost was in the time, you see, and now I've got plenty of that. I wouldn't expect to be paid. There'd be something for materials, but I've kept a lot of my tools, so I can cut the wheels and such . . . They're really very simple, clocks."

"This one is supposed to be the most complex piece of clock-work outside Germany."

Mr Mason's face, heavy, square and earnest, was not made for smiling.

"Oh no," he said gently. "As turret clocks go, I'll give you, but even an ordinary marine chronometer . . . and those are simple, really. Very simple pieces."

From somewhere a noise like a fire-alarm jangled briefly.

"I've got to go," said the guide. "That's the rota bell – it means there's another party ready to go round. But if you really think . . ."

"Shall I write to someone?"

14

"Yes. Me. Sarah Quintain. Q-U-I-N-T-A-I-N. Miss."

With the stolid confidence of an old craftsman Mr Mason took a silver propelling pencil from his waistcoat pocket and wrote on the back of his card. Miss Quintain was already at the door in the corner of the cloisters when she turned and said, "We'll need references, of course. But do write. I'd love to try and get it going after all these years."

Mr Mason merely nodded. Carefully he tucked pencil and card away in their correct pockets before moving to the edge of the arcading to gaze up through the last spatterings of the storm at the clock tower. It was a grimmer structure than either of its wings, no less fanciful but more in keeping with Byron's notion of "chiefless castles breathing stern farewells". Its archway could easily have housed a portcullis and its corner turrets were pierced with arrow-slits. The face of the tower was recessed several feet back between these turrets, not merely for aesthetic reasons, but so that the figures who danced or fought as the bells chimed could emerge from doors set at right angles to the clock face. There was one plain gothic window above the archway; above that a strange, foreshortened arch, a stone mouth, cut the whole tower from side to side, to allow the carousel that bore the dancing figures to rotate; above that came the clock face, and above that again a miniature line of battlements which screened the track along which crusader and Saracen came out to do battle; then eight feet of vertical masonry and the battlements proper. Along suitable ledges pigeons huddled from the shower, two or three of them almost wholly white, others piebald, but mainly native grey, whose genes over the years had gradually dominated the strain of the snowy tumblers that once had graced the courtyard.

The clock had stopped at two minutes past twelve, but the carousel was out of phase, with the figures to accompany the first quarter showing. Perhaps somebody had disconnected the whole striking train and let the timepiece work out its last years without its allegories. Or else, to have something worth showing the visitors, they had cranked the carousel on to this point, with the lissom figure of Spring about to vanish into the right-hand turret and the scythe of pursuing Time swung back to sever the ankles of the last lamb who danced behind her.

2

I

On a Friday afternoon in June 1937 a woman stood in the courtyard at Snailwood and gazed at the clock tower. The masonry shimmered slightly with the first true heat of summer, and the world was still enough for one to be able to imagine one could actually hear the steady tock of the pendulum, until the silence was broken by the burr and snap of a car being driven briskly down the steep bends of the drive. Thirty seconds later an open car, a dark green AC Ace, whipped into the courtyard and parked, deliberately choosing, it seemed, in all that emptiness the one spot that would unsettle the small flock of white pigeons that had gathered there to peck among the cobbles. The birds wheeled away in a dazzle of wings. The driver, a fair-haired young man, appeared to notice the woman as he climbed out, but then turned and rather deliberately lifted from the back seat a suitcase, two tennis rackets and a golf bag. The woman walked towards him, reaching him while he was still apparently concerned to place his kit in the precise position he wanted on the gravel. She held out her hand.

"Hello," she said. "You must be Harry, or Vincent."

He took her hand. Her arm was pale as ivory and bare to the shoulder.

"Ver . . . Ver . . . Ver . . ." he began.

She neither prompted him nor waited for him to complete the agony, but took the name as spoken.

"I'm Joan Dubigny," she said. "I was waiting to see the clock strike. I don't think I'll ever get tired of it."

Vincent glanced up at the tower. The hands stood at eleven minutes past three. When he turned back to Mrs Dubigny it was as though the clock had performed some kind of introduction between them, putting them now on a footing that enabled him almost to master his first appalling stammer.

"Zena's new k-keeper?" he said, meeting her glance. Her eyes beneath the plucked eyebrows were dark blue, her skin despite the heavy make-up apparently as pallid as her arms but without any suggestion of fever or debility. Her red lips smiled at him, inviting him to like what he saw, though she must have been several years older than he was, perhaps almost thirty. She in her turn looked at an ordinary young man, large-framed but carrying himself lightly, face ruddy, hair and small moustache only a little darker than straw, and with no more than a faint hint of puzzlement about his countenance to prepare a stranger for the stammer. It would not have needed the straightness of his posture or the cut of the moustache to tell one that he was almost certainly a soldier. He was in fact a lieutenant in the Royal Berkshire Regiment.

"We expected Harry to get here first," she said.

"I passed him in the town. My bus is faster up the hill."

"But your colonel must have let you off early after all?"

"My adjutant, actually. Not at all pleased about it. I g-gather Zena had wangled it with someone in the War House."

"That was me. I happen to know a rather sweet little general. Ought we to send your adjutant a box of cigars?"

"Doesn't smoke. Sweet tooth, though."

"Liqueur chocs? From Fortnums?"

"Spot on. You seem to have c-cottoned to Zena's style pretty fast."

"I love it," she said, smiling in a very different manner than before, this time widening rather than narrowing the apparent age gap between them, as if looking down on him for a whole flight up the stairway of experience.

"Here's Harry," he said.

A fawn Jowett, also open but much more gently driven, slid in under the archway, bringing with it a sudden sharp odour of unclean exhaust. The driver parked on the far side of the AC, climbed out and came round to shake hands. A family likeness could be seen if looked for, though Harry was lighter of frame and feature than his cousin, clean shaven, and with brownish hair that struggled to curl against its restraining hair oil. He moved, too, at a most unmilitary pace and looked as though he had never puzzled about anything all his days. As Vincent introduced him to Mrs

17

Dubigny the clock tower emitted a slow and painful groan.

"Hush," she said. "It's starting."

She moved towards the centre of the courtyard. The young men followed her.

"That's only the door opening," said Harry.

"Forty seconds to g-go," said Vincent. "I say, old man, I'd better have a squint at your c-carburettor. I'm surprised you made it up the hill."

"Bit of a pull," said Harry.

"Do hush," said Mrs Dubigny. "This is my first chance all day – I've been so busy with everybody coming."

"Who's everybody?" said Harry, but she held up a hand as a new groaning began, staring at the clock.

The clock face was splendid enough in itself, despite the peeling gilt on its openwork hands and on the gilt angels in its four corners who now stiffly raised trumpets to their lips and blew an imaginary fanfare. The train of Spring emerged from the door that had opened in the side of the left-hand turret. A lamb came gliding out, poised on one hind hoof, then a shepherd and another lamb. Next came Spring herself, taller than the shepherd and wearing a long dress of faded blue. A symmetrical group of shepherd and lambs slid out behind her. When Spring was at the centre of the tower the procession stopped and all seven began their dance, lambs and shepherds merely rotating but the goddess, moved by much more complex gearing, seeming to retreat and advance as she turned while the arm that held her circlet of flowers rose and fell in a gawky gesture. The last workman to retouch her paint (shortly after the war, by the look of it) had given her a pleasingly puzzled and defenceless air. A carillon of bells, preliminary to the quarters, tinkled while the figures gyrated. Then, as the quarters themselves began to clank, the dance abruptly ended. The figures slid towards the right-hand turret just as Time emerged from the door behind them, no friendly old gaffer with a scythe, but close kin to the skeleton reaper of the *Totentanz*. He moved at the same speed as they did, so that it did not look as if he could catch them, but the clockwork's choreographer had designed one last surprise. The scythe had seemed fixed to Time's torso as he emerged, but when he reached the place where the dancers had performed it swung out and forward, lunging at the disappearing lambs. The effect was to make it seem as he went through the door that he was already gaining on the dancers and would mow them down in darkness.

Mrs Dubigny clapped her hands.

"Nice to see it going again," said Harry. "It wasn't last time I came."

"It must be terrible when it goes wrong," she said.

"Nobody knows. Vincent is always trying to get a look at it but McGrigor won't let anyone into the tower. It stops. Uncle Snailwood sends for McGrigor. He says it can't be mended. Uncle Snailwood says he'll write to the clock specialists. McGrigor says 'Wait' – he'll see what he can do. Next day it's going again."

"He just hangs another half hundredweight of scrap iron on the weights," said Vincent. "You can hear – it oughtn't to groan like that. He must be making merry hay with the rods and bearings – some day soon it'll pack in c-completely."

"Oh, I remember," said Mrs Dubigny. "Vincent's the mechanical one."

"That's right. And I'm the human one," said Harry.

"I didn't mean that!"

"It's true – you've only got to see him playing a ball game – he's so damn accurate he has to be a robot. Flesh and blood hasn't a chance."

"Harry guh . . . guh . . . guh . . ." began Vincent.

"Who is everybody, Mrs Dubigny?" said Harry firmly.

"Who? Oh, you mean the everybody who's coming. All sorts. This is my first real Zena do, you know. The main thing is she's going to settle the Palestine question."

"Oh lor!" said Vincent.

"That should be interesting," said Harry. "Who's she got for that?"

"The list's in my office."

"Same as Nan used to have?"

"I believe so."

"Right. Soon as I've unpacked. Want me to sketch it out for you, Vince? You'll be expected to come up with the army line, no doubt."

"There's a Brigadier Trotman coming," said Mrs Dubigny. "He's just back."

"Oho! Quite a big fish," said Harry. "Who's she got batting for the Yids?"

"Somebody called Professor Blech."

"Has she now?"

Harry had begun to smile with eagerness, like a child who has prepared a practical joke and is waiting to see his victim spring the trap. He made a move to fetch his cases.

"And then there's an Arab prince," said Mrs Dubigny. "Yasif ibn Sorah – I hope I've pronounced it right."

"Oh, I know him," said Vincent, clearly astonished. "If it's the same fellow – I played against him in the Harrow Match."

"Probably his father," said Harry. "They all have the same name."

"No, it's the son," said Mrs Dubigny. "In fact Zena invited him in Vincent's name – that was why it was so important to have Vincent staying. My general grasped the point at once."

Vincent went red, but when Harry began a raucous and explosive laugh he joined in as if from habit.

"Come on," said Harry. "Or we'll have to stay and let Mrs Dubigny see the half-hour strike."

"I like Summer best of all," said Mrs Dubigny.

By the time Vincent had loaded himself with his case and all his sports gear the other two had started towards the house and he needed to lope to catch them up.

". . . school clock," Harry was saying. "Sometimes it used to go bonkers. According to my mother there was an episode in my dad's day when a visiting preacher insisted on working it into his sermon – you know, the usual sort of thing, we'd get 'em at least once a half, old buffers absolutely besotted about Eton, pretty embarrassing sometimes. Anyway there was everyone sitting in College Chapel while the chap orated on . . ."

He deepened his voice and infused it with breathy pomp. The cloister arches, under which they were now moving, returned ecclesiastical echoes.

". . . and we know that this great institution will continue to do its work and send out the leaders of the world as surely as we

20

know that the clock outside in Lupton's Tower will now strike twelve. We will wait and hear it."

Harry paused.

"He'd timed it perfectly," he said in his own voice. "The trouble was the clock struck a hundred and twenty-eight."

2

"It's bloody cheek," said Vincent, speaking extra stiffly because he was gripping the turn-ups of his white flannels under his chin as he worked the coat hanger up them before putting them in the wardrobe.

"Can't expect anything else from Zena," said Harry, tossing socks into a drawer. "She's like that."

They were in a bleakish room on the floor below the servants' attics. The bed frames were iron, ornamented with brass bobbles. There was one washstand, its crockery bearing the Snailwood crest but mostly chipped. This and the wardrobe and the two chests of drawers and the two wooden chairs were painted white. The only element that suggested comfort was the horsehair cushions on the seats in the window niches, and even those seemed more designed for a boy to stretch out on and read a book with his fingers stuffed in his ears all Sunday afternoon, than for an adult to sit on and feel easy. Vincent and Harry went through the process of unpacking half automatically, knowing where it was natural to put their clothes and which drawers needed a jerk to unstick them.

"She's thoroughly mucked me up with my adjutant," said Vincent. "We do most of our training at week-ends in the TA, and I've begged off a couple of Saturdays for cricket matches already. I'd sworn I wouldn't this time."

"But the order came from on high."

"Makes it worse. He can't abide political soldiers."

"Never mind. No doubt Zena will have arranged for compensation in the shape of glamour girls."

"To help solve the Palestine question?"

"Oh, I don't know. Some of these old chaps have quite boyish tastes, no matter how grey their eminences. I thought Mrs Dubigny herself wasn't half bad, for a start."

"Yes."

"Think it's any part of her duties to sleep with Uncle Snaily?"

"You've been publishing too many cheap novels."

"I hear that's why Nan left. Zena decided that she had performed that function as long as duty demanded and tried to get Nan to take over. Nan jibbed."

"Who told you all this?"

"Nobody told me all of it. Purser was full of sly hints last time I came. Nan left without another job to go to, so I heard, and she hasn't a bean of her own. Mrs Dubigny I am told is divorced. She is distinctly easy on the eye, and she doesn't look as though she'd mind."

"You can't trust Purser when it comes to Zena."

"I'm making allowances for that. Finished?"

"Don't wait for me. You want to look at that list."

"It's going to be a very interesting week-end, Vince. I'll give you a rapid crib, so you can make the correct noises while all the old buffers are woffling on."

"I'll stick to the army line, thanks. Provided the politicians will let us get on with it we can stamp on this revolt, pacify the Arabs and carry on from there."

"They aren't half making a soldier of you. Presumably that will be the Brigadier's line. I don't know much about him."

"Rifleman. Said to be a sound chap, though. Bit of an expert on camel patrols or something like that."

"Tremendously useful for settling a religious war. The point is, Vince, that this lot of politicians we've got now haven't the slightest intention of letting the army loose to pacify the Palestinian Arabs. It doesn't matter a hoot what anyone's promised the Jews in the past, they can see that if we stick to our word we're going to lose every Arab friend we've got between Persia and Gib. Lose them, lose our oil supplies, lose the supply line to India – how do you think we're going to fight a war with Germany on that basis? I'll lay you five to one in fivers that we let the Grand Mufti back into Jerusalem by this time next year. Now, a young officer who showed himself, however unwillingly, aware that this is the true situation might do himself a power of good in certain quarters."

"And a power of harm in others."

"A young officer who already has an entry into the councils of the ruling family of Sorah. The Emir . . ."

"Look, I hardly know the blighter. I hardly even played cricket with him because he wasn't at the wicket for more than five minutes. I got him l.b.w. almost at once in both innings."

"All the better. He'll be eager . . ."

"Lay off, Hal. I don't want to get involved in the politics of it. I'm a soldier, pure and simple. My job is to do what I'm told by the politicians. Matter of fact, our second battalion was in Palestine till 'thirty-five, so I could keep my end up if I had to, but this week-end I don't propose to make any noises, right or wrong, while the statesmen are holding forth."

"Okey-doke. I'll tell you my own views some time. I'm really looking forward to meeting Blech. We might get a book out of him – provided, that is, I can persuade bloody old Throck it's his own idea and not mine. I wonder who else she's roped in."

"Push off and look at Mrs Dubigny's list. I'm going to hang around here, I think. I don't feel like facing Zena till I've cooled off."

"See you at tea, then. Don't let her get your goat, Vince – she's sure to give it a go."

"I can cope."

"Good man."

When Harry had left Vincent finished putting his clothes away, re-folding every article, even those which would not spoil by creasing, and then placing it with great exactitude in the drawer. When he had finished he slid his case under his bed and did the same for the one Harry had left lying open on the floor. He went to the window and glanced out as if to check that the garden was also in its proper location, the series of long narrow terraces descending in steps westward along the slant of the hill, all planted out with hybrid tea roses in a series of geometric beds, making a strong but at the same time strangely dead effect with their rather meaty shades – meaty at least when seen from above, *en masse*, however individually perfect and subtle each single bloom might have proved on closer inspection. Lord Snailwood was visible on the second terrace, personally selecting and cutting the flowers that would greet his week-end visitors in stunning masses all around the house. Thring, the rose gardener, was with him, but only to pull the peculiar trolley built by McGrigor for the special purpose of cradling the cut flowers unblemished. Vincent watched for a couple of minutes, seeming to relax slightly from the stance of soldier pure and simple, as though the sight of his uncle engaged in this familiar ritual allowed him to make contact with the period of his life before his military training had begun. Then he turned, looked round the room, grunted approvingly and went out.

The upper floors of Snailwood – that is those above the levels complicated by the need to accommodate the Great Hall and other high, romantic vaults – were very simple in lay-out. A corridor ran the whole way round, its windows looking out over the cloister roof and the courtyard. Doors in the opposite wall led into the various bedrooms. At each corner where the east and west wings met the south front another passage, dark and windowless, slanted off to serve the room that filled that level of one of the two massive corner towers. What had been known for the last twenty years as "The Boys' Room" lay three doors down the western wing, so on coming out of it Vincent turned right. But when he reached the corner, instead of going on to the main stair or taking the circular staircase down the inner corner turret, he turned up the spur that led to the tower room. Half-way along it he paused and looked at the sepia engraving of Snailwood as it had been before the fire, its details almost invisible in the dimness, but showing when brought into the light a plain brick box of a house, a sailing barge on the Thames below, haymakers in the meadow pasture, and ladies and gentlemen, ludicrously out of scale, walking among the scarce-grown topiary of the terraces.

Without knocking Vincent opened the door at the end of the passage.

"Oh, I'm f-frightfully sorry," he said.

The tower rooms were kite-shaped, circular on the outside but square on the inner two walls. Though the space was not specially large, the thickness of the outer masonry, manifest in the deep window recesses, gave an impression of ponderous scale. It may have been this that made the child seem so small and vulnerable.

She had looked up at the movement of the door, but her face had fallen on seeing a stranger. She was about seven, primly dressed in a blue pleated skirt and a white blouse. Her dark hair curled around a pallid, mildly sulky face. She had been dressing or undressing a large rag doll.

"I just wanted a qu-quick look," said Vincent. "I used to use this room rather a lot."

"Was it your nursery?" said the child.

"Sort of. This isn't really my home, but Harry and I spent most of our school holidays here. Have you got everything you want?"

"No. It's all boys' things."

"'Fraid so."

"There isn't anywhere for Mary to sleep."

Vincent glanced at the bed – nearly full-size but still cot-like with its beechwood rail all round – that jutted from the wall on his right.

"Oh, I see, Mary's your doll," he said.

"Course she is. It's time for her rest and there isn't anywhere for her to sleep."

"I could make her a c-cradle, if you like, supposing my Meccano's still there."

"Yes, it is."

"Well?"

"What?"

"Would you like me to make Mary a cradle?"

"If you want to," said the child, not yielding anything.

Vincent closed the door and crossed to the central window, where he lifted the cushioned lid of the windowseat and took out from the space below a round-topped wooden chest, painted with skull and cross-bones. This he placed in the centre of the room, then sat on the floor beside it a few feet from the girl. When he opened the lid she did not even glance to see what was in the chest. Whoever had last been playing with the set – or sets, for there was evidently more Meccano than in the largest box sold in shops – had put everything away with extreme neatness. Though well used, so that round many of the holes the gold or red paint was worn through, all the strips and girders had been graded to size and fastened with elastic bands, the wheels matched and packed on to axles, bolts and clips sorted into match-boxes, the clock-work motors wrapped in grease-proof paper.

"I've never built a cradle before," said Vincent. "I shall have to think it out. Do you want one that rocks?"

"If you like."

"I suppose I could make it so that it rocks itself when you start the motor."

"Yes, please."

"Lend me Mary a mo to measure for size. Thanks . . . Not bad, but it's going to be a bit knobbly for her unless you can find something to make a mattress."

The child did not react or move. For a while Vincent did nothing either, apart from staring into the box while his fingers teased unthinkingly at his moustache, but there was a sense of dormant energies coming to life and focusing to a sharp-seen point. Then he took a bundle of short girders out, opened a couple of match-boxes and began to assemble an end-frame, his large fingers handling the miniature nuts and screws without fumbling, every movement looking in fact as though he had been fibbing about not having done this before, and had really been practising regularly for this moment.

"When's Mummy coming?" said the child suddenly.

"I'm afraid I don't know. Is your mother staying here?"

"We live here now. Mummy works for the Countess."

"Oh . . . Mrs Dubigny?"

"Yes."

"What's your name?"

"Sally."

"I'm Vincent. Vincent Masham. My friends call me Vince."

"She said she wouldn't be very long."

"I met her in the courtyard about half an hour ago. She was going to show my cousin something. I expect she'll come after that."

"She usually forgets."

"If I see her I'll remind her."

"I'm not allowed downstairs alone. The Countess says I might knock things over."

"I'm sure you wouldn't."

"I'm not allowed in the garden alone. The Countess says I might walk on the flowerbeds."

"That's too bad. The garden's the best thing about Snailwood. I expect she'll change her mind when she's used to you. There haven't been children here for ages. We used to run all over the garden. There are some corking trees to climb in."

"That's a boys' thing."

"I suppose so. Lend me Mary again, for a try. She *is* going to need some kind of mattress, you know."

"She's only a doll. She can't feel anything."

"If you say so."

A few minutes later, when the two end-frames had been joined by longer strips and girders to make a shape like a truncated canoe, Sally rose, went to the child-size chest of drawers beyond the bed, tugged open the top drawer and came back with a yellowish Chilprufe vest which she folded slowly, trying several methods, until she had a shape which fitted the bottom of the cradle. Settling the doll into place she sat down again, now leaning against Vincent's arm and watching while he worked at the first support.

"We'll need another of these," he said. "Would you like to find the pieces for it – just the same as I've got here?"

"No, thank you."

Neither of them spoke until Vincent had finished the second support and attached it and a motor to the base-plates.

"Now comes the tricky part," he said. "You see, this wheel's going to go round and round and push this crank and I've got to join the other end to this wheel so that it goes round for a bit and then goes back. To make the cradle rock to and fro, you see. If I'm not careful we'll have Mary whirling round and round as if she was on the wheel at a fairground – except the motor isn't strong enough for that, probably."

"Mummy's not used to having me," said Sally. "That's why she forgets. I lived with Auntie May, but then the judge said I must come and live with Mummy."

"Oh, I see. Do you like it at Snailwood?"

"If only I could go in the garden when I wanted."

"Look, just let me finish this – it won't take five minutes – and then we'll go and look for your mother and ask if I can take you out till tea. O.K.?"

"If you want to," she said, apparently as dismissive as ever. She contrived to appear as though she was watching Vincent assemble the cradle because there was nothing more interesting to do, but in another sense she was attending closely enough to impede the movement of his left arm.

"Your coat's scritchy," she said, stroking the tweed sleeve.

"Sorry about that."

"Take it off."

"Won't be a sec, and then we're going to go and ask if you can go out in the garden with me. I'll show you the secret path to Far Look-out. Now, here's the key. Do you want to wind it or shall I?"

"You."

The large spring wound with heavy clicks of the ratchet. When Vincent showed the child the lever for starting and stopping the motor she still refused to take any part in setting the gadget off, so he did it himself. The motor ran with an even whirr, but the crank clicked and clacked as the cradle jerked rapidly through a small arc.

"Not so bad for a first try," said Vincent, talking as much to himself as to the child. "I'll have to gear it down next time, but . . ."

"Hello, darling," said a woman's voice from the door. "I see you've found a friend."

The child bounced to her feet and sprang across the room. Rising more slowly Vincent saw her thud into her mother, flinging her arms round her legs and burying her head in her stomach. As she staggered with the impact Mrs Dubigny laughed and began to tousle the child's hair in an affectionate but still absent-minded manner, almost as if she had been fondling somebody else's dog.

"What have you two been up to?" she said.

"Building a c-c-cradle for Mary," said Vincent.

"Oh, that's too good of you! Do look, darling — isn't that clever?"

The child paid no attention at all but continued to cling to her mother like some parasite anchored to its host for both their natural lives.

"I wish we'd had something like that for you when *you* were little," said Mrs Dubigny. "Do let go, darling. I've got to take Mr Masham to talk to the Countess."

"He promised to take me in the garden," said Sally.

"I said we'd g-g-go and ask if we c-could," said Vincent.

"Not now, darling, I'm afraid," said Mrs Dubigny, reaching behind her back and taking her daughter's wrist to pull that arm free.

"He promised," said Sally. "Why don't any of you keep your promises? Ever?"

"Now don't be silly," said Mrs Dubigny. "Mr Masham's made you a lovely cradle for Mary, and . . ."

Sally began to cry.

"I'm so sorry about this," said Mrs Dubigny, as if apologising for some phenomenon over which she had no control, such as the weather spoiling a tennis party. "She can be very temperamental."

Vincent knelt and undid the buckle of his watch strap.

"Can you tell the time, Sally?" he asked.

"Course I can," sobbed the child.

"Look, here's my watch. It says five past four, doesn't it? I'll put it here on the table and you can look after it for me. When it says twenty-five past four – look, when the big hand gets down here – I'll come and take you out. That'll give us half an hour before teatime. Don't forget, I'm going to show you the secret path. All right?"

"You won't," whined Sally. "None of you ever do – none of you!"

"If I'm not here at half-past four," said Vincent, "you c-can k-k-keep my watch for yourself."

"Oh, no, I can't allow that!" said Mrs Dubigny.

"I will be here, so it won't happen," said Vincent, standing up again.

"But Zena . . ."

"Zena is not in my g-good books at the moment. Let's be off. You'll look after my watch, won't you, Sally?"

The cradle was still restlessly clacking as he closed the door. Mrs Dubigny stopped at the top of the circular stair and put her hand on his sleeve.

"You mustn't think I neglect poor Sally," she said in a low voice. "It's just that we're still getting used to things here. I must change Nanny's half-day. I didn't realise how busy Fridays were going to be."

"Oh . . . I hadn't . . ."

"When Nanny's here they spend a lot of time in the garden. Didn't she tell you?"

3

Lady Snailwood – Zena to the hundreds of people who knew her, and also to tens of thousands who did not – was in one of her most familiar attitudes, half-curled on a nest of huge satin cushions near the centre of the Great Hall, wearing a white Aertex shirt, white cotton slacks and a pair of strangely mannish brogues, looking tiny compared with the enormous borzoi whose ears she was fondling. She was always smaller than strangers expected and often somehow than acquaintances remembered, but this was evidently one of her days for looking frail and protectorless. It was also one of her days for a faintly Ruritanian accent.

"So here you are at last, Vincent, darling," she drawled, making it sound as though it was she alone who had organised his rescue from grim dungeons into this house of comfort. "I'm so happy the soldiers let you go."

"They weren't, very."

"Silly little men. You must take no notice of them."

"I have to. It's the system."

"Then we will change it."

"You . . ."

"Don't argue, Vince," said Harry, who was lolling some yards away on a chintzed armchair, smoking. "Zena means she thinks she would look stunning in a field marshal's uniform. That's what she's after. She's going to start by spending this week-end drilling her guests on the tennis court. You're here to teach her the words of command."

"Oh yes!" cried Zena, sitting up. "And one day I shall ride my white charger through the Arch of Victory at the head of all my armies!"

"You'll have to arrange for a war, you know," said Harry. "Enemies to conquer are the main thing, I suppose."

"They are there already. We will conquer the Bolsheviks. The new Tsar shall ride by my side – only a little behind."

"On the other hand," said Harry, "you could arrange for a Wonderland war – victory first, fighting afterwards. I shouldn't be surprised if that wasn't the coming thing in any case."

Zena lay back among the cushions, which were located where the sunlight, passing through the stained glass at the top of one of the windows, mottled the floor with blotches of colour. It would be difficult to be sure whether Zena was conscious of this effect, and whether she was wearing white to take advantage of it, but as she moved and the colours moved across her it was almost as though she was practising to become the Chameleon Woman in a fairground, effortlessly adapting her own hues to those of the cushions on which she sprawled.

"That stupid *Alice*," she yawned. "Of course England is no longer great when it is the only book our intelligentsia really care about. Darling Vince, I am so pleased your stammer is becoming so much better."

"Pretty well under control, thank you," said Vincent with no obvious effort over the guttural.

"I do not understand how you can give orders to your men when you stammer so."

"I'll show you. Parade! Paraaaaade . . . Shun!"

The commands came out full volume, in the extraordinary gargling yelp of the army drill instructor. The Great Hall was a large enough space to set up a perceptible echo. Zena put her hands over her ears.

"Please do not do that again," she said. "Now you have given me a migraine."

"Have you seen?" said Harry. "Zena's had a new picture done."

"I thought there was something different," said Vincent. "I'm still not used to the room like this . . . oh yes, there. I say. I like that much better than the John. I think that's distinctly jolly."

He went and stood by Zena's immensely elongated piano to look more closely at the portrait.

"Very good likeness of the Duke of Cats, too," he said. "I'm not sure some of those boats would actually float."

"My dear old Vince," said Harry. "If you don't watch out Zena will get you taken on as art critic of the *Morning Post*."

"Have I said something wrong?"

"Darling Vince," said Zena. "But come and tell me all about this friend who is coming to visit us – Prince Yasif ibn Sorah. Have I said that right?"

"Don't ask me. Honestly, I don't know him that well. I've an idea the chaps in the Harrow team called him Solly."

"That won't do, not with Blech here," said Harry. "Endless confusion. Vince, you're a broken reed."

"Joan dear," said Zena. "If you could be an angel and telephone the Foreign Office. Ask for Sir Hugh Swiddle-Smith. He's had lots of postings to disgusting places full of Arabs. He'll know how to pronounce the poor young man's name. Wheedle him, darling, so that he tells you things – oh, how they love being indiscreet, these starchy old gentlemen! Anything that might be useful. Say I send him twenty-seven kisses, but don't call him Hughie unless he tells you to. I'm sure you can do all that."

Mrs Dubigny had been standing by the fireplace watching Zena's attempts at Vince-teasing with a faint smile, which now broadened with complicity, subversive of the whole male order of things.

"I'll do my best," she said, and slipped away.

Zena sighed, the weight of the campaign now on her shoulders alone.

"But I made the soldiers let you go this afternoon so that you could prepare me to meet his highness," she said. "It's very important."

"I'm sorry," said Vincent. "The only thing I know for sure is that he c-couldn't pick my top-spinner. Don't imagine that's much use. The Harrow chaps seemed to like him, far as I remember. Honestly, Zena, he's your g-guest, not mine. I'll be friendly with him if he lets me, but . . ."

"He's *your* guest, Vince. That's very important. You've got to go in the Daimler and meet him tomorrow morning, because he's coming on the same train as Professor Blech. Charles Archer will go with you to meet the Professor. But it is your task to make the Prince understand that it's just an accident that he happens to be here the same time as the Blechs. Don't you understand?"

"Trouble is I don't know anything about this Blech fellow."

"He's famous for that," said Harry. "People not knowing anything about him, I mean. He's a professor of something bizarre – botany, I think. But he's a crony of Chaim Weizmann, and he's very much in with the Paris Rothschilds and that lot, and he's said to have Roosevelt's ear, and so on. Is he here by accident too?"

"Oh no," said Zena. "He's far, far too clever for that. I asked him to come and explain the Zionist viewpoint to Charles, and I suggested his wife might bring her cello and play to us, and we will take a collection for a Jewish charity. Don't you think that's . . ."

She was interrupted by the clank of the big iron latch which fastened the pair of black oak doors beneath the gallery. Purser came in and opened both leaves to admit a small procession – first Lord Snailwood, then Thring pulling the rose-trolley, and then a new footman pushing an even odder device, also purpose-built by McGrigor, a big brass tub on a pair of rubber wheels, with a brass jug and other smaller items dangling round its perimeter, giving the effect of part of the armoury of Tweedledum and Tweedledee in Tenniel's illustration to the fantasy Zena so disapproved of. Lord Snailwood added to the sense of ritual entry by carrying before him a single pink rose, half-way between bud and full bloom. He was wearing much the same clothes as in the Birley portrait, tweeds and gaiters. His scalp, tanned and mottled, glistened with mild sweat. He approached Zena and with a stilted bow presented her with the rose.

"Oh, isn't it perfect," she cooed.

"Perfection to perfection," said Lord Snailwood, speaking as though he were grumbling about something.

"How sweet you are. Has the darling thing a name?"

"The Doctor, of course. Show standard, in my opinion."

"Award of merit, dearest. But could I ask you possibly to do the other bowls first and this one after tea? We're talking, you see."

"Not possible," said Lord Snailwood. "Terribly sorry, dear, but I must do the big bowl first. Only way to get it right. Can't hope to do that with the left-overs."

"As a matter of fact," said Vincent, "I've g-got to be off. I've an appointment in five minutes."

"Ah, Vincent, glad to see you," said Lord Snailwood. "I want you to talk to McGrigor about the clock."

Lord Snailwood always spoke briskly and clearly, but still somehow gave the impression that he wasn't talking to anyone in particular, but rather to the whole room or the passing air. It was as though he lacked confidence in the interest of his remarks to be sure that any one person would want to hear them, and so preferred to send them forth at large in the hope that there might be a pair of ears within range with nothing better to listen to at the moment. Thus among strangers he sometimes evoked no response whatever; more often, because of the inherent value of words that have just passed between the lips of an earl, several of his hearers would hasten to respond, and then halt, mutually abashed. Not many of his utterances were as remarkable as this last.

"You don't say!" said Harry.

"I certainly do say," said Lord Snailwood. "I will have him up tomorrow morning. Ten o'clock, eh, Vincent?"

"No, dearest," said Zena. "Vincent has to meet the 10.43 at High Wycombe."

"A train? You mean he's got to meet a train?"

"Yes, dearest. McGrigor will drive Vincent and Charles Archer to meet the train. When they get back, which will be about eleven-fifteen, they can talk about the clock. There will be time for that before Sir John and the others come. And then in the afternoon some of us are going over to Bullington to play croquet, and the politicians are staying here."

Zena spoke almost dreamily, but it was characteristic of her that she had the time-table of the week-end precise in her mind, and was able with no fluster at all to accommodate the extra item of talk about the clock. Lord Snailwood nodded.

"Eleven-fifteen, then, Vincent," he said. "Keep an eye on McGrigor. Don't let him slip away."

"I'll do my best, sir."

"Vincent," murmured Zena. "I am most interested that you have an appointment so soon after coming to Snailwood."

"Only half an hour. I'll be down for tea."

"Come here, Vincent darling. Bend down. I want to whisper. Closer."

Though Vincent eventually knelt with his ear only inches from Zena's mouth, her whisper when it came was as carrying as an actor's. Harry could certainly have heard it, and Lord Snailwood if he'd been listening, and quite likely the pricked ears of Purser and Thring and the new footman, as they waited to perform their functions where the huge bronze urn stood empty on its stand just clear of the overhang of the gallery.

"You are not to debauch any of my maids this visit," she said. "The servant problem is quite difficult enough without that."

Before he could protest she laughed like a wicked stepmother, threw her bare arm round his neck and kissed him vehemently. He pulled free and rose, laughing too but without great conviction. His natural flush, combined with the slight struggle, made it hard to say whether he was redder than usual. As he climbed the main stairway at the opposite end from the gallery his figure came and went, framed in the series of lancet arches that partially screened it from the body of the Great Hall. Before he had vanished out of the last one Mrs Dubigny came back, her smiling lips moving slightly as she rehearsed the syllables of the name she had been sent to learn.

3

By late March the desert noon already foretold the appalling heat of summer. It seemed worse in the shade of the camouflage, but that was an illusion produced by the stifling dusk, the sheer clarity of the light beyond the awnings seeming to imply more tolerable conditions. Indeed, for a few seconds after one stepped from the darkness the illusion was sustained as the sweat scorched off the skin and boosted the body's natural refrigeration, but those who had fought through the campaigns of 1940 had learnt that the relief was not worth while.

The two Lysanders were parked in echelon, so that their wings could overlap and reduce the camouflage area. The effect was to produce a cave of additional darkness between the fuselages, perhaps faintly cooler because of the double layer of roofing, but containing an air almost unbreathably thick with paint smell and petrol smell and sweat – or more likely urine, where an aircraft-man had risked a piss *in situ* rather than make the theoretically compulsory trip to the reeking latrines.

"Smells like the monkey house at the zoo," drawled the taller of the two officers who had come into the edge of the shade and now stood silhouetted there, features and badges of rank quite invisible against the glare.

"Been here too long," said the other man. "We'll be glad to move on, sir. Look for a nice spot for us – palm trees, water to swim in, houris."

"I don't think you get houris so far west."

"The men will be disappointed, sir. How are you doing, Mason?"

There was a difference between their voices, slight but definite. The senior officer spoke casually, with a near drawl. The junior used almost the same accent, but with less confidence, as though he had only recently mastered it. His question was answered by a thud and scraping from the darkness, followed by a heavy, uninterpretable grunt.

"We're having to make do with one mechanic, sir," said the junior officer. "My A/c Airframes got the sand-squitters. Lost a stone in eight hours. But Mason's a first-class chap – I'd rely on him for anything. Only it takes him longer to get round. Be ready by fourteen hundred, d'you think, Mason?"

Again the grunt came, this time probably affirmative. Peering into the cavern it was just possible to see the hindquarters of a man who was leaning into the cabin of the right-hand aircraft.

"Come out of there, man, and make a proper report," snapped the junior officer. "Good God! What have you done with your face?"

The last words were spoken as the mechanic, after backing ponderously from the cabin, drew himself up and faced them. His head seemed to have disappeared. Only his teeth and the whites of his eyes glimmered in the dimness.

"Went and tried to wipe the sweat off of my face with my oil rag," he said hoarsely.

"You all right, Mason? I'll be up the creek if you go sick on me too."

"Sorry, sir. Just swallowed one of these bleeding flies. Stuck in my throat. Got an hour and a bit more work on her, sir."

"Ready by fourteen hundred, then?"

"'Less I find something needs attention, sir."

"Report to me at once in the mess tent if you do."

"Sir."

"Carry on then."

The two officers turned and walked into the glare at a lounging pace but still precisely in step. The senior was revealed by the sunlight to be a major in the Intelligence Corps, the junior a pilot officer. They had walked about half-way to the little group of tents when the major halted.

"This man Mason," he said. "Where's he from, do you know?"

"Somewhere in the Midlands, I think, sir. But he doesn't seem to have much of a tie with home. He never gets any mail, for instance. Worked in a garage before the war, I gather."

"Did he now? What an extraordinary coincidence. I think it

must be the same man who used to service my Jowett. D'you mind if I go and have a chat with him?"

"We really want to be off by fourteen-thirty, latest, sir."

"Oh, I won't hold him up more than a couple of minutes. I'll see you in the mess tent, if that's all right."

"Very good, sir."

Back under the camouflage awning the major stood in silence, watching the mechanic at work. Little was visible of the man above the waist as he leaned in through the cabin door doing something at floor level which apparently demanded brief, precise but effortful wrenchings. He finished and began to back out of the cabin.

"Vince," said the major.

The movement stopped.

"No, sir," said the man, mumbling a little.

"You have a most characteristic backside," said the major. "I've seen it too often poking out of the bonnet of a motor to be deceived. Come on, Vince. I've always hoped we'd meet somewhere."

Slowly the man turned round.

"Seven three oh oh nine Aircraftman Mason, sir," he said.

"All right. That's who you are now. I won't tell anyone. But listen. That appalling business at Snailwood. It wasn't you who did it. I'm absolutely certain of that."

"I . . ."

"Don't misunderstand me. Of course I never thought it was you because I know you well enough to be sure you wouldn't do anything that foul. That's not what I'm talking about. What I'm saying is that I now know who did do it, though I'll never prove it. I think I know why you cleared out, too, but . . ."

"I don't know what you're talking about, sir."

"Yes, you do, Vince, and I haven't got much time, so I'm going to go on talking as if you'd admitted it. There's nothing I'd like better than to get back to the old days, and the old relationship. I still feel that apart from Joan and Sally you're the person I care about more than anyone else in the world – you probably don't know that I've married Joan Dubigny and adopted Sally – but I can see that whatever I think there'd still be problems if you tried to come back, even after the war, so if you want to carry on being A/c Mason, I won't stop you."

"I don't see how you can, sir. That's who I am."

"I wish you'd call me Hal. Just here, where there's no one to hear. Never mind. I've got to confess I'm in a bit of a state, Vince. I've been having quite a jolly war so far – I've managed to attach myself to a slightly eccentric general who spends half his energy intriguing against other generals and the other half putting up hare-brained schemes to HQ. Just when everybody's sick of him we manage to pull off something, and then he's a hero and those in power take the chance to pack him off to some other quarter of the war where they don't know about him yet. So I've been around quite a bit, as you can imagine. Now we're here and he's got a notion that the way to stop the Hun coming to punch us back into Egypt, which they're due to do any moment, is to go and punch them first. He's right, in a way – it's almost impossible to fight a defensive battle in the desert – but it means I've got to go and take a look-see what the chances are. You know they've grabbed all our fighter cover and sent it off to Greece? These things are sitting ducks, without fighter cover."

The major slapped angrily at the nacelle of the Lysander. He had seemed to become more and more agitated as he spoke. The mechanic simply looked at him, unconsciously turning a large wrench over and over in his hands. The sweat and oil gleamed on his forehead and cheeks.

"I do wish you'd give a bit, Vince," said the major. "But if you won't you won't. Still, there's something I hope you'll do for me. Listen. It's been pretty tricky keeping Snailwood going. It was bad enough before Uncle Snaily died, but at least I had power of attorney then and the lawyers were tolerably helpful. But as soon as he was out of the way Aunt Ivy started to take the line that you were the one who was supposed to inherit and started throwing injunctions around and so on and it's become pretty well impossible. Uncle Snaily left things in a total mess, as you'd expect. Mercifully Zena's married an American and gone to live in New York, but that's the only bright spot. I've been just about able to cope, with Joan's help. But if I catch it on some hare-brained op.

my general's dreamed up – I don't mind saying I've got the wind up about this one – Aunt Ivy's going to take the line that with me out of the way you're the heir, no matter what I've put in my will. Down with aunts."

There was a pause. The major's last three words had had almost the intonation of a question.

"Sir?" said the mechanic.

"All right. I shouldn't have tried it. The point is, your mother . . ."

"Pardon me interrupting, sir. My mother's passed on."

"Not as far as I'm concerned, Vince. She's alive and kicking in my world, and more of a nuisance than ever. If I thought the only reason you'd cleared out was to be shot of her, I wouldn't have blamed you. I don't blame you anyway, damn it. But . . ."

"Pardon me, sir. Mr Toller told me . . ."

"Quite right. I'll leave you alone. But assuming I come back in one piece – and really there's no reason why I shouldn't – things have been quiet enough, in all conscience. If only they hadn't withdrawn those bloody fighters . . . Think it over, won't you, Vince? There's nothing I'd like better than a good long talk. Leave a note for me with the mess waiter, or someone, and we'll wander out under the desert stars and talk as though there'd never been any war and Zena had never come to Snailwood."

The appeal in the major's voice was very strong. The mechanic hesitated, nodded and began to turn back towards his work. He paused.

"You won't say anything to anyone about this, sir?"

"What? No, no, of course not. Fact, I've already told Toller you're the chap who used to service the Jowett. If it's any inducement to you, Vince, I've a bottle of Scotch in my kit . . . Carry on then, Aircraftman."

The major's salute deliberately mimed the total superiority of the officer caste. Back in his role, he lounged into the sun-glare and out of sight. The mechanic stood where he was, gazing apparently without seeing it at the Lysander, but there was a sense of intelligence gathering itself to a focus to consider a problem. His hand teased unthinkingly at his upper lip. Suddenly he drew a deep breath and then shuddered, as if deliberately disrupting the image that had formed itself in his mind. He returned to his work.

Owing to the exigencies of war the inquiry into the loss of the Lysander did not take place for nearly three weeks and was in any case brief. Aircraftman Mason was a witness. He produced an oily job sheet, and told the inquiring officer that he had serviced both engine and air-frame, the latter being necessary because of the illness of A/c Strong. The Lysander had been fully airworthy, though a week before the loss he had discussed with Flight Lieutenant Allison the possibility of cannibalising one machine to ensure the safety of the other, and they had agreed that there might be a need for that if spares did not arrive, but not for a couple of months or more. Meanwhile having two aircraft available when only one was needed for regular use allowed proper maintenance to be carried out on the other one, with the additional safety that that implied.

There was one brief diversion from matters mechanical.

"I understand that on the morning after the loss the mess waiter returned to you a note you had left for Major Quintain," said the enquiring officer. "Perhaps we had better hear whether that had any bearing on the state of the Lysander."

"No, sir."

"Nevertheless would you mind telling us what was in the note?"

"Well, sir, it was like this. I'd run across Major Quintain before the war. He had a little Jowett what he used to have a lot of trouble with the carburettor of – he'd get it into his head it was running too thin and he'd try and adjust it himself and make a balls of it, and then he'd think it was the timing and foul that up too, messing around, and only when the Jowett was hardly going he'd bring it along to me to put right. Happened time and again, almost like it was a game between us. Well, you see, bumping into each other there, he thought he'd like a chat about old times. There wasn't time before the flight if I was going to get the plane set up, so he said what about after. He told me he'd a bottle of Scotch in his baggage, and he left it to me to fix some place we could meet and have a nip or two. That's what the note was about."

The social difficulty, even under desert conditions, involved in an officer from another unit sharing so rare a commodity with an Other Rank while failing to do so with his hosts in the mess – though it was for that that he had originally brought the bottle, no doubt – was clear to the inquiry. Some kind of semi-secret rendezvous among the dunes would certainly have been necessary. So the inquiry moved on, reaching the obvious verdict that no blame attached to anyone for the failure of the Lysander to return, but that the actual cause of that failure – enemy action, breakdown, pilot error – could not be known until the wreckage, now several hundred miles away after the abrupt retreat, was found.

It never was.

4

Waiting for the train on Saturday morning, Sir Charles Archer leaned both hands on his black cane and stared along the railway line. Though still as an image, his pose expressed inward restlessness, or hunger; he might have been waiting for the train to bring him his bride. That mysterious smoky and oily breeze, which even on still days railway stations seem to conjure up, more like an outdoor draught than any natural wind, breathed gently past him; but he leaned into it as if it had been a gale and he on some cliff-top look-out, peering seaward. In front of him, but invisible from the platform, the long and dreary township of High Wycombe wound through its valley to the west.

"How's the army treating you, my boy?" he said suddenly.

"Very decently, sir," said Vincent. "I'm enjoying it."

"They teaching you to kill effectively?"

"I'm teaching other chaps now. I've been posted to our new TA battalion in Hackney."

"So you will march to battle at the head of costermongers and clerks. Charming. Who are they planning to let you slaughter first?"

"The c-current assumption is that it'll be the Germans."

"You'll enjoy that too?"

"I think I shall enjoy fighting."

"And accept the necessity to kill as unfortunately incidental to the fighting?"

"Looks like it. I mean, suppose I spent my life in the service and ran out a general, without ever having been involved in a proper shooting war, in theory that'd be the best thing that c-could have happened, but I'd be bound to feel I'd missed something, wouldn't I?"

"By 'the best thing that could happen' I take it you are referring to the good of the country at large."

43

"Well, yes, sir."

"Then you are mistaken. Peace is of course beautiful, but a country such as ours needs a war, approximately once a generation, in order to retain its moral strength. It needs to put forth its full energies in battle, or it will begin to lose its own sense of its destiny. The question is not whether we should fight, but when, and whom. This war that you envisage will happen five years too early, but that is not the worst thing about it. Let me ask you whether you find it natural to regard the Germans as the enemy you are being trained to kill."

"I think so, sir. Dash it, I don't mean that. It's not natural to k-kill anyone."

"It is, my boy. But go on."

"Well, the Germans . . . . I mean, we were fighting them when I was born. They k-killed my father – and Hal's. And you must have done for a few, sir."

For the first time for several minutes Sir Charles moved more than his lips. It was in any case natural for interlocutors, even near strangers, to find themselves standing in a position where they could see only the left side of his face, though no conscious effort seemed to be needed on the part of either person to make this happen. Now the large and bonily magnificent countenance swung to face Vincent, so that the great blotchy naevus that smeared the right cheek from eye-corner to jaw-bone came into view.

"It was a bad dream," said Sir Charles, his heavy purr slowing to a drawl. "I have woken up. I have woken up."

"Still, it looks as though that's what we're g-going to be in for again, sir," said Vincent. "Even if it isn't what we want, supposing Herr Hitler . . ."

"Adolf is only one man," said Sir Charles, returning to his former pose. "I've had several chats with him, and I think I know what makes him tick. He's a politician, first and last. Remember that he's got to carry his country with him."

"I saw a newsreel of the last Nuremberg rally."

"I was there, my boy. I was there. And very impressive it was. But remember those roaring mobs are not the real Germany. If only people would get it into their heads that a modern nation is nothing more nor less than an economic system, a network of industries. The people who run the real Germany are the big industrialists. I tell you, Vincent, Germany's industrialists, many of whom I number among my friends, have absolutely no intention of letting Adolf off the leash, though they will let him bark as much as he likes. I suggested as much – I put it in those very words – to Herr Ribbentrop only last month, and he laughed and agreed with me. So . . . Ah, there's the bell at last . . . I must say, I wish Zena had consulted me before dragging this young Arab in. Tell me about him."

"I've only met him once, sir, playing c-cricket. I've never talked to him alone. I'm not sure I'd be able to put my finger on Sorah on the map."

"A dot half-way up the Persian Gulf on the left-hand side. The only decent harbour on that coast, so it controls one of the main routes to Mecca from the east. They aren't supposed to tax the pilgrims, but they find ways. They have something of a reputation for luxury among the Arabs – rather like Sybaris among the early Italians – based on a specialist slave trade they run. Girls from Persia."

"There c-can't be much of that these days, sir."

"Officially, none. Unofficially . . . . you are aware that half-hearted suppression of trade in any commodity increases the profits of the middleman? If there are too many girls coming through Sorah – they're said to be pretty well children by our standards – the Emir instructs his officials to be zealous for a while. The flow slackens, and the price per child rises. You know, I find it curious to consider that this young man's education in the art of passing himself off as a gentleman should have been paid for by the sale of children to gratify the perversions of savages."

"Oh, cuh . . . cuh . . . cuh . . . cuh . . ."

Sir Charles's voice had deepened to a richly throbbing bass, perhaps only an indication of his relish in the dramatic manipulation of language. When he turned to smile at Vincent his eyes seemed to have gained colour and to twinkle with only slightly malicious charm. Or it might not even have been malice, merely inquisitiveness at the shape of a mind that could not savour an irony he himself enjoyed.

"I was teasing, my boy," he said. "The trade is very nearly suppressed, as you say. And in any case the Emir is anxious to show himself a good friend to Britain. There is an American company exploring for oil, too, and if they find it the Emir will be able to suppress the trade entirely, I imagine. No, it would be truer to say that the Prince's education in the ideal of a Christian gentleman had been paid for by a levy on the poor who make the journey to Mecca. Just as curious an irony, but less repellent. At last! Next time I see Tuffy Gallacher at White's I shall take great pleasure in twitting him on the performance of his railway."

Very slowly, almost as though the driver was uncertain that this was the right station, the train steamed in, stopping with a long, exhausted sigh.

"Your chap will no doubt be travelling first," said Sir Charles. "One cannot be sure about the Blechs."

There were not many passengers. Vincent stood back from the train, craning along the carriages, his usual look of faint anxiety now quite marked. After all it was perfectly possible that two brownish young men would alight, and then how was one to be sure of recognising a figure last seen four years ago at the length of a cricket pitch? In fact there was no chance of mistake. A porter homed on a first-class compartment and heaved out three large new cases. A small man stepped down and gazed around him.

At Lord's the Prince had looked two or three years younger than his age, lissom and soft-featured. The softness was still there but the lines had changed, becoming definitely bulbous; and he had grown a neat black beard. He was wearing grey flannels and a college blazer. As soon as he spotted Vincent walking towards him he sprang forward, hand held out.

"Hello, Masham," he said. "How are you?"

"Very well, thank you, sir. Very g-glad you were able to c-come."

"None of this 'sir' business, please. I gather from your aunt — she is your aunt, eh? — that the only formalities take place this evening."

"Zena would manage to make a c-coronation feel informal. That's all your bags? We're meeting some other people off this train . . . He's found them, by the looks of it."

Vincent led the way down the platform and introduced the Prince to Sir Charles.

"Honoured to meet you, your highness," said Sir Charles. "Allow me to present Professor and Mrs Solomon Blech."

The Prince had been on the verge of saying something, probably another request to forsake protocol. Now he underwent a marked change, almost a spasm. The effect was like that occasionally seen when an actor in a repertory company suffers an aberration and makes his first entrance under the impression that he is still in last week's play. The charming laugh, the suggestion of tennis, freeze on his lips as he stares round the gaunt set and at the other members of the cast, all visibly racked with the tragedy they have been enacting. The Prince continued to turn towards the Professor, but withdrew several inches as he did so. Blech, a short, rotund man, bowed Austrian-fashion.

"I have corresponded with your highness's uncle, the Kemalah," he said. "I hope His Holiness is in good health."

He spoke rapidly and softly, running the words together but putting a heavy stress on some syllables, apparently at random. His mien was perfectly solemn, but his small bloodshot eyes blinked frequently as he spoke, giving him a look of inquisitive delight, a child's dangerous innocence. But clearly he knew his way about the world, for the mention of the Kemalah of Sorah acted like a letter of recommendation and had the effect of allowing the Prince to translate back into the sphere of light comedy.

"That old villain!" he cried. "Still raking in the shekels, as you would say, Professor."

He turned smiling to Mrs Blech, who curtsied as she touched his hand. She was a pale, harried-looking woman, taller than her husband. She emanated a sense of suppressed nerves, as though the station platform were swarming with snappy little dogs which she had to pretend, for form's sake, not to notice. She clung to a worn green cello case. The Blechs' only other baggage appeared to be a cloth suitcase and two brown paper bags.

"I'm afraid the chauffeur's sick," explained Vincent. "I have to drive."

"Then I'll come in front with you," said the Prince, almost as though it were a social adventure to ride in front of the Daimler's glass partition. This was probably just as well, for though there were two seats in the back, each running across the full width of the car, as well as the little folding chairs that popped out of the floor – so that in theory eight passengers could fit in behind the partition – Mrs Blech would not be parted from her cello and Sir Charles, constrained by the metal-ribbed corset he had to wear, also took up a good deal of room. It was distinctly tactful of the Prince not to add to the problems by asking them to fit royalty into the jig-saw.

"I've never been allowed to drive this bus before," said Vincent as the large engine took the Daimler breathily away. "It feels more like a ship than a car."

"Or a camel," said the Prince. "You know, Masham, I'm delighted to have met you again. I have dreamed of you from time to time. That second innings! My century at Lord's! Gone! Never another chance!"

"Sorry about that."

"I do not even know that it has been good for my character, as they promised. Do you still play? I don't."

"In the army, yes. The funny thing is that I've lost my leg break. I still do the flipper and the g-googly, but for some reason my ordinary plain tweaker won't tweak."

"That is symbolic of our progress to the tomb. I say, Masham, I've often wished the Prophet had played cricket. He'd have had some interesting things to say, don't you imagine? Now tell me about this man Archer. Blech I know of."

"Sir Charles? Oh . . . well, he's a journalist and an MP, but he's a bit more than that. There's a small g-group in the House who follow him, but I don't think they have much effect. Still, he has a lot of influence in other ways. He had a terrific war, you see. In the end he was so badly blown up that he has to wear a sort of steel corset thing all the time. And he's a marvellous public speaker. Even so, it's difficult to say why people think he's important, but they do, and so he is."

"What is his interest in Professor Blech?"

"He wants to talk to him, I imagine. He's not well off. He makes his living by his journalism, and that depends on knowing what's g-going on. Apparently Professor Blech is the chap to tell you about the Zionist view on the Palestine problem, so . . ."

"He is an enemy of my people, Masham. I say, this car makes a remarkable amount of smoke."

"That's the trouble with these sleeve-valve engines – they're famous for it. But as a matter of fact I think there must be something a bit rummy with the transmission. I noticed it c-coming in, but I thought it was only that I wasn't used to the fluid flywheel. Now it seems to be g-getting worse."

Soon it became clear that something was indeed wrong with the Daimler. The soggy suspension, combined with the fluid flywheel, always gave an illusion of smoothness, almost of floating on a mildly swelling ocean; but as they climbed the steep road on to the chalk escarpment south of High Wycombe they trailed behind them exhaust smoke blue as a thunder cloud. The car slowed and slowed until it could barely have overtaken a bicycle, and the needle of the fuel gauge dropped visibly. At last the scaly pattern of roofs that snaked along the valley fell out of sight and they moved into the uplands, only to wallow more noticeably as they picked up speed. The morning was bright and warm, the road almost empty. In the rear compartment Professor and Mrs Blech sat in opposite corners of the back seat, Mrs Blech with her eyes closed as if already desperately trying to master the car sickness which the Daimler almost instantly induced in certain passengers. Professor Blech completely ignored her distress, leaning forward and speaking with great volubility and many small gestures to Sir Charles, who sat sideways on the front seat, twisting stiffly round to listen. In the driving compartment the Prince had returned to the subject of Palestine, speaking now with a low dispassionate voice which contrasted strongly with the boyish dash with which he had referred to his two disastrous innings at Lord's.

"But didn't we g-give our word to the Jews?" said Vincent. "The Balfour Declaration and all that?"

"You gave more than one word, Masham. You have promises to keep to us Arabs also. You are soon going to have to break at least one promise. Why should it be the one you gave us?"

"There must be some cuh . . . cuh . . . cuh . . ."

"Compromise? You mean you think it fairer to break both promises, rather than keep one and break one? I tell you bluntly, Masham, how it appears to the Arabs. Herr Hitler is chasing his Jews out of Germany. You do not want them here. If they have a country of their own you can keep your consciences clean by telling them to go there. You are deeply anti-semitic people."

"Oh, I don't . . ."

"Remember I have lived here now almost ten years. There were a few Jews at Harrow. Not only the boys but also many of the masters openly despised them. Some of them despised me also. I have heard myself called a nigger by a grocer's son – behind my back, but he intended me to hear – yet believe me such behaviour was made easier to bear because I could see that it was superficial compared with the dislike of the Jews."

"I'm afraid we had a bit of that at Eton, too. I think it was only rather stupid boys . . ."

"Sir Oswald Mosley is not stupid."

"Yes, but . . . really he only says those things because his party must have somebody to attack. In private – he's been to Snailwood several times, you know – in private he plays all that down. It's only when he's ranting on a platform."

"It is still part of his policy that the Jews must have a national home. Is that part of Sir Charles Archer's policy also?"

"I believe so. Last year he was pushing Madagascar . . ."

"That is rubbish. The only place the Jews will agree to go to is one that contains Jerusalem – which is one of the great holy places for the followers of Islam. Was not Abraham our father? Why should the Jews have Jerusalem? Tell me, Masham, why?"

"I don't know. I suppose that's one of the problems. I mean it's difficult for us to understand anyone feeling so strongly about something like that. No one I've talked to in the army is at all k-keen on the idea of fighting the Palestinian Arabs, but one has to keep order, you know."

The Prince checked his answer, nodded and smiled, now looking considerably older than Vincent.

"One has to keep order indeed," he said. "Explain to me, Masham, about this aunt of yours. I don't mind telling you hers was a rather peculiar invitation, but as I am at Oxford to study politics my tutor suggested it would be worth the experience to come. I have already met a few of your notorious English aunts. Would you say Lady Snailwood is a typical specimen?"

"Zena? G-g-good lord, no!"

Still trailing its fuming cloud the Daimler swung down the tight curves of the drive and sighed to a stop beneath the battlements of Snailwood's east façade. The arrival was not particularly well timed, as they passed the Sunbeam coming from the other direction after depositing the guests from the Marlow train. Under the *porte-cochère* – for that was all it was, though imposingly tricked out as part of the fortifications – stood the loose pile of their luggage, with Purser beside it evidently supervising its removal. He gave a furious glare at the approaching Daimler, picked up the lightest available case and stalked out of sight. The only figures left beneath the ponderous frontage were Sally Dubigny and a vapid-looking woman whose outfit – grey felt hat, grey quasi-military coat, flat-heeled shoes – though not exactly a uniform would at once have declared her to be a nanny even if there had not been a child in sight.

The guests climbed from the Daimler, first Sir Charles, then Mrs Blech – lemon-coloured and holding a handkerchief to her mouth – and finally the Professor still talking volubly over her shoulder to Sir Charles.

"One moment," said Sir Charles, turning and beckoning dramatically to the nanny, as though he himself had posted her there to cope with precisely this contingency.

"Mrs Blech is going to be sick," he said. "Take her somewhere, will you?"

"But Sally . . ." began the woman.

"Quick!" snapped Sir Charles.

"I'll look after Sally," said Vincent.

"Excellent," said Sir Charles. "And I'll take care of his highness. Well, get on with it, nurse! Now, your highness, Professor, I had better explain to you that one of the minor delights of staying at Snailwood is to watch the progress of the campaign between our hostess and her butler, the redoubtable Mr Purser . . ."

The group broke up, the nanny at last moving decisively,

putting her arm round Mrs Blech's waist and supporting her up the steps. Sir Charles stayed where he was, to allow them time to get clear and also seizing the chance to give his set-piece entertainment on the subject of the Snailwood Feud, its alliances, treaties and betrayals. The Prince began to laugh almost at once. Professor Blech composed himself into that attitude of acid patience which serious foreigners learn to adopt when confronted with exhibitions of native childishness.

"Why don't you get in the car?" said Vincent to Sally. "When I've got the luggage off we'll drive it round to the stables."

"Can I steer? Daddy always lets me."

"If you like."

Even had Vincent taken his hands off the wheel there would have been little danger of Sally hitting anything. The Daimler appeared far sicker after its halt. Sluggish and reeking, but still ineffably sedate, it nosed round the corner tower, along the north front and the main entrance to the courtyard with the clock tower above, and at last in through the double doors of the old Coach House, dim-lit by grimy lower sections of lancet window high up on its inner wall. Vincent switched off the motor, but Sally stayed on his lap, vigorously heaving the large wheel to and fro. During the actual drive she had been entirely submissive to his movements, making no effort to steer of her own accord.

"C-come on, young lady," he said. "I have to look after my g-guest."

"I like it here. Let's stay a bit longer. You're warm."

"A bit too warm, thanks. C-c-come on, miss — Nanny will be wondering what's bec . . . bec . . . happened to you."

"I hate Nanny. She's too new . . . I like you, Vince."

Suddenly she took her hands off the wheel, squirmed round and hugged him by the neck in a gesture almost as violent as that with which she had seized her mother in the nursery the previous afternoon. Vincent sat rigid. The child, more tentatively, as if aware of moving into treacherous ground, placed her lips against his cheek and kissed him wetly. He did not respond until she lowered her head and twisted it to and fro against his jacket, like a puppy nuzzling its way to warmth. With a jerk Vincent raised his hands, took Sally round the rib-cage and wrenched her loose. She screamed.

"You're a silly little guh . . . guh . . . guh . . ." he said, shoving her across and dumping her in the passenger seat. Her scream became a sob. He paid no attention, but opened his door and stepped out on to the running board. Lord Snailwood was standing by the rear mudguard, sniffing in a puzzled way at the oily air.

"Ah, Vincent," he said. "Looking for you. You heard McGrigor says he's sick?"

"Yes, sir. That's why I'm driving the Daimler."

"Sent a note by that daughter of his to say he won't show us the clock. Vincent, I tell you I don't care for the way this motor is beginning to smell. McGrigor insists it's only because of the shirt-valves, but I suspect she's blown a gaskell, eh?"

"I don't think so, sir. The engine could do with a tune, but I think the real trouble's something to do with the transmission. If you'd like . . ."

Vincent had stepped down as he was speaking but was still holding the door. Now Sally emerged, her face blubbered. Without looking at either of the men she edged along the running-board, climbed down and walked between them, sniffing loudly. Lord Snailwood stared at her but said nothing. As soon as she was out of the Coach House she broke into a stumbling run, crying as she went. Vincent was about to follow when Lord Snailwood said, "No, no. Must talk to you about the Daimler. Thought for a long time McGrigor's not been looking after it. Same with the clock. Mark you, don't think he's sick at all. Swinging the leg, that's more like it. Afraid of being found out when he shows you what he's been up to. What's that you were saying about the transition?"

"I'll just take a dekko, sir. Hold on."

As if it were a relief to be dealing with the certainties of the world of machines Vincent took a large hand torch from the front pocket of the car, crouched down and swung himself further still, keeping his knees just clear of the floor by supporting his weight on the runningboard and on the knuckles of the hand that was holding the torch. Its beam shone yellow over the underside of the chassis, darkening perceptibly as the brief initial impulse of the exhausted battery died. A drop of clear oil fell from the bell-housing from which the transmission shaft emerged. Another fell almost at once, and then another. The big timbers that covered the inspection pit glistened with wetness. Vincent twisted slightly, swinging the fading beam towards the rear to pick out glistening spots along the chassis and an area of blackness on the exhaust pipe where it curved into the silencer, still perceptibly giving off a faint fume from the hot metal. He rose and dusted his hands.

"Well?" snapped Lord Snailwood.

"The oil seal's g-gone on the fluid flywheel. There's a pretty serious leak. That's why she's losing so much power. Most of that smell isn't exhaust — it's oil from the leak being blown back on to the exhaust pipe."

"How long has this been going on, eh?"

"I don't know, sir. The leak's pretty serious. She wasn't pulling too badly when I started off this morning, but she hardly made the hill out of Wycombe on the way back. It might have g-gone all of a sudden. Or McGrigor might have known about it and just k-kept topping the oil up till he found a chance to replace the seal."

"Dammit, he ought to have done it at once."

"It's a fair size job, sir. Most owners would send the c-car back to Daimler to have it done."

"Rubbish. What do you think I employ a trained mechanic for? Find me something to kneel on, will you? I see I'll have to look into this myself. Give me that torch, Vincent."

"The battery's dead, sir. I'll fix up the . . ."

Vincent was interrupted by Lord Snailwood snatching the torch from his hand, pressing the switch several times to and fro, and finally glaring at the glass, behind which the bulb now glowed so faintly that the actual shape of the filament was discernible as a gold coil. Here was a dereliction whose mechanics the Earl could grasp. He switched off and tossed the torch on to the driving seat, then gave a curious little hop, as though he had been bitten from behind. It might have been the first step in a vehement dance of rage to which he could never give full expression.

"I tell you, Vincent," he said in a slow, hoarse voice, "this is the last straw. The utter last straw. Where is that secretary woman?

She shall type me a letter. I won't stand it any more. Zena filling my house with wogs and sheenies. Black spot all over Ophelia. McGrigor refusing to let me look at my own clock. They've no right to expect it. What do you say? They've no right, eh?"

"I daresay I c-could pick the lock of the tower and take a look at the c-clock without McGrigor."

"Pick the lock? Rubbish! I'll fetch my own key!"

"I thought McGrigor . . ."

"Course I have a key! I'll go and fetch it at once, hey? What do you say to that?"

"Better to wait till after the noon strike, sir. It'll have to be wound, then. It would save making two visits."

"Oh, very well, very well. Now look here, Vincent – what I want you to do is take a thorough look at this fly-piece thing and let me know how long it's been leaking. Then find that secretary woman and bring her to my study. She shall write me a letter dismissing McGrigor, and I'll show you where I keep the keys, eh? Then get hold of that new fellow – name's slipped my mind for the moment, you know, dash it, you saw him helping with the roses last afternoon – where was I?"

"You want me to show him how to wind the c-clock, sir."

"Course I do. You don't have to tell me things like that!"

"Yes, sir."

"Well, get on with it. Got to know about the car before I sack McGrigor, dash it. Got to be fair on the fellow. Caesar's aunt, hey? So I'm relying on you, Vincent."

"All right, sir."

"It's the last straw, I tell you!"

Lord Snailwood threw his arms above his head and brought them down in a gesture such as Moses might have made when smashing the Tables of the Law. He turned on his heel and stalked out, wheeling at once in the direction of the courtyard.

Left alone, Vincent drew a deep breath, held it and then blew the air up his face, shaking his head as he did so. He fetched an inspection lamp from the workbench which ran along the wall opposite the doors and opened the side of the bonnet to clip the leads to the terminals of the accumulator. He looked only briefly at the engine before fetching a tarpaulin and spreading it beside the car and in under the runningboard. He took off his jacket, lay down and wriggled in beneath the car with the lamp. After a minute he slithered out and with a tyre-lever prised up one of the timbers over the inspection pit, rolling it aside, then lay on his belly to peer into the cavity. Even in those black recesses gleams of gold and green showed how much fresh oil had dripped down over the recent weeks. Vincent rose and after another sigh, another blow of cooling air up his face, put things back as they had been and left.

Mrs Dubigny was standing in the courtyard, on almost the same spot where she had been the afternoon before, but now she had Sally in her arms. The child's face was buried in her mother's shoulder and Mrs Dubigny was patting her spine in a manner that was no doubt intended to be calming, but at the same time was vaguely chiding, chiding that there should be any need to be calmed. Seeing them Vincent squared his shoulders and walked steadfastly across the courtyard. Mrs Dubigny withdrew her gaze from the clock to smile at him.

"I say," he said. "That's my fault. I'm terribly sorry. I managed things wrong. Sally g-g-got a bit too friendly, and . . ."

"Oh, she's a terrible flirt, aren't you, darling?" said Mrs Dubigny. "You mustn't worry, Vincent. It's something that happens at this age. I expect I was just the same."

But as she caressed Sally's back she glanced at Vincent with a frown of warning and mouthed, inaudibly but clearly, "She misses her father."

"Of c-c-course," said Vincent.

The doors to right and left of the clock face opened with their premonitory groan.

"Do look, darling," said Mrs Dubigny. "It's going to strike. And honestly you're getting too heavy for me to carry for ever and ever."

She lowered Sally to the ground and turned her firmly to face the world. Sally glanced only briefly towards the clock, then stared at Vincent. She had stopped crying. Despite the tear-streaks her expression was now unreadable.

"You've got a dirty face," she said.

"Sally! Manners!" cooed Mrs Dubigny. "But I'm afraid it's true, Vincent. What on earth have you been up to? Oh, hush . . . it's starting!"

With its usual judder of effort the clock began its show. A calf slid out, then a milkmaid and a second calf. Then came Summer, buxom and beflowered, followed by the second milkmaid and her beasts. The bells jangled their intricate tune and the figures danced in the sunlight until Time emerged to break up their round and shoo them through the further door. A white pigeon wavered down to perch below the clock.

"Have you noticed how lovely the second milkmaid is?" said Mrs Dubigny. "Isn't it funny how that sort of thing happens? I don't suppose the man who painted them did it on purpose – I mean I expect he thought he was making them all as beautiful as he knew how, but his brush slipped or something and he made that one perfect by accident."

"I hadn't noticed," said Vincent. "I'll look next time."

"God must be a bit like that, don't you think? Doing his best, I mean, but really needing a fluke to get anyone as beautiful as Zena? The rest of us are the best he can actually do on purpose. Now, Sally, I want you to make friends with Mr Masham and then we'll go and find Nanny."

"I want to stay with you."

"I can't, darling. Didn't you hear his lordship? I've got to find Mr Masham and bring him to his lordship's study, and bring my pad, too, to write a letter. Have you any notion what that's all about, Vincent – he seemed in the most fearful bate?"

"He wants you to write a letter sacking McGrigor."

"Oh lor! But that'll be the end of the world, won't it?"

2

We are fortunate in having a contemporary account of what it felt like to be a guest at a Zena week-end "do". In the summer of 1936 Harold Nicolson had written to V. Sackville-West about precisely that experience: –

"My own dearest,
"For once I can say with sincerity that I wish you had been here – I

think even you would have enjoyed yourself, scrum and all. And that despite the garden being a perfect waste of all the opportunities one could wish for by way of natural vistas, nooks, surprises and changes of level. Considering how you and I have laboured to achieve our effects in the near-flat wilderness of Sissinghurst, what could we not have accomplished here? Snailwood is interested in nothing but roses, and has laid out bed after bed, pruned to their gawkiest – though I admit that in season the blooms do look splendid inside the house, arranged in great vases by the hundred. This is Snailwood's only achievement – he does it all with his own hands. *A propos*, one rather delicious detail: do you remember my showing you a photograph of the John portrait of Zena? It was in last year's Summer Exhibition and now hangs here, strident but striking, portraying Zena with a sheaf of blossoms. It turns out that she has never arranged a twig in all her life. The whole thing is, like so much of modern art, (or so it seems to me) nothing more or less than a great tease.

"Eighteen to luncheon on Saturday – fairly political, with most of what people are beginning to call 'the Snailwood gang', though Charles Archer is in America. I had been hoping to try and make up a coldness which arose mainly from my getting in a huff about what he wrote when I left the New Party. Foolish of me. I *am* a lightweight and there's no reason why Charles should not say so, but still I did mind. In addition there is an exceedingly cultured American banker called Hoffman who had read my Murrow book and told me a couple of things about M. I am glad not to have known at the time of writing; his exceedingly half-cultured wife, the type of American woman who helps one understand why their divorce rate is what it is; Ducky Boone and Lady F.; Snailwood's sister Ivy Masham, quite as appalling in the English fashion as Mrs Hoffman in the American; an impressively intelligent young publisher called Harry Quintain who won my heart at once by being able to quote three or four lines of *Out with a Gun*. Admittedly he might have mugged them up (flattering, in a different way, if he did) but how was he to know that of all your poems that is my favourite? He is Snailwood's nephew, favoured by Zena, I am told, to inherit; but there is another nephew, Ivy Masham's son, of whom I know nothing other than that he is a soldier with a stammer. It is said that Snailwood leans more to him. Quintain appears to me just such a young man as I might have been had I not joined the Diplomatic Service. He is looking for an opening in politics, and – finances permitting – will attempt to contest a seat in 1940. His politics are not mine, but would mine be if I were his age, now? The pull of what you might call intelligent Mosleyism – and having been so involved in M's tragic career I can truly assert that that was not always a contradiction in terms, but may well turn out to have been the great missed turning of the 'thirties . . . Why am I writing you all this? It does not interest you in the least, except in so far as it interests me. You would have loathed the Saturday luncheon. But I should have liked you to meet Quintain. I will tell you about Zena.

"She is an impossible creature, capricious, self-regarding, ridiculous, but quite clever enough to perceive that these vices can be presented as delightful foibles if well managed. That is her art – management. Of herself, of others. If she has never arranged a flower, she has been greatly successful with bunches of people. She is not your Nancy Astor type of hostess, bossy and incompetent (I remember an afternoon at Cliveden when five of us were forced to go boating in the rain in a skiff that would safely carry no more than three). Instead of bouncing about, stopping people doing things that they are enjoying and forcing them to do things they do not enjoy, Zena lies on piles of cushions, looking – but that is not her main secret – extremely beautiful. Her guests are attracted to her by natural force; and then somehow, without being bossed, they find themselves doing precisely what suits them. You, my darling, would not have needed to express a preference for dogs and privacy to find yourself walking alone with an affable young borzoi.

"I must not give the impression that Zena spends her whole day as an odalisque. It is simply her process of getting things started. After that she rushes about, taking part, teasing, coaxing, aware apparently of the exact moment when some process is about to diverge into tedium and . . . do I mean interposing herself? Yes, that is just what I mean. Imagine one of those old movies we used to take the boys to – do you remember? – the heroine bound to the railway line – the express approaching – the cowboy spurring to the rescue? Tedium is that express, Zena that heroine, and every man jack among her guests that cowboy. Where Nancy would get out her megaphone and order the express (vainly, in my experience) to go elsewhere, Zena contrives that it is we who, to all appearances by sheer luck, divert it. It is a pleasure to have realised this and study how she works. If only she would not fool around with politics. And I would guess that inside the family her machinations may not always achieve happy results.

"Let me tell you about Saturday night. Zena, typically, refers to the whole week-end as a 'do' and to the big party on Saturday evening as a 'superduperdo'. I grumbled to you in my last letter about having to find my trivial decorations because Zena had contrived to attract some princeling to her table. It all seemed drearily *démodé*, more appropriate to one of my father's ambassadorial unfestivities before the War. And when I stole into the office of Zena's secretary to crib the list of guests (for as you know I am not above doing the sort of preliminary mugging-up of which I accused young Quintain) my heart dropped to my boots. I foresaw an evening of no mere tedium, but of inexpressible embarrassment. It appeared a quite impossible 'mix', some fifty people, not one of whom had ideas or interests in common with more than three or four of the others.

"And yet it all 'went'. The formality, the decorations, the tiaras, the bows and curtseys to the princeling, somehow these were converted from trappings of outworn formality into – I don't know – fancy dress, I suppose. It is Zena's combination of gusto and irony that achieves this. The gusto may verge on hysteria, the irony become self-parody, but a balance is found. It is as if inwardly we all were saying that because we are unashamedly 'modern' we can amuse ourselves by cavorting in this antique mode. And then the 'mix'. Of course like does not necessarily mean *like*. Have we not two millennia of Christian thought to prove that no arrangement is so certain to induce sullenness than to place side by side the advocates of two heresies different in their own minds but indistinguishable in those of others? One sees this among the Communists also. Stalin will shake the hand of Rockefeller while his agents are hounding Trotsky round the world. This truth does not normally operate in the social sphere, but it does when Zena wills. Fifty or so incompatibles, we sat down to an eight-course dinner, and everybody as far as I could see 'got on'.

"I sat between . . . but I mustn't forget to tell you about Zena's dress. It was designed for her by Schiaparelli, who if she did not excel herself I think can be said to have exceeded herself. Enormous puffy sleeves, each containing more material than the whole of the rest of the frock; the back completely bared, as if for the attentions of a tattooist . . ."

And so forth. It is fair to say that Mr Nicolson seems to have struck a good week. By no means all of Zena's guests were so captivated.

3

"The fellow had become impossible," Lord Snailwood told the area surrounding him. As most of the Saturday luncheon guests were within that area, other conversation had become subdued. Lord Snailwood, having dictated and signed the letter dismissing McGrigor, seemed unable to let the matter rest. It was as though King Edward III had met the burghers haltered and trussed for hanging beneath the walls of Calais, had proclaimed to all in earshot his determination to show no mercy, but then because of some error in timing had been forced to reiterate his indignation for an hour on end until Queen Philippa should put in an appearance and melt his steely resolution. Sadly, the residents and regular visitors to Snailwood showed little wish to beg for McGrigor's reprieve, many past discomforts, major and minor, having been attributable to the fact that Lord Snailwood would let no one else service cars, repair overflowing cisterns, conjure with the central heating, or tamper with anything that could be classed as machinery anywhere on the estate.

"The war, of course," said Lord Snailwood. "He's still got pieces of shrapnel under his skull. Accounts for his temper. Used to be a first-class man in the old days. Came to my uncle to help with the railway. Walked over from Swindon, he'll tell you, and was going to walk back if he didn't get the job. Nothing to

McGrigor those days. Walked down from Inverness to Swindon in the first place, but found he couldn't take the racket in the boiler sheds. Been on the estate ever since, not counting the war years. He'll keep his cottage, of course, and draw his pension, but I wish I knew what had gone wrong with the fellow. Used to be such a first-class man. Do a repair, and it would be stronger than before it broke – last for years. And damned ingenious too. Told you about the rat trap in the generation room?"

Suddenly the Earl's voice ceased to be a grumble, took on an enthusiasm only otherwise heard when he spoke of his roses, as he repeated the many times told account of how McGrigor had used a large rat trap, triggered by a five-shilling alarm clock, to switch off all the lights in Snailwood every night at 10.05 sharp, so that the private generator could recharge the accumulators overnight. Though he did not say so, it was clear to his listeners that part of the charm of this device was the emphatic signal it gave to house guests and visitors that it was time to go to bed, or to take their leave. The gadget had ceased to be needed with the installation of mains electricity in 1931 but remained the prime evidence for McGrigor's ingenuity partly because it was simple enough for the Earl himself to grasp its principles, and partly because it had continued to function for years on end, unlike so many of McGrigor's later contrivances, whose very complexity and waywardness had involved them in ceaseless breakdowns and at the same time ensured that only McGrigor was able to understand their foibles. Lord Snailwood appeared to see no discrepancy between his present outrage at McGrigor's failure to maintain the Daimler and his own past fervour in defence of his employee's devices. The story about the rat trap concluded with a pause for emphasis, into which Sir Charles Archer moved with more firmness than tact.

"I tell you what, Snailwood," he said. "We're all in your position."

"What the devil do you mean, in my position? You've rooms in Albany. Nothing to go wrong there. I'd like to see how you'd make out if you had to depend on McGrigor to maintain the lifts."

"Oh, yes, superficially some of us are pretty comfortable, but I was talking about the country as a whole. Has it ever struck you that one of the ways in which we differ from the other civilised nations is that we had our Industrial Revolution two or three generations earlier than they did? The result is that we are now much further along that road. For a long time now the whole machinery of Britain has been wearing out, becoming less and less efficient, repairing itself with solutions that are little more than ingenious patchwork and last for shorter and shorter spans because of the decrepitude of the fabric at large."

"Indeed, indeed," interrupted Professor Blech. "And like this poor Scotsman you admitted splinters of foreign matter under your skulls during the war, so now you have this unpredictable temper."

Even so early in the week-end Sir Charles must have established that in the Professor he had found a conversationalist, or at least a monologist, as formidable as himself, but he was long used to dealing with heavy metal among Zena's guests. He accepted the point with a nod and a smile, but managed to make it seem that he was chiefly grateful for the chance to draw breath.

"And now we are proposing to embark on another great war," he said. "Have you asked yourselves who will be building our tanks, repairing our ships, manufacturing the aeroplanes to defend our skies against wave upon wave of dive-bombers? The answer, my friends, is that it will all depend on McGrigor!"

"Do you really think it will come to that, sir?" said a tall young man who had been sitting on the very edge of the sofa and gazing with great attention at whoever happened to be speaking. While it had been Lord Snailwood he had merely gazed. For Sir Charles he added a small repertoire of nods. Professor Blech's interruption had evoked a miraculously balanced expression of appreciation of the point and polite doubt of the good taste of a foreigner in making it. The young man's name was Flitwick-Johnson. He was a fairly regular guest at the Saturday luncheons, because he was a leader-writer on the *Sunday Clarion*, one of Sir John Dibbin's newspapers, and so it was often necessary for him to stay at Bullington in order that he should receive Sir John's intimate direction for tomorrow's clarion blast. He preferred to be called by the initials of his surname. Nobody knew his Christian name,

63

but according to Harry Quintain his wife was permitted, in moments of endearment, to refer to him by his hyphen.

Sir Charles, sitting because of his corset on a throne-like upright chair, began to speak with his usual emphasis on the pointlessness of the proposed conflict. Unlike Lord Snailwood he had the knack of appearing to speak to a single person, in this case Flitwick-Johnson, while commanding the attention of a wider circle. This included Lord Snailwood, who at the start of his own harangue had been in the process of taking the sherry decanter round but for the last ten minutes at least had stood holding it while his guests did their best not to display their empty glasses in too obtrusive a manner. Now Purser, who had finished satisfying the more complex needs of the cocktail-drinkers, came over and with a murmur of apology took the decanter. Lord Snailwood glared at him as if the momentum of sacking McGrigor might carry him on to dismiss his entire staff. Purser appeared not to notice.

At last Sir Charles made the mistake of asking a rhetorical question, immediately answered by Professor Blech, who having established this bridgehead proceeded to advance rapidly into Sir Charles's front along several main routes of thought, but concentrating on the manner in which Germany's own economic impetus, its downhill career, would inevitably carry it into war. The Professor's mode of speech, rapid and hushed, allowed members of the listening circle to withdraw from the engagement and start their own conversations.

Lady Dibbin, a small but broad woman whose masterful air and flattish, sallow face gave her a look of Napoleon in a white wig, had some months before attended a concert at which Mrs Blech's quartet had performed. She beckoned her husband over to the further sofa so that he could bear witness to the pleasure they had both had. Mrs Blech, recovered from her car sickness and now only naturally pale, treated these approaches with reserve, perhaps as a means of controlling her own chronic jumpiness, or perhaps because she had heard of Lady Dibbin's reputation for arranging charity concerts and was unwilling to begin to commit herself and her colleagues. Sir John, a fleshy, purring man, showed no impatience to be back in the political argument, though Sir Charles had now counter-attacked by conceding the inevitability of Germany fighting a war of some sort, but arguing that the natural enemy was Russia, and that British and French commitments to nations such as the Poles and Czechs should not be of a sort to prevent this happening.

Two of the Bullington visitors turned out to know one of the Snailwood guests, a cheerful tanned girl called Nancy Blaise, and the three of them began to recall the highlights of *Yes, My Darling Daughter*, which they had seen together at the St James's Theatre the previous week. Several other guests, though they had not apparently seen the play, found the recapitulation of its merits and defects more interesting than the political argument. Zena, lounging as usual on a pile of cushions on the floor, was by now telling Brigadier Trotman about her childhood – or rather about one of her childhoods, as the events and even the country seemed to vary from week to week. For Brigadier Trotman it was a castle in the south of Poland; he had admitted only a slight knowledge of Poland, the result of a four-day visit to the Baltic. The south, Zena assured him, was very different.

The size of the Great Hall, and the number of guests, meant that there were several other groups beyond the central ellipse whose vague foci were Sir Charles on his throne and Zena on her cushions. One of these consisted only of Harry and Mrs Dubigny, sitting on a chaise-longue between two of the windows, Mrs Dubigny doing most of the talking and Harry laughing a great deal in a rather curious fashion, throwing his head about and opening his mouth as if to emit the explosive guffaw which she had heard the previous afternoon in the courtyard, but in fact making almost no noise at all. She seemed to appreciate the display. Whatever she was telling him – some long anecdote of comic disaster, to judge by her grimaces of mock dismay – evidently stimulated her also. Though she remained pallid as ever the slight aura of tragedy that had hitherto hung round her as the survivor of the wreck of a marriage was gone, as was the apparent age difference between herself and Harry.

Vincent was in the group remotest from the centre. Its other members were Prince Yasif and Mrs Flitwick-Johnson. They had originally split off because Mrs Flitwick-Johnson wanted to look closely at the new Rex Whistler. She was a thin but soft-featured blonde who kept her large blue eyes a little more open than is usual. This and her small round mouth and receding chin gave her a look of innocence, but not the innocence of a child, rather that of some animal whose mode of life seems sinless because it has been fixed by the weird decrees of evolution. In Mrs Flitwick-Johnson's case, had she been that animal, the mouth and chin would have suggested an adaptation for the painless sucking of juices from a host-animal, and the large too-round eyes another adaptation for nocturnal hunting. Nevertheless she would definitely have been considered a beauty in most gatherings; the Prince clearly found her attractive; Vincent showed little of the unease he had on first meeting Mrs Dubigny. When they had studied the Whistler the Prince had deliberately led them further apart, and now he and Mrs Flitwick-Johnson were leaning against Zena's absurdly elongated piano, while Vincent faced them and took very little part in a conversation about which English painters the Prince should think of buying supposing he were to start a collection. Mrs Flitwick-Johnson showed a thorough grasp of the values involved, aesthetic and financial.

Over in the central group Sir Charles had countered Professor Blech's thrusts by opening hostilities on the home front.

"Mosley's muffed it," he was saying. "The moment he put his chaps into uniform he went off course. He's a brilliant man, but he's no notion of what our people will stand. That's the prime art of the politician, you know. If you haven't got it you're like a carpenter who has no feeling for timber, however sharp he may keep his tools. A chap like that will cut you out a plank and it will fit its space and look a treat – until you put a load on it. Mosley's still got a lot of the right ideas, but he's trying to work against the grain of England. In many ways he's a better man than Adolf, but England is not Germany. I have no doubt that this country will be ruled by a dictator in ten years' time – sooner, if we don't manage to keep out of fighting Germany – but it will never be Mosley we put in the driving seat."

"What about Churchill, sir?" said Flitwick-Johnson.

"A spent force, an empty man, a wasted life. No, none of the present crew – nor myself, in case that was what you were thinking. Just possibly I might fit a position analogous to that of

Doctor Goebbels. But whether the man comes from the right or the left . . ."

"Why must it be a man, Charles?" said Zena over her shoulder, without apparently interrupting her own close attention to Brigadier Trotman's account of a camel race near Bizerte. Sir Charles, unready for this thrust from a presumed ally, snorted.

"You have a knack of making serious questions frivolous and frivolous questions serious," he said. Zena, her eyes wholly on the Brigadier, answered with a lazy movement of her shoulder blade. Blech, regrouped, flooded forward into the breach, leaving Sir Charles silent, bolt upright on his throne; his right hand, which had been readied for some oratorical gesture, closed its fingers stiffly upon nothing.

A few minutes later Purser announced luncheon.

5

"There's masses of room for your bike in the Coach House," said Miss Quintain. "I expect you'd like to put it under cover on a day like this. Out through the arch, turn left, past the No Entry sign – that doesn't apply to you – and through the second pair of double doors. But if you'll let me show you the clock room first – I've only just time. I have a visitor coming and it's absolutely vital I should see him. Now."

Miss Quintain had a large iron key in her hand. She led the way beneath the arch of the clock tower, inserted it in a door in the right-hand wall and after a slight struggle to turn it tugged the door open. A narrow stone stair circled up into darkness.

"As I told you on the telephone the pigeons have been getting in for I don't know how long," she said.

"I've brought a load of plastic bags," said Mr Mason.

"Splendid."

"Very good stuff for starter. for compost heaps. Quite as good as anything you can buy commercial."

"I'll tell Mr Floyd. And then of course there was the fire . . . oh, dear! It's always far, far worse than one remembers."

Miss Quintain had stepped off the stair into a room that filled the whole square of the tower and rose another twenty feet to a plain stone vault pierced with a number of slots through which dangled ragged ends of rope. The room was quite well lit by the lancet windows in its north and south walls, and it was almost empty, apart from the hummocky mounds of bird-droppings and a jumble of ironware stacked along the right-hand wall – mostly round weights, called "cheeses", but also oddments of metal – a ploughshare, a huge rusted cogwheel, several flat-irons and other shapes less distinguishable beneath the pall of droppings. The dried-out body of a young starling lay on one of the heaps. In the far corner the floor seemed to have given way.

"Better not come any further just now," said Mr Mason. "Weights came down in the fire, I take it?"

"Yes – how did you know?"

"See where the ropes burned through. Else you'd have them hanging, like that one."

He pointed at the wall to the right of the window, where a loop of rope hung almost to the floor with the pendulum vertical beside it.

"That'll be the going train," he said. "What turns the hands. Someone's had the sense to take its weights off, but they wouldn't be so heavy. Ruddy great weights you'd need to turn the carousel. Should have been hung in a chute, for safety, case something like that happened."

"It was dreadful. They came clean through the floor and the arch below. There was a man standing underneath who got killed. I must have seen it happen, but I didn't realise. I had the arch repaired when we opened for visitors, but it didn't seem worth doing the floor."

"Least it smells dry."

"I think it smells awful."

"There's awful and awful. You don't need to stay no more, Miss Quintain, seeing how you're in a rush. I can look after myself if you'll just give me the key. I'm used to all this, you know. There's a lot of vicars, for instance, who've never been up their own towers – too old, or too scared. I can find my own way."

He spoke with gentle confidence. His was not a bedside manner but something of that order, designed to comfort and reassure and at the same time to emphasise his own especial competence in this field. Miss Quintain, hitherto immensely brisk, relaxed slightly.

"Oh well, if you really mean it," she said. "Would you like to come over to the kitchen at eleven for tea or coffee?"

"Thank you, but I've brought a flask."

"Lunch, then?"

"I usually cut my own sandwiches."

"I've got to see you some time. I did as you suggested and looked into the insurance, and you don't seem to be covered. You're not strictly a workman, and you're in an area excluded under the policy for visitors. But if you really don't mind signing an indemnity . . ."

"That's all right. I'm getting on. You might say there's not all that left of my life to be worth insuring."

"I'm very grateful. I've been in such a rush with this man coming that I haven't had time to get Mrs O'Rourke to type the thing out, but she'll have it ready by lunch. Really it would be best if you came then, as I'll be busy with visitors all afternoon. We have lunch in the old kitchen, twelve-thirty sharp. I'll send Jo-jo over to show you the way. She'll enjoy that."

"Thank you, then."

"You can bring your own sandwiches if you don't trust our food, but it's very good. Don't forget to lock the door when you go out."

Mr Mason grunted and watched Miss Quintain leave, then took a pair of galoshes from the Laker Airways bag he was carrying, put them on and began to move with six-inch paces around the floor, shuffling the muck aside to test the planking beneath. He kept well clear of the hole. After a while he left, went down the stairs, locked the lower door and crossed the courtyard to where his motor cycle and side-car stood. Leaning his weight against the handlebars he wheeled it round and under the arch, where he stopped to unload a shovel, brushes, a blue metal tool-case and a bundle of black plastic dustbin-liners. Then he pushed the bike out and round to the left. With its side-car it was a fair weight and it might have been easier to start the machine and ride it, but somehow this did not seem to suit Mr Mason's style. He did things his own way. His actions expressed a willed personality, long conformed to. The slow, forceful trundle of the bike gave an impression of certainty, almost of remorselessness, of aims it was useless for anyone to try and frustrate.

He wheeled the bike well into the Coach House, straightened and looked round. A two-year-old Marina Estate and a five-year-old Rover 2000 stood near the open doors, and by the closed ones a newish Landrover, a beat-up little 2Cv, and a small Fordson tractor hitched to a flat trailer loaded with drums of weed-killer. Sideways behind these three stood a much larger shape, swathed in dust sheets. Mr Mason walked through to the inner wall to inspect the workbench, trying the vice, lifting a file from its rack and testing it with his thumb, rapping a power socket with his knuckle. The process brought him close to the shrouded vehicle, and casually he lifted the dust sheet to expose the front of it. Above the radiator grill gleamed a series of parallel scooped hollows into which a child might lay her fingers, caressingly, to relish the warmth within. Mr Mason grunted, jutted his lower lip out, blew air up his face as if to cool himself after the effort of shoving the bike, and let the dust sheet fall.

At twelve-thirty Miss Quintain was waiting for him outside the kitchen door under the cloisters. The air was still, and soft with odours of baking for the visitors' afternoon teas in the Orangery, but her attitude seemed unusually tense as she stared out over the courtyard, glittering in sudden sunlight after yet another May downpour. At the sound of Mr Mason's footfalls she turned and came quite hurriedly to meet him, but it would have taken her eyes a while to adjust to the shadows of the cloisters. When they were a few paces apart she stopped abruptly and turned her head away.

"You oughtn't have . . ." he began.

"What did you do to Jo-jo?" she said in a low voice.

"The kid? I yelled at her to get out. Sorry about that. Didn't hear her coming, and there she was, right out in the middle of the floor. That's the upper floor I'm on about. I reckon the beams are sound, they'd have to be, to carry the weights, but I can't say for the planking and after what we'd been saying about the insurance I was scared . . ."

"*You* were scared! You seem to have frightened the living daylights out of Jo-jo."

"Sorry about that. Maybe she was jumpy before I yelled, coming up all that way in the dark. And the smell and all. Matter of fact, she gave me a bit of a start. For half a sec it was like one of those figures had begun walking around."

"Oh well, I expect that explains it. Usually she's tough as old boots, not afraid of heights or strangers. And you probably don't realise what a state you look – you'll need to clean up before you eat. I'll show you where."

"It's a dirty job."

"I suppose so."

*   *   *

When he came into the kitchen Mr Mason's face glowed with scrubbing, giving him an absurd look of the culprit schoolboy, though otherwise he showed no sign of guilt or bravado. Miss Quintain rattled off the names of the half-dozen women who were eating at one end of a large scrubbed deal table. The child Jo-jo, blonde and tanned, a tough and perky-looking little specimen wearing a red T-shirt, sat huddled against one of the women. Mr Mason seemed to take no notice of her stare.

"There," said the mother. "There's nothing wrong with the gentleman, and you're a silly little scaredy-cat."

"I shouldn't have yelled at her," said Mr Mason. "I was telling Miss Quintain, I don't know as that floor's safe."

"That's all right," said the mother brightly.

"I only said he . . ." complained the child – already, as if from habit, preparing defensive positions for the coming change of role from sinned-against to sinner.

"Personal remarks," said her mother.

Mr Mason sat down, and the child continued to stare at him as he opened the plastic box he had brought and took out sandwiches made with brown commercial bread, the filling too thin for one to be able to discern what it might be except by taste, and possibly not even then.

"*Do* try one of Mrs Floyd's rolls, Mr Mason," said another of the women, pushing a shallow basket across the table. "She bakes them for the Orangery and we get the ones that don't come up to standard, though I must say if *I* could bake bread as good as Mrs Floyd's rejects I'd think I had every right to be pleased with myself. Oh, come on, do! They're fresh, and there's *always* more than we can eat. And we brew our own cider, too, don't we, Jo-jo? (Jo-jo's a *great* help with the bottling.) Only we're not allowed to sell it. This is *quite* a good brew, though I say it myself. *Please* try, Mr Mason."

Reluctant but polite, Mr Mason accepted a wholemeal roll and half a glass of cider. When he tasted them he contrived to express his appreciation with no actual words and a minimum of facial change, but it could not be said he seemed in any way churlish; the reserve and stolidity were clearly part of his personality, a personality that implied considerable inner coherence. He ate slowly and replenished his glass with water, explaining that he was not used to drinking at midday. When he had finished he put back in his box the half-sandwich whose space in his stomach had been usurped by Mrs Floyd's roll.

Meanwhile he took very little part in the conversation, which was almost wholly to do with the running of Snailwood in a manner to extract for them all a reasonable living by means of a steady throughput of visitors. The roles of the women became clearer. Jo-jo's mother was Mrs Floyd, cook to the enterprise and also the head gardener's wife. Mr Floyd himself – a man with something of Mr Mason's stamp, but smaller, younger and with close-cropped dead-white hair – came in at one o'clock with his assistants, two young women, one on the lumpish side of buxom, the other dark and lanky. They settled further along the table and ate with almost angry hunger.

The woman who had spoken of the bread and the cider – and continued to speak with equal flow and enthusiasm of every other subject that emerged – was called Mrs O'Rourke and doubled as manageress of the Orangery and secretary to Miss Quintain. Two others were official guides. Mrs Robson was primarily a cleaner, married to the estate handyman, who was at this moment taking Miss Quintain's morning visitor back to the station. The two last performed a number of functions, such as issuing tickets at the garden gate and the front door and waiting in the Orangery. They all lived on the estate, either in what had once been the gardeners' cottages or in flats in the old servants' quarters on the upper floor of the main house. Some were married, but apart from Mr Floyd and the handyman the husbands had jobs unconcerned with Snailwood. No doubt there were various complex arrangements balancing rents against wages. The lunch in the kitchen on Open Days was a routine, a functional occasion rather than a gathering of kindred spirits, but the fact that all the talk concerned the efficient running of Snailwood, the maintenance of order in the face of the chaotic impulses of visitors, gave an impression of great single-mindedness.

Though Miss Quintain owned the house and estate, her attitude was in no way dictatorial and there was no obvious deference to her. The only exception to this came when the subject of that morning's visitor emerged briefly. Mrs O'Rourke brought the matter up, the unmitigated eagerness of her conversational style making it hard to tell whether this was a subject of special interest. But Mrs Floyd paused as she raised a cream and pastry gâteau to her lips, it being impossible to cope with so explosive a mouthful and at the same time listen attentively, though the others had all ceased talking. Miss Quintain answered with no especial brusqueness that the man had been quite sympathetic; perhaps she would have been more expansive if Mr Mason had not been there. In any case she immediately turned to him and asked how he was getting on in the clock room.

"Too soon to tell," he said. "I've hardly begun clearing the mess out. Then it'll be a matter of testing the main beams – you're going to have two tons, two and a half tons, bearing on them once I've hung the weights back on. There was the fire, of course, and then how long was the roof leaking, would you know?"

"Most of the war, I should think. They must have done a temporary repair, but Lord Snailwood was very ill for a long while, and by the time my stepfather took over the war had almost started. My mother managed to wheedle a grant out of the Ministry of Works in 1950 to do the main roof, and there was enough left over for the clock tower then."

"Let's say the temporary roofing lasted half that time, then. Five years before it began to leak, and a couple more before it was bad enough to notice . . . Your main beams should be sound still . . . if they're not, I don't know . . . it could turn out more than I can tackle alone . . . in any case half the carousel timbers is going to want replacing . . ."

"I know," exclaimed Mrs O'Rourke. "That's what you get in fairgrounds."

"Right. Just a big turntable to carry the figures round, only this one's got to be the biggest ever made. Thirty-two figures it carries, counting the little animals. Four for the seasons, eight for the dancers, sixteen little animals and four Father Times."

"Four Father Times!" said Mrs O'Rourke.

"Well, there'd have to be," said Mr Mason patiently. "I don't see how you could work it otherwise. You could have him coming out on an arm each time, I suppose, but not if he's got to follow the others on round. Much simpler gearing, you see, if there's four of him, only it does mean having this ruddy great turntable . . ."

"I say!" said Mrs O'Rourke. "I've just had a super thought! Perhaps we could get it in the *Guinness Book of Records* if it's really the biggest in the world!"

"That's the reason for the weights, you follow," said Mr Mason, uninterested in the possibilities of publicity. "I reckon you'd need getting on for half a ton to pull the carousel round alone. Then some middling ones to drive the figures, and another lot for the other set of figures above, and some for the quarter chimes, and one for the hours, not to mention the going train – that's what we call the part that drives the hands, the going train. Devil of a lot of winding every twenty-four hours."

"Oh dear," said Miss Quintain. "Every twenty-four hours? I shall have to think about that . . . Beryl, dear, did you remember to bring that document for Mr Mason to sign?"

Mrs O'Rourke jumped to her feet, miming guilt.

"Stupid female!" she said. "I've got it all beautifully typed but I've gone and left it in the office. I'll run and get it, shall I? Won't be a tick, honestly."

She picked up her plates and took them to the sink, but instead of leaving at once she became involved in a conversation with the stouter of the two assistant gardeners, who had taken her plates over at the same time. Miss Quintain watched her for a moment, sighed and shrugged. The other diners were rising, and Miss Quintain was piling her plates together when Mr Mason spoke.

"Excuse me asking," he said. "I hope you won't take it personal – it's only that Quintain's not that common a name, spelt the way you do, I mean."

"I've never heard of any others," said Miss Quintain. "It used to be with an O like everyone else, only my grandfather – my step-grandfather, really – decided to be different."

"I ran across a Major Quintain during the war. He spelt it your way."

"You didn't! Major Henry Quintain? Bucks Light Infantry?"

The change of tone was instantaneous and very marked. Explaining about the spelling of her name Miss Quintain had let a trace of amusement mingle with the brisk, sphere-controlling competence of her normal mien. Now her eyes opened wide and she stared at Mr Mason as if he were the bringer of miraculous news.

"He was 'I' Corps those days," he said. "Initial H. something, though. H.B. was it?"

"H.P. But it *must* have been Harry. Where was this? When?"

"In the desert. It wasn't the sort of place to have a name. Right at the end of March 1941."

"But that was when he disappeared! The thirtieth of March!"

"Right. We'd stopped belting along after the Eyeties and we'd just been sitting out in the desert three or four weeks south of Msus. We sort of knew Rommel was coming, but we didn't know when. Major Quintain came down to our unit because of us having a spare Lysander ready to go and went off on a recce flight. I suppose you know he didn't come back, and next morning we were legging it for Alexandria fast as we could run. That's the only time I ever saw him. I'm sorry. I expect I oughtn't have mentioned it. I didn't want to upset you."

"Oh no," said Miss Quintain. "It's a bit of a shock, but . . . anything about Harry, anything at all. Was he happy, Mr Mason?"

"Far as I could see, ma'am. I wasn't in the mess with him, being only an A/c One, but I heard him telling Mr Toller he was enjoying his war."

"Toller was the pilot?"

"Right. He didn't come back either. Far as I know they never found the Lysander."

"No. I longed to go and look for it as soon as the war was over – I must have been about sixteen – but my mother wouldn't let me. She'd made up her mind to stop thinking about him as soon as the telegram came. I remember her opening it in the morning room – Purser brought it in – it was almost the end of the holidays – I remember her reading it slowly and folding it up and her whole face seeming to close. All she said was, 'Well, that's that.' We'd been happy . . . less than two years, I suppose, before he had to go away for the war . . . I . . ."

Miss Quintain smiled suddenly and shook her head.

"Some other time," she said. "I've got the guide rota now. Try and remember anything you can, Mr Mason. Anything. He was only my stepfather. I changed my name to his as soon as I was twenty-one. My mother wouldn't let me before. He was rather important to me, you see."

6

". . . the imaginary landscapes of childhood, the Arabia of the
mind," gabbled Professor Blech, gesturing at the groves and fields
below the terraces as though they were that Empty Quarter.
Harry, walking beside him, glanced across the line of march to
catch Vincent's eye. The twitch at one corner of his mouth might
have been a gloss on the Professor's words or gesture, a calling-of-
attention to meanings unknown to the speaker. Vincent nodded,
serious. Neither the Professor nor Brigadier Trotman, walking
between the cousins, appeared to notice the exchange. The smoke
of their cigars hung above the roses in the still, post-prandial air.
There was half an hour before the croquet party could set off for
Bullington; the Professor, no doubt, would have been equally
happy to stay indoors and expatiate at ever greater length to the
Brigadier on the military aspects of the Palestine problem, as well
as any other aspects or problems that could in any way be annexed
to it; it had been Zena who had told the cousins to "show them the
way round the garden", as if it were possible for visitors to
become lost, or even be ambushed by bandit Buckinghamshire-
men, among Lord Snailwood's phalanxed roses.

"Far are the shades of Arabia," continued the Professor, "but
taking shades in the sense of ghosts they are very close to the
hearts of your ruling caste. Those languid gentlemen in the Foreign Office possess a *Selbstbildnis*, an inward image – as it might
be the opening sequences of a motion picture – showing them
their true selves – tanned, hawk-eyed, scrawny with travel, speaking impeccable Arabic, as they sit at a fire of camel dung in a circle
of Bedouin, accepted as brother of the desert, comrade of immemorial blood loyalties, et cetera, et cetera."

"Sandy Arbuthnot," said Harry.

"Knew the fellow he was based on, as a matter of fact," said the
Brigadier.

78

"Of course you did, of course you did," said Blech, almost crowing with delight. "Just as every old India hand knows the man on whom Kipling based his Strickland."

"You seem remarkably *au fait* with our less intellectual writers, Professor," said Harry. "Have you made a special study of our childish tastes?"

"To a certain extent I share them, Mr Quintain, but it is of course not merely a matter of taste that dictates your choice. Rather it is a celebration of images, the *lares et penates* of your national household, which unlike other nations you keep in a dark corner behind the chimney and do not take out for public worship, indeed as with us Jews and the *teraphim* which appear to have performed a somewhat similar function up to the time of King David, you will often deny that these gods exist or existed or were ever anything more than children's playthings. For other nations such symbols are embodied ideas – Jerusalem, the swastika, the flame on the tomb of *le Soldat Inconnu* – publicly perceived, even in certain cases deliberately invented to perform the function of worship-object . . ."

"Never cared for any of that," said the Brigadier. "At least we don't go making bloody fools of ourselves over some sort of intellectual fiddle-faddle."

"Undoubtedly your notorious distrust of ideation has tended to keep you out of trouble of certain sorts," said the Professor. "But has it not been at a cost? Does it not for instance strike you that before our young friends here are three years older they will be fighting a war of ideas in a world dominated by the opposing ideas of Communism and National Socialism and Fascism, and yet to guide you through this holocaust you have chosen a Prime Minister, and he himself has chosen a cabinet in which there is not one single man who, despite a certain share of intelligence, could be called a man of ideas – all jurists, administrators, technicians?"

They had reached by now the limit of the normal "stroll round the gardens". The nature of the whole site of Snailwood precluded more than a few variations on this circuit. The platform, part natural and part artificial, on which the house was built extended towards the river as a paved terrace. To the west of this, running along the slope of the hill, lay the three garden terraces, the outer two quite extensive and the middle one smaller but containing a belvedere dating from before the present house. The levels dropped by several feet between the terraces, and the far steeper slope from north to south meant that in order to achieve those levels retaining walls had had to be built. You went out with one such wall – ancient brick, about twelve feet high – on your right, and came back through the Lower Garden – a rather haphazard series of spaces and enclosures and one or two pools – with the second wall on your left, deep-buttressed and where the ground dipped to the Great Lawn almost thirty feet high.

The out and the return circuits were connected at a few points by almost ladder-like flights of steep stone steps running down the retaining wall, but a much grander marble stair at each end made it natural to walk the full round. The western stair, which the party had now reached, was flanked on its further side by several old holm oaks, whose sombre glittering leaves composed a screen and finish to the vista as effective and apparently impenetrable as a cliff. The strollers were half-way down – the Professor had in fact halted on the platform at that point as if to emphasise by inaction the superiority of the idea to the deed – when the leaves by the balustrade at the bottom of the stair began to heave and rustle as if a large animal were fighting free of them, or as if the ambush which Zena had feared were about to be sprung.

For a moment it seemed that the animal was the likelier explanation. Through the outer leaves a form emerged, roundish, grey, hindquarters rather than head, not any known specimen of British fauna but just possibly an escaper from Whipsnade. The illusion lasted a couple of seconds until the figure had fought clear of the branches, turned and straightened to become Sally's nurse, pink-faced, clutching her hat to her head, and additionally flustered to see four gentlemen advancing on her line abreast down the stair, giving her no chance to erase the impression of a maenad struggling from the clutches of an oak spirit.

"Something wrong?" called the Brigadier.

"Oh, please could one of the young gentlemen help?" said the nurse. "She's gone and got herself stuck up a tree."

"Long way up?" snapped the Brigadier.

"Out of *my* reach. If only . . ."

"Fort Two," murmured Vincent to Harry, running back up the steps.

"Ladder," said the Brigadier, like a magician commanding an object to appear out of thin air. Perhaps in his own mind he was telling one of the cousins to fetch one, but Harry was already half-way up the stair and Vincent had reached the top, where he pulled a branch aside and disappeared as neatly as a ghost walking through a panelled wall. A moment later Harry did the same trick. Deprived of suitable subordinates the Brigadier strode up the steps two at a time and made off along the terrace.

Professor Blech smiled at the nurse, who seemed on the verge of weeping, more likely with irritation than worry or fear. He too climbed the steps and pulled the branch aside, holding it for her as if it had been a door.

"*That's* where the dratted thing is," she sniffed as she went through.

Inside the wall of leaves was a cavernous space raftered with long dark branches like the necks of dragons. Some yards down the steep slope Vincent and Harry were standing, looking up into the next tree. The child was almost on a level with Blech and the nurse. She was lying on her chest with arms and legs clenched round a horizontal branch and her face pressed against the bark. Though her body might have been in a coma with the terror of height, her eyes were fixed on the cousins, staring as if they had been predators rather than rescuers.

"She can be ever so wilful," said the nurse. "I did tell her she wasn't to."

Blech remained silent. No doubt he had opinions on the role of will in the development of the psyche, and on acrophobia, and the instinct to climb trees in despite of it, but he seemed aware that he was now in the sphere of action, rather than what he chose to call ideation.

"It's your fort, dash it," said Harry.

Vincent laughed and walked to the trunk of the tree, still further in from the steps. The branch to which the girl was clinging rose from the main boll only just above the ground, running out at an angle until it was ten or twelve feet high, and then flattening out for a while before arching down to spread its weight of leaves into the sunlight. Along this inner length there was only one large bifurcation, and no other branches ran near it.

Vincent leaned against the trunk to remove his shoes, then climbed in stockinged feet on to the branch, stood, steadied himself and walked up the slope with small and careful steps, arms spread for balance. As he moved further from the centre the branch swayed with his weight, rustling its lowest leaves against the marble of the balustrade. Sally whimpered, craning past her shoulder to watch him come. Once on the level he moved faster, reaching her in four or five ballet-like steps. He steadied himself, bent his knees, laid his palms on the branch, took his weight on his arms and slid his legs clear so that he could sit beside her.

"Come on, Sally," he said softly. "I told you not to try it without me to help, but you're a brave girl to get so far."

Gently he put his hands round her rib-cage to lift her but she tightened her arms round the branch and screwed her eyes shut.

"C-come on," he said. "Show us how brave you are. Up with you."

He had to reach down and pull her left arm free, much as her mother had done to loosen her embrace the previous afternoon. There was a slight struggle before he dragged her up and set her, rigid as a doll, on his lap.

"There you are, you see," he said. "Now do you want to sit on the lookout seat like I did, or would you rather c-climb straight down?"

"Down," she whispered.

Vincent looked back along the branch and shrugged.

"Easier if I go on out," he said, speaking downward to Harry. "If you went up on the bank there, ready to take her . . ."

"Right-o."

"Put your arms round my neck, Sally, and don't wriggle."

Vincent had to move her arms, one by one, to the position he wanted. Then on his palms and the seat of his trousers he worked his way sidelong to the start of the downward slope, where he swivelled and half-climbed, half-slithered down the limb, now dividing into a rough fan of branchlets. His weight had the leverage to depress the whole branch so that a ragged slot appeared in the wall of leaves, letting in brightness. A little above his head a section of another sideways-running branch was worn smooth on its upper surface, the last trace of Fort Two, whose master used to sit there, peering unseen across the silent gardens.

Harry reached up. The child looked at him with her usual half-sullen stare but then, before Vincent had quite settled himself to cope with the problems of transferring her weight out and down, she loosed her hold, wriggled, slid, and would have fallen if he had not grabbed her upper arm. She continued to wriggle, more violently now.

"Catch, then," said Vincent, heaving her outwards and letting go.

She dropped the eighteen inches into Harry's arms and the moment he lowered her to his chest she buried her head in his shoulder and clung to him with her customary ferocity of embrace. Harry laughed and strummed the fingers of his free hand along her spine. Vincent sat looking at them, unsmiling, then swung himself to the ground and went over to collect his shoes. All five moved out into the sunlight.

"Thank you ever so much," said the nurse. "Now let go of the gentleman, Sally. We've got to go and find your mummy, haven't we? Mrs Dubigny's going to be ever so busy later, seeing to everything for the party, so she said she'll have Sally now, 'stead of after tea which is her usual time. Now, Sally, you mustn't be a naughty girl or Mummy won't be pleased."

She spoke in exactly the same brisk, fretful tone to both child and adults, as if not expecting to be understood or obeyed by either. Sally's response was to hide her face in Harry's shoulder.

"Tell you what," said Harry. "I'm not going over to Bullington. I was proposing to take the Jowett out for a spin and see what Vince has done to her. I could take Mrs Dubigny and Sally along. Would you like that, Sally? You can sit in the dicky and let the wind blow your hair about."

At last Sally straightened up. Her nod was firm, almost commanding.

"Right you are," said Harry. "Come along, Nanny – we mustn't waste any of Mrs Dubigny's precious time. Sorry to leave you, Professor – I could listen to you till Doomsday. Have fun,

Vince. Knock spots off old Dibs for me. If I meet the Brig I'll send him round the other way."

Hefting Sally on to his hip he marched off along the terrace with the nurse at his side, the pace he set making her walk seem more flustered than ever. Professor Blech, blinking in the sunlight, smiled at Vincent.

"A peculiarly English episode," he said. "I wonder whether it would have been improved had the creature to be rescued been perhaps a cat . . . You no doubt noticed the appropriateness of the Brigadier imposing a military solution wholly inappropriate to the circumstances?"

"He c-c-couldn't have known, sir."

"Exactly. It is often supposed that intellectuality by its search for the unifying theory imposes a strait jacket upon action, whereas the pragmatic approach allows flexibility uninhibited by preconceived notions. But such pragmatism is the slave of history. Whatever worked last time will always be tried again and not be discarded until it has been proved to work no longer. This is the rationale of your notorious muddling through – to suffer a series of defeats at the hands of enemies who during the period of peace have made innovations based more or less on theoretical concepts – for it is the function of theory, after all, to provide as it were a map of the future, or in the case of more sophisticated theorisms a series of maps of possible futures, interlocking, cognisant of the moral, political, cultural dimensions, et cetera, et cetera of what may seem on the surface purely military problems – you follow me?"

The Professor, aware by now that he stood in no danger of Vincent attempting to take control of the conversation, had altered his style sufficiently to invite occasional comments. He was not a rapid walker. Had he been going round the garden alone (and therefore presumably in silence) he would still surely have moved with shuffling irregular steps. He had the gait of a man who in his own home is seldom out of bedroom slippers. Conversation slowed him down still further. Every few paces he would pause, perhaps to devote all his energies to the choice of a word or the flow of a gesture, or else, as now, to turn and peer at Vincent for response.

"At least it's worked so far, sir."

"It has *usually* worked so far thanks to factors other than military – economic and to a lesser extent cultural. But the economy of Britain is like an old house, impressive from a distance, but full of intimate rots and crumblings, affecting the lives of those who inhabit it – the culture, you follow me – in ways that they do not perceive or if perceived they do not understand. It will be too late when they perceive what is happening, has happened, to them, for such a building though its decay may be imperceptibly slow, collapses when its hour comes with awful suddenness, so that win or lose there will be no rebuilding *this* world when you have done your fighting. It will have passed away. Even the lessons that you have learnt, and learnt so late, by your mistakes, will be valueless. Meanwhile . . ."

They moved on, with many pauses, through the Lower Garden, a more gently sloping area set with a number of mature specimen trees and underplanted in Victorian times with rhododendrons, now mostly through their flowering and in any case often having reverted to the *ponticum* stock on which they had been grafted. There was some variation on this pattern, but on the whole one passed through a series of mown glades of varying size, aware of the increasing height of the wall on one's left, though it was often hidden, and rather less aware of the Thames beyond the meadows on one's right. Even on this bright June afternoon the hummocky splodges of dark green rhododendrons seemed to cast thunder-shadows beneath the trees.

This did not perceptibly oppress the Professor. He began to expound the discrepancies between the purely military theory of the Wehrmacht and the social, economic and cultural theories of National Socialism and his arguments against the widely held belief that when war came the military thinkers would automatically get the upper hand. Vincent paced beside him, responding when invited to at only just sufficient length to show that he had understood what was being said, but without giving any definite signs of impatience or boredom. Gradually they approached the Great Lawn. It was necessary to get at least this far because Lord Snailwood, hearing of the expedition, had insisted with unpredictable vehemence that the Professor should see and appreciate the Rose Wall. Just before reaching it — indeed the lawn could already be glimpsed beneath the gawky branches of a belt of ornamental cherries, its pale width shimmering in the sun — they came to a small glade, almost an enclosure, close beneath the wall, up which a steep flight of narrow steps ran slantwise to the terraces. The cherries surrounded the place, several varieties but none having any visual interest except during their brief frenzy of blossoming, which this was not. In the centre of the glade stood a low rectangular plinth of stone, possibly from its acanthus pattern at the corners a remnant of the eighteenth century, having then supported some statue — recumbent, to judge by its shape — but now no more than a slab. Somehow its emptiness gave an extra sense of vacancy to the space. If there had been no slab the glade would have seemed simply a glade with nothing in it. The empty stone signalled the void, gave it a mysterious meaningfulness, as if it had been something willed.

The Professor appeared not to notice the effect, but perhaps the habit of observation was stronger in him than he let show. As they passed the stone Vincent reached out his left hand and touched it with his fingertips in an apparently casual gesture. The Professor made one of his frequent halts but accompanied it by actually stopping the flow of discourse.

"What is the stone?" he said.

"'Fraid I don't know. It's always been there."

"You touch it for luck?"

"Well . . . I suppose so . . . oh, not really. It was part of a g-game Harry and I used to play round the g-gardens."

"Games have great importance to you?"

"I've been lucky. I was born with an eye for a ball, so I've had plenty of fun. But when people k-keep telling you they're first-rate training for life . . ."

"You mean you have not found it so?"

"Well . . . I don't know. Not directly. But what you've been talking about — theories and all that . . . it seems to me the only thing that makes sense is to treat it all as a sort of g-game. Nobody tells you the rules. You find them out by playing. And anyway they k-keep changing."

"And what is the object of this game?"

"There isn't one, as far as I can make out – apart from becoming a reasonably c-competent player."

"And when your regiment is posted to Palestine and you find yourself patrolling between the villages of armed Jews and the villages of armed Arabs, you will be the referee, I take it, of a rather dangerous game?"

"Something like that. The important thing is we've just got to do the best we can. Provided everyone realises that . . ."

Vincent stopped, because something seemed to be happening to the Professor. His nods and blinks increased in rapidity and violence, as if he was on the verge of a fit. If so, it was a fit of words. It would be hard to say why a man of his experience should choose to expend so much emotional and intellectual energy on a companion so unrewarding. Very likely his excitement was not concerned with Vincent, but was a response to earlier stimuli – the discovery that the political clout of the Snailwood Gang was less than their pretensions, or some marital contretemps between himself and the enigmatic Mrs Blech, or even, as is sometimes the case with such verbal self-asserters, a semi-automatic pressure release like that which in nature causes a geyser to spout its jet of mud and steam with exact regularity, in which case the Professor was due to let off a great gush of verbiage somewhere around two-thirty p.m. that Saturday, and merely happened when he did so to be talking to Vincent in the glade that contained the empty stone.

"The best you can, the best you can," he said, varying the note of distaste and scorn. "What is this *best*? An irrelevance because what you will be refereeing will not be a game, because even in the mind of the most illiterate villager the conflict is a conflict of ideas, while your *best* has nothing to do with ideas, but is the best of the games player, the graceful shot, the daring tactic, the sporting gesture, all purposeless apart from the game, the true definition of a game, *pace* Herr Wittgenstein, being the negative one of an activity unconcerned with the function of ideation. Ideation is as natural to man as breathing. Ideas are what he lives and dies by and for. In Palestine you are attempting to interpose yourselves in a conflict between two fanaticisms, but you are acting and speaking and writing as though these fanaticisms were the aberration and your impartiality were the civilised norm. But fanaticism, my young and peculiarly unknowable friend, is the norm whereas the so-called virtues of civilisation, the virtues of the games player, calm, phlegm, tolerance, fairness, respect for the customs and prejudices of other players, et cetera et cetera – these are the aberration. Civilisation, intellectual progress and so on and so forth lead not as you suppose towards your ideals but away from them, towards that fanaticism which feeds on the idea. I am myself a fanatic, because I am a Zionist, and Zionism is an idea. It is not part of the rules of any game, nor is the Arabism which opposes it. But you, you referees, ignore both Zionism and Arabism and propose to go and see fair play in a game you call the Palestine Question, promising yourselves that all will be well provided the players remember that you are doing the best you can. Again I cry, what *best*? How is this measured? *Doing* I understand. Doing is action. Action on the throne of ideation, the rationale of anarchy, because each action creates fresh circumstances in which action must again take place, action for this *best*, but never with any scale of theory against which to measure better or worse, and again you must act and again fresh circumstances surround you and again you act, always for what you tell yourself is the best, and never perceiving that in your trampling round and round you have worn a hollow in the ground and the hollow has become a pit and the pit has become a darkness, a darkness of your own making but one in which even you cannot perceive that what you are now doing for the sake of this *best* has become monstrous. At last, too late, a light shines into the pit, and you see. And then you hide your face and run away. This is how your whole Empire will end, in Palestine, in India, in Africa, even in Ireland – first you will breed your monsters, your Minotaurs of the labyrinth whose windings are the track of your attempts to follow the illusory thread of the best. Then you will run away."

The geyser had spent its force. The Professor stood, staring at Vincent from beneath his fluttering eyelids, as if to see whether the jet of words had managed to dislodge one grain or pebble from his stony façade. Vincent smiled.

" 'Fraid you're right, sir," he said.

"Ah."

"I mean I shall have to run away . . ."

He indicated his wristwatch.

". . . They're just due off for Bullington and I'm driving one of the c-cars. Sorry to leave you, sir. It's been very interesting to hear your point of view. Look, the Rose Wall is just through there, sir, and you'll be able to tell my uncle you've seen it. It really is worth a visit, this time of year."

"Remember, action is meaningless without the substratum of the idea."

"I didn't have to think to g-get Sally out of the tree."

"But she still has her terror of heights."

2

The process of loading the cars disturbed the white pigeons. They circled the courtyard, waiting to have their kingdom to themselves. There was a wood pigeon among them.

"Stranger in your midst," said Prince Yasif.

"Smollett will get him with an air rifle next week if he doesn't push off," said Vincent. "He goes through the nest-boxes after they've fledged, too, and knocks off any which don't come up to scratch."

"So that's how you keep them so jolly white."

Vincent answered by gunning the motor of the AC, quite mildly, but the raucous little silencer made the whole courtyard echo. As if taking advantage of the noise the Prince leant closer and said in a low voice, "I'm afraid your aunt is offended with me."

"Zena? Why should she be?"

"Because I refuse to play her game. I refuse to stay here and talk with men who are my enemies as though our quarrel could be settled as if it were a business deal. You know, Masham, quite suddenly, without telling you, a lot of people are going to stop playing your game. What will you do then?"

"You've more in c-common with old Blech than you think. He was saying almost the same thing to me only ten minutes ago."

"Yes, of course. Enemies have their enmity in common. How fast will this bus go?"

The Prince's changes of role were extremely abrupt. Evidently he was still uncertain what part he was expected to play in the Snailwood comedy, and whether he wanted to oblige. Vincent made the engine snarl again.

"Wind her up to eighty," he said. "That's not really her strong suit. She c-corners like an angel, and she's an absolute dream of a g-gear-box. Like to see? Tell you what, we'll let the Sunbeam g-go and then we'll g-give them the fright of their lives, passing them on the drive. Right?"

The Sunbeam was already moving sedately towards the arch. Vincent followed at the same pace and drove gently round the level sweep of drive behind the house. Then, at the first steep bend, just as the Sunbeam was disappearing into the trees, he double-declutched, roared the AC up the short straight, whipped round the next bend and accelerated out with rear wheels slithering wide and the gravel of the drive battering into the banked rhodo-dendrons. Immediately ahead of them, like a wall across the road, loomed the back of the Sunbeam. Vincent blared his horn. Still in low gear and now almost at peak revs the AC rushed at the inadequate gap. Smollett (younger than McGrigor and always more tolerant of "the young gentlemen", in fact often something of an ally in their boyhood campaigns) swung the bigger car tight against the inadequate verge. The AC slipped through. Vincent raised a hand in thanks, took the next bend just slowly enough not to pepper the Sunbeam with spurted pebbles, but then whirled away up the hill. Prince Yasif laughed. Vincent nodded, unsmiling.

"Wish I'd had old Blech with me," he said.

"Why? Oh, I see . . . You know, I might have fun with one of these in the desert. I could hunt oryx from it."

"You'd need a special air filter. I don't think she'd like the sand."

"You shall come and talk to the makers for me."

"Right-o."

As Vincent slowed at the lodge gates a car showed up in the mirror McGrigor had put there to allow one to turn into the road with something like safety. He stopped and waited as the Jowett swung into the splay of the drive and halted beside him. Mrs

Dubigny was in the passenger seat, laughing as she held a wide hat, quite unsuitable for an open car, down on to her head. Sally was in the dicky, laughing too, her eyes weeping with the rush of wind and her knuckles white where she clutched at the rib of the folded canvas roof.

"Better?" said Vincent.

"You're a magician, Vince. Hey presto – new car! Zena gone yet?"

"Just coming up the drive."

"That's all right. I promised to get Joan back before she left. Now come on, miss – you're going to steer us down the drive, aren't you?"

Harry turned round to lift Sally on to his lap. Mrs Dubigny, still laughing, waved as Vincent turned into the lane and whipped away.

"Your cousin seems to have hit it off with the secretary bird," said the Prince. "Or are they old friends?"

"Never met before yesterday."

"These quick courtships!"

"We aren't all like that."

"I say, Masham, I think I'd like your advice. You remember I was talking before luncheon to Mrs Flitwick-Johnson about collecting British artists?"

"I'm the last person. I don't know a thing about art."

"It's not the pictures, my dear chap. It's about an acceptable way of paying somebody who is not a professional for advice."

"I suppose it depends who."

"Mrs Flitwick-Johnson. She appears to be very up in the subject, wouldn't you say?"

"She g-gave that impression. She won't say no, you know. Harry tells me the F-Js are probably pretty strapped – Dibbin's famously mean with his staff."

The Prince assimilated this news with a smile and several little nods.

"In that case a commission . . ." he said. "Ten per cent, would you think? Fifteen?"

"Ten sounds masses. I bet Harry'd be able to find out. Shall I ask him?"

"Please. And then I can pay you the same when you help me buy my car."

"Oh, that's all right. I'm not short. Give you a hand any time."

"And I the same," said the Prince.

He settled back into his seat and sat, smiling quietly to himself, while Vincent spun along the lane, on to the main road, and down the hill to Marlow Bridge.

3

"Medium mallets on the Near Lawn, Taylor," said Sir John. "Mediums for the tennis court, too, but take a couple of the lights down in case the ladies would prefer them."

"Very good, Sir John."

The chauffeur — immensely smart, in fact turned out with something of the unreal perfection of a dressage horse — actually saluted as he snapped his black-booted heels together, but slipped away without any obtrusive military stamping.

"Have you played this game before, your highness?" said Sir John.

"I am looking forward to learning."

"Dolly shall teach you. We'll put you with the handicappers."

"The handicappers?" asked the Prince with a slight edge to his affability, no doubt through long experience in the need to cope with the unthinking affronts which English society almost ceaselessly offered to someone in his position. Sir John's eye gleamed.

"The tennis lawn is the handicap," he explained. "Some would call it a sporting surface."

"It's a beautiful lawn by anyone else's standards," said Mrs Flitwick-Johnson. "And it's much more fun than the other one. All you do there is watch the experts taking two-hour turns."

Sir John smiled. Criticism at this level was permitted, at least from Mrs Flitwick-Johnson. She did not in any case give the impression that she would hesitate to make her opinions known.

"Zena and Donkin can be the other pair on the tennis court," said Sir John. "Now on the Near Lawn we might get an even match if Masham and F-J make a pair. F-J plays at plus three and

Masham I should think about plus seven, so we need someone around plus twelve to play with me . . ."

His voice remained dry, almost toneless, as he surveyed the half-dozen contenders for that awkward honour but the faint, almost nacreous light in his eyes suggested his much gossiped of relish in the exercise of power.

"Miss Blaise," he decided.

She nodded, perfectly self-possessed. Though only in her early twenties there was something about her boyish, outdoor air that made one feel she really belonged in the previous decade.

"When I told you this morning I played I was only talking about vicarage lawns," she said, "I've no idea what my handicap is."

"Twelve," said Sir John. "Ten each side, and no need to mess around with bisques."

"Oh, I see. I'm *your* handicap."

"Exactly."

Sir John nodded to the others, the sultan dismissing the un-chosen, and led the way, at first down the endless-seeming vista of sharp-clipped yew hedges that stretched in front of the house, but then through an opening on to the croquet lawn. The chauffeur was already there, stacking four mallets tentwise, like piled rifles; a gardener in plimsolls was pulling a lightweight roller clear of the playing surface; under the shade of a striped canvas structure, suggestive by its shape and colour of the pavilion in which a knight might have prepared for the jousting barriers, a parlour-maid and a footman were laying out teacups, plates of small sandwiches and biscuits, as well as glasses, jugs of soft drinks, and champagne in Sheffield plate ice-buckets. A crescent of folding chairs flanked the pavilion. Despite the greater sportingness – and hence, at least for the uninitiated, excitement – of the tennis court, guests were expected to watch the solemn, chess-like manoeuvres on the Near Lawn. Sir John, after all, regularly took time off from sacking his journalists, hectoring the governments of the world through his newspapers, and pursuing public and private vendet-tas against his numerous enemies in order to compete for the Coronation Cup, twice reaching the semi-final round. And if he was not, by those standards, quite best in the country his lawn almost certainly was – mown daily to a millimetre of fine grass, rolled to a perfect level, lying between its yew hedges and ornamented only by a pair of stone eagles on either side of a flight of steps that led nowhere – giving, in fact, an impression of blankness so virgin that it might have been some kind of supernatural canvas waiting for the fierce, creative brand of the world-artist.

It would be hard to say whether Sir John's pairing-off of Prince Yasif with Mrs Flitwick-Johnson had been a deliberate piece of mischief, though he would have needed considerable intuitive powers to have spotted that anything was afoot. But in the case of Vincent and Flitwick-Johnson it is quite likely that he was interested in something more than a balanced partnership of two contrasting styles. The contrast was there. Flitwick-Johnson was a very fair player, having modelled his game on his master's, cautious, defensive, highly tactical; if a ball or hoop was within what he regarded as his range he would almost certainly bring the shot off, but beyond that point he would not attempt it if any other line of play offered. Given the opening he could build his turn into a series of safe shots, thought out several moves ahead and leaving the next player very little to go for.

Vincent, on the other hand, was prepared to try anything, often regardless of the consequences either of success or failure. He took the game seriously in the sense of using all his considerable flair for ball games in the striking of each shot, but not in the sense of thinking it worth spending much intellectual energy calculating moves. Rule 40 (b) of the Laws of Croquet reads: "*Assistance to Partner*. A player may not only advise but may assist his partner in the making of a stroke in the sense that he may set the balls for a croquet stroke and indicate the direction in which the mallet should be swung." Flitwick-Johnson showed himself as prepared to render such advice and assistance as Vincent was unwilling to take it.

The laws contained a further cause of friction. At the beginning of a turn either ball of a partnership may be played, but only by the player to whom it belongs. Often it is obvious where the advantage lies, but more so to a player of Flitwick-Johnson's temperament than one of Vincent's. After a while Flitwick-Johnson gave up, and allowed a system to develop whereby he and Vincent simply took turns to play, unless the advantage in not doing so was too obvious to be ignored.

Naturally Sir John took note of this. The afternoon seemed to have arranged itself totally to his satisfaction: fine weather; obsequious guests to watch him play; a pretty partner to nurse round the hoops; opponents good enough to give him a game and enough at odds with each other to give him tactical leverage to exploit and a growing antipathy to observe. That the indirect frustrations and humiliations of his employee were perhaps a particular relish might be deduced from the way Sir John led the applause when Vincent, after briefly lining up a shot two-thirds of the length of the court, paused, concentrated, swung and brought it off. It must indeed have been galling for Flitwick-Johnson that it was not he, the dedicated worshipper at the shrine, achieving these miracles, but a chance-come non-believer, there for an afternoon's pastime, who would soon go, taking his miracles with him. Still, anyone employed in journalism by a magnate such as Sir John must be hardened to galls.

This was shown about half-way through the afternoon. For some time Sir John had concentrated on helping Miss Blaise through the hoops, neglecting his own progress; now thanks to a miscalculation on Flitwick-Johnson's part the chance came for him to catch up. Flitwick-Johnson watched him run a couple of hoops and walked over to Vincent.

"He's on for a good while now," he said. "Something I wanted to ask you."

At once he began to move away towards the eagle-guarded steps, well out of earshot of the guests round the pavilion. Vincent, visibly with slight reluctance, followed him.

"Something you can tell me," said Flitwick-Johnson, frowning his heavy brows into a line. "This chap who calls himself Prince Yasif – he's your chum, I gather?"

"Yes," said Vincent.

"What do you know about Sorah – the place, I mean. Not the person."

"Oh . . . precious little. No idea where it was till Sir Charles told me."

"Archer? When did he say this?"

"This morning."

"Did he tell you anything else?"

"A bit about trade. A tax on pilgrims, and the Yanks have started looking for oil."

"Slaves?"

"Not much of that now."

"A market for child slaves from Persia?"

"He t-t-told me that. Then he said he was t-teasing."

Vincent showed his normal reluctance to discuss such subjects, perhaps slightly modified by a feeling that the domestic economy of Sorah was safer ground than the proclivities of the Prince himself, or the finances of the Flitwick-Johnson menage and the commission a picture collector should be expected to pay for the advice of a friendly amateur.

"Very strange," said Flitwick-Johnson, tapping his mallet gently against the pedestal of an eagle. "The problem is as follows. Archer passed much the same information to Dibs at luncheon. Dibs suggested to me on the way back that I might do a piece on this trade, which would fit in very well with the *Courier* line on the Near East – you are aware that we support Zionism, and so are willing to publicise evidence that the Arab states are not suitable allies for a civilised nation. The question is the reliability of the evidence. Is Sir Charles trying to use us? We don't like that. His interest in Zionism is somewhat different from ours. He is obsessed by the chimera of Britain's need to avoid a war with Germany. I call it a chimera because such a war is in any case unthinkable, but Archer regards it as thinkable and therefore is determined to make it impracticable. The alienation of the oil-producing states by support of Zionism is not in Archer's mind too high a price to pay, provided it makes war with Germany impracticable. The same motive, you see, would explain Archer's attempting to plant libellous material in the *Courier*. Better, from his point of view, if it's untrue. You follow me?"

"Yes. But why would he bother to tell me?"

"Exactly. That suggests a quite different set of motives. Dibs has told me one or two things about Archer – I'd better not pass them on in detail – which suggest that Archer's interest in this alleged trade in children is not exactly . . . shall we say objective?"

"I thought your paper supported him."

Flitwick-Johnson raised his eyebrows, as though Vincent had brought in something quite irrelevant to the conversation.

"Of course, of course," he said. "But Dibs likes to keep tabs on anyone whom he has dealings with."

"That's rather a rummy way to treat one's friends."

"Friends? Oh, I see what you mean. Especially his friends, in Dibs's case. He has a safe of files in his office, nothing to do with the paper's. Photographs, too. I understand he bailed Archer out of some problem a few years back, something to do with a house in Paris. So it didn't get into the English papers, you know. I must say Archer has been extremely careful. I mean, this was the first I'd heard of it, and I hear most things. I'd simply assumed, like everyone else, that Archer's tastes were fairly straightforward, and your aunt was his mistress, and so on."

Flitwick-Johnson's dull eyes could almost have been said to sparkle as he spoke, no doubt indicating the journalist's special fascination with news he is not going to be allowed to publish. Vincent turned abruptly away, saying as he did so, slowly enough to control his stammer, "She is not my aunt. Can't you fellows get anything right?"

"It isn't her relationship with you that's in question. I'd be glad to know about her relationship with Sir Charles."

"I've no idea. Looks like my turn c-coming up. Sorry I c-can't help you."

Flitwick-Johnson at once switched his attention to the lawn. He evidently had the ability, useful in a journalist, to regard the varied strands both of his own life and of the world in general as quite unconnected with each other, so that there was no need to make any argument in one of his articles, or piece of behaviour on his own part, compatible with last week's article or this morning's deed. Now he watched Sir John lining up his last sequence.

"What's he up to?" he said. "He could run eight and peel Nancy through and then . . . Oh, I see! The old devil!"

Flitwick-Johnson's own ball, blue, lay close by the hoop to the left of the stone eagles. Towards the further end of the lawn Sir John lifted his own ball, yellow, placed it beside Vincent's, black, and straightened, studying angles. Making a minor adjustment to the lie of the balls he studied the angles again, bent over his mallet and struck his ball briskly. It barely moved a foot, but Vincent's rolled towards the edge of the court, coming to rest four feet beyond the corner hoop. Sir John walked round behind it, looked along the line it made with the hoop and returned to his own ball, which he tapped nine inches to the left. He glanced at the result, nodded and raised an arm to his opponents to indicate his turn was over, then walked off, smiling. Two or three of his guests clapped knowledgeably.

"Playing it rough, eh, Dibs?" called Flitwick-Johnson.

"My turn," said Vincent.

"No, hold on a moment. I can see . . ."

Vincent paid no attention but walked off towards the further end of the court. Flitwick-Johnson almost scampered to catch him up.

"You'd much better let me have a go at red," he said. "It's only half the distance and if I miss I'll be out of harm's way. But if you have a go at me and miss, Nancy can run sixth, hit yellow, run One Back, yellow again and I'll be lying down by Two Back for her . . ."

"I'm going to have a go at yellow."

"But you're wired! Dibs left you wired on purpose. Mine's the only ball you can see. Didn't you notice him smiling?"

By this time they had reached the corner where the black ball lay. Flitwick-Johnson was right. Sir John had left the balls so that the corner hoop lay directly between black and yellow, and also screened red, which was poised ready to run the near centre hoop.

"Have to jump it," said Vincent.

"Honestly, Masham . . ."

"I'm not g-going to let him g-g-get away with it."

It would not be true to say that Flitwick-Johnson's face turned white – it was never in any case of a particularly healthy colour – but he certainly swallowed with some violence.

"Now look here . . ." he said.

"Be a good chap," said Vincent, smiling, apparently quite confident and even happy with the sudden certainties of action. Flitwick-Johnson swallowed again.

"For God's sake watch out for the lawn," he muttered.

Vincent grunted and studied the stroke. After a few seconds he straddled his ball with his feet rather further forward than for a normal stroke. He made only one brief practice swing, then brought the mallet head through a sharp arc so that it was still travelling downward when its upper edge struck the black ball. The ball, compelled thus to bounce, successfully leapt the hoop but also cleared the yellow ball by a couple of feet, running on to smack briskly against the red. Clapping broke out from the pavilion, but stopped abruptly as Sir John, so far punctilious about the courtesies of the game, strode on to the playing area.

"Bit of a fluke, really," said Vincent cheerfully. "I was g-going for yellow."

"Questionable stroke, in my opinion, Dibs," said Flitwick-Johnson, gabbling slightly.

"Nonsense," said Sir John. "But let's see what Masham's done to my turf."

"Bit of a dent, I'm afraid," said Vincent. "Couldn't help it. I was so jolly close to the hoop."

He stood aside. Just where he had struck the ball the nap of the grass was spoilt by a sudden scar, almost an inch deep, shaped like the imprint of a giant fingernail, where the corner of his mallet head had bitten into the turf. Sir John palped the wound with the point of his shoe, then turned and beckoned to the gardener who had been rolling the lawn when they first arrived and who had since been standing alone in the corner of the hedges opposite the pavilion, watching the game. He came forward carrying a large trug full of tools, from which he selected a garden fork with curved tines. Prodding this into the turf at various points around the indentation and levering downwards he gently raised the soil at the centre against the sole of his shoe. When at length he straightened and stood aside the surface was as smooth as it had ever been, though admittedly the grass that composed it had rather a bruised look. Once more Sir John pressed his foot gently around the place.

"Sorry about that," began Flitwick-Johnson. "I tried to talk him . . ."

Sir John looked at him bleakly.

"No real harm done," said Sir John in his normal deadish tone. He glanced half sideways at Vincent.

"You didn't leave me much else, sir," said Vincent.

"Don't do it again," said Sir John. "Black to play. You've just croqueted red."

He walked back to the pavilion.

The match ended unexcitingly. Flitwick-Johnson's game seemed to fall apart, as if he had quite lost interest. Vincent made some untidy progress. Sir John led his side out easy winners, and then took everyone off to watch the end of the game on the tennis court, whence laughter and cries of excitement and despair had now been coming for some time.

4

"What on earth did you get up to at Bullington, Vince?"

"Played croquet. Lost."

The sun, shining through the west-facing window of "The Boys' Room" laid a slab of strong light across the beds. Harry lay on his, smoking, with his pale and hairy legs emerging from the split of his orange silk dressing gown to rest with crossed ankles on the brass bed-end. Vincent, wearing only underpants and dress shirt, as yet collarless, was standing in shadow, arranging studs, cufflinks and waistcoat buttons in drill order on the chest of drawers.

"That all? According to Zena you've somehow got us all in dutch with old Dibs."

"What did she tell you?"

"Just that. All sweetness and light when the croquet started. Icicles when it ended. Dibs perfectly civil, but told her something had come up which meant he wouldn't be able to send his quota over for the dance this evening. It was only going to be half a dozen of the young, so it won't matter all that much."

"Prince Solly's not going to be too happy. He's hit it off no end with Dolly F-J. Perhaps Dibbin's trying to break that up."

"Zena says it's something to do with you. She's just guessing, Vince, but she's pretty hot on that sort of thing – and if she's on to anything she'll do her damnedest to see Uncle Snaily hears about it. I imagine that's why she was so eager I should ask you."

"The only thing that happened was that I made a small dent in Dibbin's lawn."

"A hole in his holy turf! Vince! On purpose?"

"I didn't just go out and bash it with my mallet, if that's what you mean. I had to jump a hoop, and I was a bit close. I realised I'd probably take a divot, but I didn't mind. That ass Johnson had just told me some stuff about Dibbin that put my back up, and then he – Dibbin, I mean – left me on play with a thoroughly sneaky set-up and went off smirking the way he does. I just wasn't going to let him get away with it."

"I wish I'd been there."

"And Johnson kept wittering round trying to stop me, telling me it wasn't the thing. How should *he* know? He's an ass."

"He's going to be editor of *The Times* one day."

"That won't stop him being an ass."

"What had he told you about Dibs? I'd have imagined fawning loyalty to the great man was his line."

"That only made it muckier. He couldn't see any harm in Dibbin keeping a secret file on Charles Archer."

"Well, of course he does. He's that sort of person."

Vincent, who had been pushing his studs into various patterns with his fingertips as they talked, now turned and took a cigarette from the open case on his bedside table. Holding it unlit between his fingers he spoke with slow emphasis.

"I don't think being 'that sort of person' lets anyone off."

"Let's try one of your fags ... Thanks. Being that sort of person. I don't know. Look at it the other way round. Suppose Herr Hitler ... No, he's too monstrous a monster ... Suppose old Dibs, just once in his life, has done something completely uncharacteristic. Suppose, for instance, he has performed one generous action. Don't you think he gets extra credit for that because it was so much harder for him? When he stands before St Peter, I mean ... Really this is the basic moral question ... Did F-J tell you what Dibs has actually got in this file?"

"Mucky little hints. Something about a house in Paris. Children."

"Oh, *that*. I wonder whether Dibs has got anything which

actually proves Charles . . . You know about *l'affaire Panquelin*,
Vince?"

"By the sound of it I'd rather not."

"It affects you, distantly. You remember that rumpus a couple
of years back when Uncle Snaily tried to tell Zena he wouldn't
have Charles in the house any more? That was because some
busybody in Boodles had explained to Snaily about the
affaire . . ."

"Johnson says everybody believes Zena and Charles are lovers."

"So I've heard. I suppose it's possible, but I very much doubt it.
Zena's far too much of a narcissist to want to be anyone's lover,
unless it suits her in other ways. I'm not saying she's frigid. In fact
my impression is that she gave Uncle Snaily a very good time for
quite a while — a real change from Aunt Clara — but I think
Purser's right and she's now decided that she's paid off her debt
for having him make her a countess. Have you noticed what a
tricky temper he's in?"

"I was there when he made up his mind to sack McGrigor.
D'you think some fellow in Boodles has told him about Charles
and Zena?"

"Possibly. Purser says that yesterday morning he came down
early to breakfast and tore up all the toast. He swore that if Purser
had been his fag he'd have beaten him till he blubbed, making him
toast like that. Purser blamed it on Zena for ordering a new kind
of bread. You know, I can't help feeling sorry for Uncle Snaily
after all those years with Aunt Clara, but I must say I hope he
doesn't make Joan's life impossible here."

"Yesterday afternoon you said . . ."

"I wasn't far off, either. I don't mean he's come padding along
to her room yet, but she tells me there've been Snailyish gallantries
which hint at that possibility."

"What's her reaction?"

"Not very enthusiastic — though one must make allowances for
what she would tell another admirer."

"That's you, I take it. You certainly seem to have hit it off with
her."

"To put it mildly. That's why I'm in such a benevolent mood

about the sexual affinities of everyone else in the neighbourhood. I positively glowed with pleasure when Zena told me about Dolly F-J making huge blue eyes at your dusky friend all round the croquet lawn."

"He's going to ask her to advise him on his collection of British artists he's decided to start. I said you'd find out what sort of commission he should pay her."

"Dolly will leave him in no doubt. How is F-J taking this romance?"

"He hasn't had much time to be aware of it."

"Dolly will tell him, first thing. And, you know, my guess is he'll rather relish it. He's a very curious bird. Will you do something for me, Vince?"

"Depends what."

"Squire Nan Blaise around a bit this evening. Do you mind?"

"Nancy's all right. Wouldn't have thought she'd have much trouble finding partners."

"No . . . it's just a bit awkward, you see. Short of being positively embarrassing, but . . . well, I asked Zena to have her along."

"I see."

"No, it's not like that. I've only met her a couple of times. Zena started it by telling me she wanted a bit of younger talent round the place this week-end, and I put Nan's name up. Just inquisitive about her, much as anything . . . but now that my main aim is to spend every minute I can wangle, night and day, with Joan, I don't want Nan to feel left out."

"Night and day?"

"It may come to that. My impression is Joan's fairly easy-going."

Vincent, who had been sitting on the edge of his bed smoking his cigarette, got up sharply and stubbed it out on the wash-stand.

"I'll take Nan off your hands," he said. "She's all right."

Harry seemed to pay no attention to his cousin's mild agitation. In any case he was presumably used to behaving as though it didn't exist, a phenomenon it was friendlier to ignore, similar to the stammer.

"You know," he said dreamily, "nothing is ever as straightforward as it seems. It is the superficially complicated desires such as old Dibs's with his ballet girls, or Charles's supposed inclinations, which are really easiest to grasp. Whereas meeting a nice girl and wanting to go to bed with her always seems to become an immensely complex experience, almost at once – more complicated if you bring it off than if you don't. I appear to myself at the moment to be in love with Joan; but what I want from her is honestly much the same old Dibs wants from one of his dancers, without the fancy frills he goes in for. And when old Dibs has got it he probably doesn't give it another thought, beyond looking back on it with a good deal of relish, I suppose, rather the way you or I might look back on a reasonably cooked meal or a passable night at the theatre. But if Joan and I . . . it's possible I'm mistaken, of course, and it will turn out to have been no more than a night at the theatre, and not necessarily a very successful one. The whole notion of being in love may be only a way of appeasing one's residual conscience, but one can't say it feels like that. No amount of introspection will analyse the notion of love away, or so it seems to me, and I must have been in and out getting on for a dozen times, with varying degrees of satisfaction . . ."

"Why do they do it?" said Vincent, angrily.

"Girls go to bed with one? That indeed is an intractable mystery. They'll tell you so themselves – without being asked."

"No. People like Dibbin. Or Charles, supposing . . ."

"Rather a drearier mystery. I believe that according to Freud it's the inability to cope with one's mother at the emotional level that sets it off. Not very useful, even if true. In Dibs's case I'd guess it was just another aspect of his general power mania. He is stimulated by making his fellow human beings do things which would normally repel them. He needs that sort of stimulus to get going with a woman, that's all. I suppose Charles might be nearer the Freudian pattern – always, as you say, supposing. I've never heard anything about his parents, but, well, wouldn't you say there's still something of the terribly clever schoolboy about him? And that war hero stuff?"

"It wasn't stuff, Hal."

"I wasn't . . ."

"He did it. He earned his gongs twice over. He could have got himself invalided out after . . ."

"You'd have taken the same line, wouldn't you, Vince?"

"Hope so. You can never be sure till it happens."

"True, Vince, true. I withdraw the word 'stuff' and all imputations implied therein. But doesn't it strike you as odd that Charles has never held office?"

"Better off out of it. He can say what he likes."

"I don't believe it's been his choice. He would like power. In certain ways he's not enormously different from Dibs. But he's never been offered power because everyone recognises he won't be any use in a team. In political terms, he's unable to accept the responsibilities of the adult world. The vision of oneself as the solitary hero is something most of us grow out of before we're twenty, but Charles never has. Remember who Peter Pan loves?"

"That sickening girl. Forgotten her name."

"Wendy. I do think it's possible Charles . . ."

"If it is it's no excuse. You keep saying people can't help it because they're like that. You said it about Zena yesterday. You said it about Dibs. Now you're saying it about Charles. D'you mean it, Hal? I want to know. Or are you just talking?"

"I mean it, I think. But it doesn't really make a lot of difference, Vince."

"It seems to me it makes all the difference in the world."

"Not really. Let's suppose, just for the sake of argument, Charles is physically attracted to little girls. Let's suppose, further, that the reason for this is either (a) that he had a perfectly frightful mother or (b) that instead of getting a packet in his spine in 'eighteen he got a bit of shrapnel through his skull, which affected his personality. Now in case (b) we would feel a good deal of sympathy for him, especially if he managed his problems the way he seems to, with a certain discretion, though ultimately it would depend of course on the effect of his activities on the other partner. Small girls aren't necessarily innocent little wax dolls – young Sally, for instance, when she clings to one like that, has at least half an idea what she's up to."

"Rot."

"Oh, I don't know. It isn't only for the fun of holding the

steering wheel that she wants to sit on one's lap and drive. But to get back to Charles. What I'm trying to say is that I don't see any moral difference between case (b) and case (a). After all, you've got as good an idea as anybody what it's like to have a tricky relationship with one's mother. You aren't going to tell me that's your fault, Vince . . ."

"Let's talk about something else."

"Right you are. Remember you began it by asking. May I go back to Joan?"

"If you like."

"Her husband was a soldier too, you know?"

"Was? I'd gathered . . ."

"Yes. Still with us, unfortunately. Resigned his commission."

"Want me to find out why?"

"Drink, apparently."

"What's he up to now?"

"Farming in Kenya."

"Not much help with the drink problem, I'd have thought."

"He wants Joan to send Sally out to live with him."

"Oh. I suppose she . . ."

"No, she's rather tempted. She's not a very dedicated mamma. It must be a bit of a shock, Vince, to have a child, to bear it out of your own body, and then find out you don't love it, aren't even specially interested in it. I say, I wonder whether that was what happened to Charles."

"What happened to Charles was that he enlisted in 1914. He got blown up in 1915. He spent eight months in hospital. He then wangled his way back to France and got blown up again in 1918. He is in pain a lot of the time and discomfort all the time because of that corset contraption he has to wear. His politics are tosh, but he's a very brave man. You might at least give him the benefit of the doubt."

"Henceforth. Promise. After all in a year or two we'll be going through all that ourselves. Looking forward to it, Vince?"

"Not a lot. We're nothing like ready for it, for a start. And there's bound to be conscription, which means getting swamped by hordes of civilians. You sound almost keen."

"Almost is right. In fact there are moments when I find myself thinking Rupert Brooke wasn't quite as awful as I have to pretend he is. He did actually feel like that, though it didn't turn out anything like he'd imagined, and it won't in our case, either. Still, I know in my bones the world is due for a bloody great shake-up, and it'll be hell while it happens, but interesting all the same to be there – something one shouldn't miss. A ghastly, harrowing play you've still got to see because otherwise you'll never be in the swim any more. You shake your head?"

"Simply no comprenny."

"Does it ever strike you, Vince, what different people we are?"

"They've never stopped telling me. Aunts and people."

"Down with aunts."

"*Gott strafe Tanten.*"

"*Les tantes à la lanterne.*"

"Et cetera. You think they're right this time?"

"Mm . . . but I sometimes wonder what we'd have been like if we hadn't had each other to be different from."

"Much the same, I'd have thought."

"I can remember at Summerfields, when you made First XI from Middle School, I came to a quite conscious decision in my own mind that I wasn't going to compete. It seemed easy at the time, but all sorts of other things flowed from it. I suppose we would have been about ten – you don't think ahead much at that age. For instance, Mummy kept all my school reports. I was looking through them last winter. The first couple of years they were so-so. Then the ushers who actually taught me started getting enthusiastic, but at the same time G. B. began adding little notes saying I was in danger of becoming a bad influence. So I must, even then, have worked out that if I wasn't going to bother about games I'd better be good at my books – I mean, that would have been reasonably obvious. But as for becoming a professional Bolshie, I don't believe a ten-year-old would have sorted out that by rejecting part of the *mores* of his society he would find himself cast in that role. Then at Eton, there I was, still a Bolshie, and a tug to boot, and making another conscious decision that it was necessary to get elected to Pop. Therefore another layer of personality had to be invented – relaxed urbanity, intellectual sparkle and so on – all because when you were still in shorts you could bowl leg breaks and had a natural cover drive."

"I think you'd have turned out much the same if I'd been a rabbit."

"I don't know. There are times when I seem very conscious of my own personality as being largely my invention. I'm not saying I'm unique, mind you. Look at Purser. If he hadn't decided to be a butler he would have been a very different kettle of fish, don't you think?"

"Same goes for all of us, only we don't spend our time brooding on it. If you don't start dressing you'll be late for the gong."

Harry didn't stir.

"By and large I agree with you," he said. "Personalities are our own invention, but with a lot of people the process is unconscious. Even Uncle Snaily has decided somehow or other that he is going to be what he is. In a sense he is not responsible, because he hasn't been aware of deciding, let alone of the consequences. But in another sense they are his decisions, and the moral responsibility is his."

"He's changed."

"You think so? I've seen him more recently than you, so I suppose I don't find the difference so marked. If you're right, it might mean something new has happened, such as Zena booting him out of her bed. You know, by most people's standards he's led a peculiarly sheltered life. You'd think he could have grown to almost any shape he wanted, and yet he chose to finish up like this. The only things that have happened to him are Aunt Clara, and then Zena, coming and going so to speak. All three events could be considered trauma inducers in their very different ways. Of course that's the really interesting thing about anybody, how they adapt their personalities to events beyond their control. Do you remember the caddis flies in the tank in the nursery – dropping chips of broken bottle into the water and seeing how the little wrigglers built them into their tunnels, and if you gave them a wrong-sized chip they'd produce a bent tunnel? Especially at the start. Suppose God goes and drops a wrong-sized chip on you. You'd have to build it in somehow."

Vincent was adjusting his braces so that the trousers of his mess uniform hung as he wanted them, pulled tight by the elastic tapes beneath the heels. The process was carried out without apparent thought, a merely physical concentration in the movement of the fingers.

"Three minutes to the gong," he said.

"You could say God dropped awkward chips on both Charles and Dibs," said Harry. "Dibs has produced a horrible twisted tunnel out of his, but Charles hasn't done too badly."

"Two and a half minutes."

"I am utterly content in my present posture. The world is the exact shape I would wish it. No mere moving of a clock face can force me to change it. You can be on time for both of us, Vince. Tell Zena McGrigor has taken my sock suspenders to balance the ball-cock in Uncle Snaily's bog."

"McGrigor's been sacked," said Vincent, slipping easily into his scarlet jacket, which until he put it on had looked strangely too small for him.

"So he has. How peculiar. A great event, almost unnoticed."

"How long will you be?"

"I haven't the faintest idea. I am lying in a great daze of love like a perfect hot bath. I shall get out when it becomes too cold to be fun. Till then time has no meaning for me. The metronome has swung too far over, and stuck. McGrigor's been sacked. There's no one to wind the clock."

"Mrs Dubigny won't be happy about that."

"Perfectly right," said Harry, swivelling himself round to sit on the edge of the bed and stretch, dark against gold sunlight. "The figures must continue to dance, for Joan's sake. I shall dance among them, and so will you. I'll be down by the second gong. Don't worry."

7

At the workbench in the Coach House Mr Mason was cutting a
wheel. His shape was a hunched darkness against the yellow cone
from his lamp. The electric motor sang, its note dropping as it
took the load, descanted by the whine of the cutting-wheel. A few
sparks, invisible in the lamplight, shot slantwise into being across
the shadow cast by the bench. Mr Mason's attitude implied total
concentration, without any tension. When he had cut a notch he
did not rest, but undid the clamps, raised the marker, turned the
wheel to the next point, fixed marker and clamps, checked briefly
and then moved the cutter firmly against the metal to begin the
next notch.

Miss Quintain, approaching him from behind the Rover,
waited during this process, perhaps assuming that he would reach
a point when it was natural to interrupt him. She continued to
wait during the five minutes it took him to complete the next
notch, and then as he withdrew the cutter stepped forward and
touched him on the elbow.

He stayed quite still for several seconds. It was as though she
had offered a stimulus to a creature of such slow reactions that it
took that time for the nerve impulses to reach the brain. And when
he moved to switch the motor off it was still with an almost
dreamy stolidity.

"Good morning, Mr Mason. How are you getting on?"

"Slow but sure. How long have I been at it now? Getting on five
weeks. Jack Robson's coming this afternoon, help me hang a
cradle from the roof so I can get at the clock face. That's what
usually stops one of these clocks, you know, running dry where the
leading-off rod – that's the shaft to drive the hands – comes through
into the open. Suppose I don't find much wrong there, all it'll need
is a good grease up. I've one more wheel to cut like this – that's another morning – and the weights to hang and that'll be the going
train done. I could have the hands turning for you next week."

"That's marvellous. What about the figures?"

"Ah, now. First there's the striking train – two striking trains, really. The one for the hours is not so bad, but by the bells for the quarters is where the water came in worst when the roof was leaking. Some of the bell-cranks are rusted pretty near solid. There's several weeks' work there. After that you come to your figures. Them at the top – the noon strike – are not so bad – but down below you've had your carousel standing out always in the same place, all weathers, how many years is it? Getting on forty. If it hadn't been oak it would have been all crumbled to powder years ago. When the clock's going, you see, the carousel turns and there's time to dry off before it gets out in the rain again. Now I've that whole section to replace the timbers of. Then there's another part burnt in the fire, and the rods for all the figures, half of them's buckled, and there's gearing under the ones as have stood out in the open – I've not had a chance to look at them so far, so there's no knowing how bad that's rusted . . ."

"It sounds a great deal of work."

"We knew that all along, didn't we? Oh yes. Put wrong in a night, take a life to set right, as the saying goes."

"Not really a life, I hope."

"Well, getting on a year. If all goes well – remember that, Miss Quintain, I'm saying if all goes well – I'll have her running for you about March."

"Oh dear. I'd been . . ."

"One thing you're going to have to ask yourself is do you want to have a man going up the tower day in day out to wind her up. The alternative is I fit you auto-winders."

"How much would that cost?"

"I've got the catalogues at home. I could get you some figures out, but not far short of seven hundred each, I'd reckon. Call it four thousand quid."

"Oh, dear. Would I be strong enough to do the winding?"

"Needs a man, really."

"That means Jack Robson again, and . . . oh dear. I think you'll have to let me know about the auto-winders. Don't let's worry about it now. What I really came to say is that the weather forecast's tolerable for once, and it's Monday so I don't have to think about visitors. I was going to suggest we took our lunch out into the garden and you can tell me what you remember about meeting Harry."

"It's not that much, Miss Quintain. I could tell you now, really."

"I'd like to hear it down in the garden. Don't worry about it not being much. The smallest scrap is worth while. I'll get Jo-jo to take a basket down to the Rose Wall – she'll like that – then you and I can go round the long way. If I meet you out on the terrace in front of the morning room at half-past twelve . . ."

"Half-past twelve it is."

Miss Quintain had already half turned to leave when she spoke again.

"You see," she said. "About the auto-winders. I suppose I could afford them, but . . . I don't want to be rude, Mr Mason, but it all depends on whether the clock is really going to work. I can't have it going for a bit and stopping and being mended and going for a bit and stopping again, like it used to. The whole house used to be full of things like that – just working, but not really. I can't afford that any more."

Mr Mason had his hand on the lever to raise the marker. He moved it slowly up before he spoke.

"When I've finished," he said, "she'll go. Provided you keep the rain out and the pigeons, she'll go without anyone touching her for as long as she's been stopped. But give her a minor overhaul every ten years – I'll leave you a list of what needs looking at – and she'll go as long as this house has stood, and longer."

"That's what I'd like," said Miss Quintain. "I might afford the auto-winders if you'll promise me that."

The spring of 1980 had been late and chill, and the summer started little better, so that any fine day seemed a festival. Miss Quintain came out on to the terrace already smiling. She was wearing a brown apron sewn with large pockets, and carrying an object like a walking stick but with a miniature hoe instead of a ferrule. She raised this to Mr Mason, half in greeting, half in explanation.

"It's one of the last Lord Snailwood's gadgets," she said. "He adored gadgets, though they tell me he could hardly wind his own watch without breaking it. All the outhouses are stacked with the ones that didn't actually do what he wanted them for. This is one of the exceptions."

Miss Quintain spoke of her predecessor in an odd tone, amusement predominating, but also an impatience that came near contempt. She hooked the handle of the implement into a special loop at the side of her apron and took out of one of the pockets a note-pad and pencil, then looked slowly round the terrace and made two or three notes. Out of doors her personality did not really alter, but showed itself in a new aspect. Her reserve, her slight over-precision of speech and gesture, became an expression of her relationship with her plants; she not only knew their names and needs but had chosen their individual sitings so that by flourishing there they should express the laxity, freedom and forthcomingness that might have seemed lacking in her. The stone lion at the eastern end of the terrace had its haunches swathed in trails of some spring clematis, now over, which made its air of total indifference and haughtiness decidedly comic, as though it still believed it owned the garden, when the garden now owned it. The plants in the cracks between the flagstones were some of them in theory weeds, some not; the distinction here seemed unreal.

"I do a tour of inspection once a week," said Miss Quintain. "Otherwise things get out of hand without my noticing. I want you to see it with me because a lot of what I've done was really Harry's idea. This way."

She walked to the top of the flight of steps at the western end of the terrace and stopped there. Though the lie of the land precluded any major alterations to the architecture of the garden at this upper level, it was still immensely changed since Lord Snailwood's day. Then, at this time of year, the visitor standing on the steps would have looked out over a sea of regimented rose bushes, echoed on the northern wall by close-pruned climbing roses. Beyond the end of the first terrace he would have seen the further half of the third, also massed with roses, reaching to the wall of holm oaks almost two hundred yards away, and as he walked in that direction and so brought into view the areas hidden by the fall of the ground he would have discovered nothing but yet more roses. Miss Quintain had retained only the perspective of distance down the centre, framing it between columnar cypresses beside the further steps, but blocking out the rest of the vista with an irregular planting of shrubs. A herbaceous border, deliberately old-fashioned and now at the peak of lushness, ran along the northern side of the terrace, the bulging brick retaining wall behind it swathed in intertwining climbers. The southern side was very plain, a brick balustrade, punctuated with urns, trailing a few silvery tendrils.

"We're very late this year," said Miss Quintain. "Lady North-cliffe's beginning to make a good show at last."

She pointed to a clematis displaying large blue plates of bloom. Mr Mason grunted. As he followed her round, gazing non-committally at the green upthrusting hummocks in the border, his reserve, different in kind from Miss Quintain's, seemed accentuated. The garden might have been a foreign country and he a first-time visitor, fastidious not to offend local custom.

"Harry left me a lot of notes, you see," said Miss Quintain. "Start with something formal – most people's idea of a garden – flowers, and a view. Then, suddenly, clutter."

They had reached the flight of steps to the central terrace. She pointed down, a gesture dramatic by her subdued standards. There was no lawn, now. The whole space around the little belvedere was planted, except where narrow stone paths criss-crossed it in a diamond lattice. The eye's first impression – that something of practically everything was crammed into the area, from monstrous silvery thistles to almost lichen-like blotches of rock-huggers growing in the pavement cracks – was soon modi-fied by the discovery that despite the uproarious growth the commonest colour of growth itself, the ordinary green of grass and leaf, was almost entirely missing. Even on a dull day the terrace would have declared itself appropriate to hot sun. On this fine morning it reeked of southern aromatic hills. Down among its density, with the view across the river deliberately hidden, isola-tion combined with the immense nostalgias of smell to produce in almost any visitor a sense of being an invader into privacies, privacies somehow connected with time, and with lost remem-brance. One would not have been surprised to discover on the steps of the belvedere a brown-skinned child playing her invented game with a pattern of pebbles on the stones; but then, not finding her there, to experience a vague feeling that this was just as well because the child's existence precluded one's own. That world was lost to one.

"It's my favourite bit," said Miss Quintain. "I do it all myself, because I don't like the idea of anyone else forking around in it."

"The smell reminds me . . . I can't say what."

"It's meant to."

Mr Mason looked at her with a glance of definite suspicion.

"We needn't take any time over it now," she said. "I'm going to have a go at it this afternoon. Now this is Mr Floyd's stamp collection."

The final terrace allowed the view in again. The steepening contour narrowed the site and heightened the retaining wall to the north. This, with the flanking holm oaks, provided as much shelter as one could ever hope for on an English hillside. Various half-tender climbers, abutilons and such, mounted the wall, in front of which on irregular raised beds the so-called stamp collection grew, plantsman's stuff, mostly unremarkable at a distance though often immensely attractive seen close to. Mr Floyd and his fatter assistant were hand-weeding one of the beds, and when she reached them Miss Quintain stopped to talk. Mr Mason at once moved away and stood by the balustrade (much more entangled with creepers and climbers than that on the upper terrace had been allowed to become) where he gazed at the view, making no discernible movement until Miss Quintain came over to him.

"Now, just quickly through the Lower Garden," she said. "We mustn't keep Jo-jo waiting."

Despite her words, Miss Quintain stopped near the end of the terrace and gazed at the cliff of glittery leaves presented by the holm oaks.

"One of my gardening friends keeps telling me to grow some rampant great roses up through them," she said. "It might look stunning, but . . . I feel they've a right to go on as they are, be what they've always been. They haven't changed, whatever else has. What do you think, Mr Mason?"

"I'm with you," said Mr Mason firmly. "My experience, things are best left let be, 'less you can see they're going adrift. I don't imagine there's much can go wrong with a tree."

"You know, the real reason why I don't want them full of roses is that there's rather a good climbing tree in there. It wouldn't be any use if it were full of rose stems. At one time I thought I might label the climbing trees for visiting children, grading them for difficulty, but the insurance people wouldn't let me unless I got all the parents to sign an indemnity. Too much fuss."

Miss Quintain nodded, confirming the rightness of her decision, and strode briskly forward and down the flight of steps by the oaks. Mr Mason followed more slowly, moving not exactly cautiously but with a definite attention to the process natural to a man both heavy and elderly, and aware of what a fall down such a flight might do to him.

No longer constrained by the terracing the Lower Garden spread irregularly towards the river. The boundaries that divided section from section had been devised to appear accidental – a snaking line of trees by a stream, or a seemingly immemorial ha-ha – and though each section had what Miss Quintain explained as an "idea" of its own, the result gave the impression of having been arrived at as much by the quiet vote of the plants as by the dictatorship of the gardener. Conversation for a while diminished to a few horticultural mutters addressed by Miss Quintain to herself as, now making a definite effort to hurry, she inspected and took notes.

Mr Mason showed no sign of boredom or impatience, but gave few hints of interest either until they reached a strange enclosure quite unlike anything else in the garden.

Coming along beneath the wall that retained the upper terraces they were confronted by a twelve-foot yew hedge. Through a gap so narrow that it seemed a mere slot came a glimpse of unnatural blue, as of the painted sides of a swimming-pool or an amateur water-colourist's attempt at a Mediterranean sky. Miss Quintain led the way in. The hedge turned out to enclose a precise circle, about thirty feet across, with the wall running at a tangent on its northern rim. At the centre was a statueless pedestal. A narrow grass path ran round the edge of the enclosure, and all the rest was a single flowerbed planted with a poppy-like flower whose blue, now that the eye could sort it into its individual saucer-bowls, no longer seemed unnatural, only unlikely.

"That's something," said Mr Mason, apparently impressed for the first time.

"*Meconopsis grandis,*" said Miss Quintain.

"Why did you choose to shut them in this way?"

"Just an idea. One likes to be a bit different. In other gardens they tend to be where people spot them a long way off and go rushing across to see what on earth they can be. And besides – it's something to do with that stone thing – Harry used to call it the Bloodstone. I remember, during the war, one of the cats got run over by the postman. I stole it so that I could have the funeral here, not really for the cat's sake – more for the Bloodstone's. Harry used to say it was a place for oaths and undertakings. You sealed them with a sacrifice. I suppose you could say I've shut the stone off and given it these poppies to keep it happy. Now lunch."

She led the way half round the circle, looking at the blue poppies as she went, not smiling but expressing a distinct sense of relationship, an almost maternal bond, between herself and these particular plants. She vanished through a slot in the far side of the circle.

They had come to the enclosure through an area of light woodland, but now emerged on to a wide lawn, featureless, so as not to distract from the famous Rose Wall at its northern edge. The child Jo-jo was standing near the middle of this space, wearing as usual jeans and a T-shirt. She had her weight on one leg and was tracing arcs on the grass with the toes of her other foot, like a bored dancer. There was a basket on the grass beside her.

"You're not very easy to impress, Mr Mason," said Miss Quintain, a hint of pique at last spicing the dry amusement in her voice. Mr Mason stopped looking at the child and gave his consideration to the wall. The roses were old, types old enough for whoever had planted them to believe that a single luxuriant June flowering was all that could be expected; the individual specimens were also old enough for some of the bigger branches of their frame-work to be almost as thick as a man's arm. The main tone of the flowers was of cream flushing into pink, the unopened buds sometimes clear red at their tips, the lax, due-to-fall petals almost white. They spread fifty yards along the wall, climbing its height to the balustrade of terrace above, and had been pruned so that in front of the main curtain of blossom long trailers looped down almost to the ground, like the fore-running foam of an enormous wave.

"Very pretty," said Mr Mason. "Very pretty indeed."

"It's almost the only thing I've kept. You know, I rooted out over nine hundred of old Lord Snailwood's roses. I couldn't stand them. But this . . . I suppose you could say he got it right by accident – and anyway you've got to keep something from the old life of the garden. It would be wrong not to."

At the sound of their voices Jo-jo had looked up and now came across the lawn carrying the basket, letting its weight pull her slight body sideways more than was really necessary, as if to emphasise the burden she had carried for them.

"You've been ages," she said. "I'm ever so hungry. I almost started."

"I'm so sorry," said Miss Quintain. "Are you going to have your picnic with us? Why don't you take it up into Hangman's Tower? I'll keep an eye on you."

"Oh, all right," said Jo-jo, dumping the basket, snatching off the napkin that covered it and beginning to rifle through its contents. "There's two rolls each. Can I have the ham ones? Ooh – *straw*berries! The lemonade's for me. I don't need a mug."

Fully self-centred, she pushed the rolls in through the neck of her T-shirt and let them fall to her waistband, stuck a bottle top-down into a pocket, chose the best of the little plastic boxes of fruit and after popping the largest berry into her mouth said a mushy thank you and ran off to an old stone pine that stood some forty yards away across the lawn, its bare stiff-curving limbs with their large-mottled bark looking as though it was waiting to be painted by Cézanne. She disappeared round the trunk, emerged a moment later in the first fork, climbed another six feet and then out to a horizontal crotch where she settled and began to balance the items of her meal along the branch beside her. Though she looked entirely safe and confident, Miss Quintain watched her closely and did not speak until she was still.

"Her mother doesn't approve her going up so high, but I'm afraid I encourage her. You know, it's extraordinary how little there is left of Snailwood that belongs to the old days. I only half do. Robson's father was Lord Snailwood's valet, and that's all. I sometimes wonder if I'm not using Jo-jo to try and re-live my own childhood, showing her the best trees and telling her their names. Harry showed me, of course – they're all part of an extraordinary game he used to play with his cousin. We can still see her from the bench."

Mr Mason bent stiffly to pick up the basket, then followed her to where a large variegated maple closed off the cliff of roses. He took a flat cap from his pocket and with it dusted the slats of the garden seat that stood in front of the tree; they sat, with the basket between them; Miss Quintain answered the child's wave. The apparent stillness was threaded with birdsong, and leaf-shift, but all so peaceful that the odd tumbling petal, the first of that summer to fall, seemed to whisper as it touched the grass.

"Tell me about meeting him," said Miss Quintain.

Mr Mason took some time to answer, apparently absorbed in rearranging the tomato slices in his roll so that they wouldn't squirt when he bit.

"I've kept wishing there'd been more to it," he said. "You're going to be disappointed . . . Well, I was with 208 Squadron. March 1941 it was. I don't know how much you know about that bit of the war . . ."

"I've read everything I could lay my hands on. Naturally. General O'Connor had made a tremendous advance and destroyed the Italian army almost by accident, but he'd had to stop beyond Benghazi. And then Rommel came and pushed us back because Churchill had insisted on half of our army going to Greece."

"You can never stop in the desert," said Mr Mason, earnestly. "That's the logic of it. If you don't go forward you've got to go back, because there's no defensive positions for hundreds of miles. And Greece and then Crete. That was a right old . . . I won't say it. Well, there we were. 208 Squadron was reconnaissance. My crowd was on detachment, right down on the southern flank, no more than a dozen of us to fly and service a couple of Lysanders. Know about them too, I dare say?"

"I've seen the one in the RAF museum. A high-wing monoplane, very slow. A sitting duck, they told me."

"That's not fair. Used right you couldn't ask better than a Lysander. Take off and land on a handkerchief. Pretty well stand still in the air if you wanted it. Vulnerable, I give you, but it wasn't ever meant to be used without fighter cover."

"All the fighters had gone to Greece, though."

"That's what you get in a war. We weren't that worried. Been sitting in the same bit of sand for more than a month and getting sick of it. Just sending up one of the planes every day for a look round and not finding anything and coming back. I was engine maintenance mechanic, but our A/c Airframes was sick so I was working alone on one of the planes, March 30th it would have been. Bloody hot for March it was, too. I had my head in the cabin when I heard a couple of blokes gabbing away behind me. One was Pilot Officer Toller. The other had a lah-di-dah sort of voice I knew wasn't one of our crowd, but as I'd been told to get the plane ready for a recce with an 'I' corps officer I guessed it might be him. After a bit Mr Toller had me out to talk about when I'd be finished, and from that I gathered they were expecting to go a bit further than usual – something this major wanted to look at, special. He didn't say much. Matter of fact I don't think he said anything direct to me. Just stood around, lounging out in the sun beyond the camouflage. I could see he was a gentleman, just the way he stood."

"Did he look happy?"

"I heard him say to Mr Toller he'd been having an interesting war. He had that drawn look, though – lot of the staff got to look that way – it's the strain, I'd imagine. Or he might have been jumpy about the flight. He'd have known about there being no fighters."

"But not specially excited?"

"No . . . not that I could tell."

"And that's really all?"

"I told you it wasn't much."

"You're sure?"

Mr Mason, who had been speaking more slowly even than usual, and with a heavier presence of his unplaceable Midlands accent, merely nodded.

"If that *is* all, why did you remember his name? Why did you ask me about him?"

"Ah well, there was the inquiry, you see," explained Mr Mason, apparently not noticing the definite sharpness in her voice.

"Tell me about that."

"Well, I was surprised they bothered. I said it was March 30th, didn't I? March 31st Rommel hit us, wham, and back we were going like blown leaves all the way to Egypt. Three hundred miles in six days. Flew the one Lysander back and the rest of us came out clinging to the one truck after the other one had hit one of our own mines not done twenty miles. Only just made it to the coast road in front of the Germans. They didn't hold the inquiry till we'd settled down back in Egypt, and because I'd prepared the Lysander for the flight I had to give evidence. That's how I came to hear the major's name. I couldn't say why it's stuck – unusual way it's spelt, much as anything. But I've always had a head for names, and when you spelt yours out to me that time I asked you about mending the clock, it rang a bell. They spelt it out loud like that at the inquiry, you see, more than once."

"I see."

"I'm not keeping anything back from you. I've no call."

"Oh, I'm sure you're not. I've been keeping something back from you, though, Mr Mason. I didn't want to put ideas into your mind before you'd told me everything you remembered. You see, Harry wrote my mother a letter that afternoon, before the flight."

Mr Mason turned his head slowly to look at her.

"He'd an hour or two to wait," he said. "Something to do. Take his mind off the flight, I expect."

"It wasn't like that. Just one page, and very excited, almost incoherent. He said something extraordinary had happened and he was writing to her to get over the shock. He was going to tell her all about it when he'd had time to talk it over, but whatever happened it might make all the difference at Snailwood. He didn't explain anything more than that."

"Not much to go on."

"More than you think. My mother used to show me most of his letters, even when . . . well, Harry didn't mind what he wrote."

"I know what you mean. There was a lot of them like that, writing to their wives, never mind it had to go through the censor."

"Exactly. Harry would put in jokes about that in the margin. My mother would laugh aloud and pass them across the breakfast table to me. I think she enjoyed seeing me blush. But she never showed me this one. I knew it had come, and I knew where she hid things, so I stole it and copied it out and put it back. I couldn't understand it all at the time, but later on several things happened which make me almost certain that Harry had met his cousin Vincent."

"Ah. The one you told me he used to play the game with."

"That's right. Vincent Masham. For reasons I won't go into Vincent disappeared about a year before the war. My mother would never let Harry talk to me about him. The only way I knew he existed was because of the game. That's why she hid the letter, of course. And that bit about Snailwood. Vincent's mother – we all called her Aunt Ivy – was a perfectly poisonous woman. Her world began and ended with Vincent, and when he disappeared she decided to make things as difficult as possible for Harry. But if he'd met Vincent and persuaded him to do something about Aunt Ivy . . . You see?"

"Vincent Masham? Nobody of that name in our crowd."

"He wouldn't have called himself that."

"Apart from Mr Toller the only other officer was Mr Allison – thin and tall and droopy. Don't know what became of him."

"He was killed in Italy. I found that out."

"Mr Toller was a perky little fellow."

"No. In any case I don't think it would have been an officer. Vincent was very good at machines. He'd very likely have been doing something like you. He was a big man, very good at games. To judge by his photographs – I'll show you when we go back to the house – he had blond hair and rather a red face, I think. He used to have a moustache, but he could have shaved it off."

"He'd still have stood out like a sore thumb in a crowd like ours. It's the voice, more than the face. Anybody talking the way I heard your stepfather would have been ragged blind about it."

"Harry left me a long letter, partly about Vincent. Usually he had a stammer, but he could control it unless he got excited. And he was quite good at what Harry called oickish accents."

"Come again?"

"Apparently it's Eton slang for anyone who talked differently from the way they did."

"Ah . . . I reckon we'd have spotted him."

"He'd have had three or four years to practise."

"That's so . . . Tell you what, Miss Quintain. I told you I'd a good head for names. I think I could get you out a list of everyone was with us in 208 – that wing 208, at least."

"That would be marvellous. And how old and how tall they were, if you can remember."

"'Scuse my asking, but are you aiming to find this Vincent Masham?"

"Yes, of course. I know it's a very long shot, but I think he might tell me much more about Harry than you can, Mr Mason. And there's something else . . . I don't know. In any case, we'll look at some of the photographs when we go back up."

They fell silent. The serious part of the interview seemed suddenly over. Miss Quintain, who had hardly eaten a mouthful so far, methodically disposed of a roll. Mr Mason, who had used food almost as punctuation to his story, sat watching Jo-jo as she scrambled around the tree. The fingers of his right hand caressed his jaw-line with slow, unconscious strokes.

"Were you a clockmaker before the war?" said Miss Quintain.

Mr Mason withdrew his hand from his face and looked at it as though it were a stranger's.

"I was just a general mechanic," he said. "Garage hand and such, up Leicester way. Joined up a bit before the war. When I was demobbed . . . well, I didn't know what to do with myself. I'd been all right in the Air Force, but now I'd lost my moorings, you might say. Got into a bit of trouble . . . well, 1948 I found myself in Lichfield, no job, no family, all at odds with myself inside. More than once I'd thought quite serious about jumping off a bridge or something. I wandered into a big church. They used to keep churches open then. No one around, but I heard thumpings up in the tower, so up I went. Tell you the honest truth, I was hoping to meet the vicar or someone, bum the price of a meal off. What I found was Sid Lauterpracht – little man, bit of a hunch to his back – having a go at the clock. I asked him for a bob or two, and he said no, but he'd pay me to fetch and carry for him a couple of hours seeing his regular man was off sick. That was my turning point. That was when I started to come back. I got interested in the gearing of the clock and when I asked a couple of questions Sid could see I knew what I was talking about, so he took me on temporary while the other fellow got over his influenza. I stayed thirty-two years and ended up owning the business.''

"It says Lauterpracht and Mason on your card.''

"Sid passed away, you see, 1959. Mrs Lauterpracht was wanting to keep the firm going, so she took me into partnership. Matter of fact, make sure of me, she went and married me. Funny when you think she hid the spoons that first night Sid brought me home to sleep on the sofa.''

As soon as he spoke about his wife a certain joviality, vague but perceptible and probably intended to be perceived, tinged Mr Mason's voice, revealing a side of his life hitherto unsuspected. He took a wallet from his inner pocket and withdrew a photograph, which he looked at for a couple of seconds before passing across. It was a snapshot, evidently taken in some public park. To one side was part of a flowerbed, planted with scarlet tulips and blue forget-me-nots. On the tarred path a woman was hunkered down, facing the camera but not looking at it as she attempted to coax a pair of mallard to eat from her fingers. She was more than plump, but just short of that state of fatness where the rolls of flesh oscillate according to their own harmonics with the movements of the body. The yellowness of her hair could not be wholly natural. She looked about fifty-five, immensely strong and healthy, and though concentrated on her battle of wills with the ducks, expressed an attitude of easy cheerfulness towards the world.

"Did they?'' said Miss Quintain, handing the photograph back.

"They did not,'' said Mr Mason. "I tell her I carry it round to remind me of the only time I remember she didn't get her own way.''

He started to gather his share of the picnic mess back into the basket. Miss Quintain stood up and shook the crumbs out of her apron.

"I forgot to ask," she said. "What sort of state was the Lysander in? I'm sure it was as good as you could make it, but I don't suppose the desert was particularly kind to aeroplanes."

"You're right there. But all things considered she was in pretty good nick. I've always reckoned they must have run into an Italian fighter. Me, like you say, I'd done the best I could."

8

The form for one of Zena's "superduperdos" (which, by the way, did not take place every week-end of the season, though there was almost always some kind of house-party at Snailwood – one week-end in three would be nearer the mark) was for some thirty house guests to have gathered at least by teatime on the Saturday. Another thirty would arrive for dinner, but not expecting to stay the night, and between ten and eleven the numbers would double again with the arrival of guests for the dance, most of whom would have dined in parties of a dozen or more in neighbouring houses, though a few might have motored down directly from London.

To somebody merely listening – a tramp, say, who had slipped over the wall to doss down on the soft drift of leaves beneath the magnolias – the confused mess of noises might have sounded like some machine undergoing a series of ultra-slow gear changes, the guests being as it were the work into which the machine was biting, the arrival of a couple of already excited carloads consti-tuting a knot in the grain of the night and causing a sudden rise in pitch, but each main stage going jerkily up from a quiet-seeming hum to straining clamour which could only be relieved by setting the machine to work at a lower ratio.

By half past seven the five-piece orchestra was out on the terrace in front of the morning room, tuning up before the guests arrived. The morning room itself had been cleared for dancing. The Great Hall, which under earlier Lady Snailwoods would have been used for that purpose, was unaltered, a large space in which groups of various sizes could sit out and – Zena's reputation by now strongly suggested – intrigue, in any sense of that word. The gardeners had set lamps out all along the terraces and hung them here and there among the trees below; with dusk they would be going round to light them. The tables for supper were laid in the

Orangery. Smollett, the second chauffeur, was out in the court-yard, ready to supervise the parking of cars. Now, with the house guests still dressing and the first gong not yet sounded, it was a period of quiet, of the gears going through neutral before the machine took up the next load.

Vincent stood at the landing of the stairs and looked down the Great Hall, his expression blank. Despite Zena's chintzes and cushions, despite Lord Snailwood's spectacular roses, despite the evening light, golden but as yet undimmed by dusk, the large space did not manage to feel mellow or cheerful. It was still an unsatis-factory room, not merely in the sense of being impractical, but also in its aura. In the absence of living inhabitants one seemed to sense the frustrations of earlier Snailwoods who had tried to live in this room, or if not in it, with it. Vincent appeared to be merely waiting for the gong, a warning to the guests but to the members of the household a signal that Zena expected them to be on hand to cope with any problems that might arise.

Footsteps whimpered on the treads of the upper flight. Vincent turned to see Mrs Dubigny coming down, wearing a cream satin dress, its plainness compensated for by exaggeratedly vivid make-up. She smiled at him with a warmth that was clearly not for him alone, an expression of pleasure with the world at large enhanced by the prospect of a party. She blew a kiss over his head. He looked to discover its target.

The high gothic windows, clear glass below and armorial bearings above, divided the evening light. At floor level things gleamed or glowed, but above that a darker palette prevailed, not dark enough for one to be able to say that the faces of the two spectators in the gallery were lost, or even unrecognisable, only that they were not immediately obvious. Sally blew a kiss back to her mother. The nurse did not smile.

"Poor Sally has such nightmares," whispered Mrs Dubigny. "It's long past her bedtime but she keeps on crying for me. I told Nanny she could come along there and watch the guests arrive. I do hope I don't have to go up to her – Zena does hate it so. In any case I mustn't let it become a habit, must I?"

"They make children g-go to bed much too early. Harry and I used to talk half the night."

"It's nice you're such friends – in spite of being so different."

As she spoke – her tone of general amusement with events sounding for once artificial in its exaggeration – Mrs Dubigny laid her fingertips on Vincent's arm, perhaps merely to feel the nap of his scarlet mess jacket, but at the same time giving the impression that she would like to test whether the man himself was composed of the same materials as Harry – with whom, presumably, she had already made a number of slight, preliminary, accidental-seeming contacts. Vincent looked her solemnly up and down, as if in turn attempting to decide by inspection whether she was good enough for his cousin.

"Everybody's different," he said.

"Yes, aren't they? But you don't have to be so gloomy about it. It's fun."

Discussion of the advantages of human variability was prevented by the entry of Prince Yasif, not down the stairs but through the double doors beneath the gallery. He was dressed for dinner, strikingly, in Bedu robes, which until he spoke had the effect of altering his personality from one of softness and affability to one of definite and even slightly sinister severity.

"Ah, there you are!" he cried. "Just the chappie I was looking for!"

They met at the foot of the stairs, Mrs Dubigny stooping into an experimental curtsey as soon as she was down. The Prince laughed, clearly excited.

"We don't have to start on any of that yet," he said. "The show's not on the road for twenty minutes, what?"

"Are you going to sweep us all off to your tent on your camel?" said Mrs Dubigny, managing to give the word "us" a gender implication beyond the normal resources of English grammar.

"Vince's camel, actually," said the Prince, grinning to show his disappointingly yellow teeth. "I say, old chap, I've been trying to use that contraption in the hall, but I haven't any change. Can you . . ."

"There's a telephone in my office," said Mrs Dubigny. "Provided we don't let on to Lord S."

"Oh, no, no, no, no," said the Prince. "The hospitality of the host is paramount. I must not abuse his trust, you know."

"That's OK," said Vincent. "Purser has a box of change in the pantry just for that. Hold on a tick."

"I'll come with you," said the Prince. "Mustn't keep Mrs Dubigny hanging about, you know. I expect she's masses to do."

"All done, please heaven," said Mrs Dubigny.

She watched the two men leave through the smaller door beneath the curve of the stairs, her hand moving to her mouth as if she was attempting to conceal a smile. She converted the gesture into another kiss to her daughter, answered this time by a stodgy wave, then walked across the room to smell the immense mound of scarlet roses in the bronze urn. The band by now was playing a definite tune, "I've got a thing about you". The drub of the first gong rumbled from the entrance hall.

Lord Snailwood's only serious resistance against Zena's invading armies – his Thermopylae, so to speak, eventually outflanked by Purser keeping small change in the pantry – had been the installation of a coin-box telephone for the use of guests. It stood in its own booth in the entrance hall, and despite the inconvenience – felt by Bernard Shaw to be a positive outrage – of guests having to pay for their own calls, it did at least give total privacy, at least from the ears of other inhabitants at Snailwood, though one cannot speak for the operators at the Marlow exchange. Perhaps it was this aspect that made the Prince prefer to use the otherwise demeaning system.

As they made their way back from the pantry Vincent said, "What's that about my c-camel?"

"Your car, old man. I was hoping you'd let me borrow it this evening."

"You're off?"

"No, of course not. I'll do my stuff here. But, tell you the truth, Dolly Flitwick-Johnson was teasing me about not being a proper desert Arab, and I told her I'd show her I was tonight. Now I learn she's not coming, and it's struck me I wouldn't be missed for an hour or so if I nipped over to Bullington. I might even manage to bring her back for a dance. Do you think that would be all right with our hostess?"

"More a q-question of if it's all right with her husband."

"Oh, he's in town, writing a leader for tomorrow's paper."

"I don't think Zena ... She's having a tiff with Dibbin. Honestly, you c-can't tell how she'll react to anything. But you c-can have the AC if you want. I'd better just nip out and see Smollett doesn't box it in when the g-guests arrive."

"Splendid. And you can show me the controls. Meet you out in the courtyard in five minutes?"

"Right-o."

No power on earth, possibly no power in heaven, could have made Smollett smart. If Sir John Dibbin's chauffeur had had the dressing of him, had his buttons and shoes been burnished by other hands and every crease of his uniform been sharp-pressed, there would have remained something in his appearance recalcitrant to such influences, something earthy, shambling, vague. He was one of those men inadequately described as having no ambition, but in Smollett's case this certainly did not imply physical laziness – he was a steady workman, a competent rough mechanic and a very safe driver – and probably not moral laziness either, but rather an inner stability, an acceptance of his own relationship with the world as satisfactory in its present form, and therefore in no need of "bettering". Harry claimed that McGrigor was Snailwood's representative of the urban proletariat, and Smollett of the rural; it was true that even at the wheel of the Sunbeam he retained an archetypal peasant air, a look of concern more with the seasons than the years. This characteristic tended to cause those giving him instructions – especially Lord Snailwood – to repeat them several times.

Vincent found this process in train, his uncle and Smollett standing beneath the clock tower, Lord Snailwood speaking in the softened tone he used when trying to give the impression that he was the only man keeping his head in a panicking multitude, but by his physical twitching and quivering producing exactly the opposite effect.

"Ah, there you are," he said, as though Vincent had been late for a long-fixed appointment. "I've been trying to get it into Smollett's head about the floodlamps. At least I could rely on

McGrigor not to make a potmess of that. Nine sharp, Smollett. At the nine strike, press the switch on the left of the one which isn't the other one. Got that clear?"

"Yes, my lord."

Lord Snailwood made an exasperated click with his tongue, as if the answer had been negative. For a moment it looked as if he was about to begin the process of explanation again.

"And Smollett's going to have to wind the clock from now on," he said. "Vincent, I'm relying on you to give him a lesson in that before you go."

"Right-o, sir."

"It struck the three-quarter all right. No trouble there."

"There shouldn't be."

"Still . . . I was going to stay and watch the hour . . . tell you what, you keep an eye on it. Let me know. Must have it going for the photograph. Don't want to get all these people out, tell them they're going to see something special, and it doesn't . . . Smollett, listen to this. You're to parade here, ten sharp, and Mr Vincent will show you how to wind the clock. Well, what is it?"

Vincent had made a minor gesture of interruption. Lord Snailwood glared.

"If Smollett's free after the photograph, sir. The noon strike weight has to c-come down before we wind it."

Vincent spoke as if giving the information for the first time, there being little chance of Lord Snailwood having remembered it from the day before.

"Oh, very well, very well. Not ten, Smollett. Twelve. Twelve. Get that into your head."

"Very good, my lord. Twelve o'clock."

Lord Snailwood produced his whinnying snort and strode away, each pace produced by an apparently involuntary twitch of the relevant leg.

"'Scuse my asking, Master Vince," said Smollett. "Then it's true as his lordship has writ to McGrigor?"

"'Fraid so."

"I'm sorry to hear that, Master Vince."

"It's McGrigor's own fault, really. He's let the Daimler g-get into a rotten state, you know. And his lordship wanted him here this morning to show me the c-clock, but he sent a message saying he was ill. That was the last straw. But really he's been asking for it for ages."

"McGrigor's genuine ill, Master Vince. Brought it on hisself, I dessay, but it's by dragging up day in day out to wind thissair clock he's done it. Been at him years to show me how, I have. Last six months he's been sneaking that Mildred in, help him with the big weights, after she brung him his dinner up. She told me. Monstrous heavy, some of them weights."

"I know. I wound 'em yesterday."

"Same with thissair Daimler. Take her down to Mowbry's, I been saying. But he's that worried of losing his place soon as his lordship finds out there's others can do what McGrigor's been doing. He's near on seventy, Master Vincent."

"All right, Smollett. Thank you for telling me. I heard my uncle say he'll k-keep his house and his pension, but I'll talk to Master Harry and we'll see if there's anything else we can do. Now listen. I've a friend who wants to borrow the AC later, so don't box her in. If I move her up here, that won't be in your way, will it, and he c-can just run her out."

"That'll be all right, sir. Shall I need to know the gentleman?"

"You'll know him all right. He'll be out in a tick for me to show him the ropes. I'll leave the k-keys under the seat. Right?"

"Very good, Master Vince."

Vincent had just re-parked the car when Prince Yasif showed up, moving more slowly now, even meditatively – a priestlike gait natural to his robes – but still with that air of charged excitement and relish. Vincent was moving to meet him when he stopped and pointed upward. Vincent came on, but watching over his shoulder as the clock went through its rite of autumn in the appropriately golden light, the tanned harvesters dancing with sheaf and sickle, outsize rabbits (their seasonal association rather obscure) gambolling fore and aft, and Ceres, classically crowned with a tower but also usurping functions of her sister Pomona by brandishing a huge apple as if it were a bomb and she an anarchist weighing it before hurling. Vincent reached the Prince and turned to watch in greater comfort as Time savaged the dance away. The white pigeons crooned and burbled.

"It is a king's toy," said the Prince. "When the Americans have found our oil and Sorah is truly rich I will build a clock like that. I will send workmen to copy it."

He sounded entirely serious about the proposal.

"You'll have to change one thing," said Vincent. "I suppose I'd better warn you, by the way. After church tomorrow we all parade out here to have our photograph taken and watch the noon strike."

"That's all right, old man. Shall I dress up again?"

"The problem is what happens when it strikes. You see, a Saracen and a c-crusader appear and fight and the Saracen is beaten. His head c-c-comes right off."

The Prince's thoughts were evidently elsewhere. He took some moments to understand.

"No," he said.

"'Fraid so."

"This cannot be altered?"

"Don't think so. I daresay I might stop it happening, disconnect that part. Now I know where my uncle k-keeps the k-keys I c-could nip in some time tonight and ... Actually, Solly, it wouldn't be very popular. My uncle's g-got a thing about the noon strike. If it fails, the Snailwood line will fail. Stupid, really. It fails at least a dozen times a year in any c-case."

"No, not stupid, Vincent. I could, I suppose, absent myself from the photographing ... No ... I shall simply think of something to laugh it off. Thank you for warning me, old chap."

The Prince's hand, which in a perfectly natural and unconscious gesture had closed on the hilt of the curved dagger at his belt, relaxed its hold.

"Now, one quick driving lesson, eh?" he said.

2

Professor Blech danced with both skill and gusto. As soon as the band, now huddled into a corner of the morning room, struck up the first notes of a foxtrot, before any of the after-dinner guests had arrived and while the other senior males were as yet barely half-way through their cigars, he was in the middle of the room with his wife, he beaming with pleasure, she expressionless but equally adept, sweeping across the as yet uncrowded floor in a series of manoeuvres so near to exhibition standard that the two or three younger couples who had been attracted by the music hesitated a while before joining in. When they did, the Blechs managed for a while to treat them as part of the performance, obstacles in the course to be overcome with maximum grace, until the crowd became too thick for one to be able to follow the movements of any individual couple.

As the evening progressed the strength of the Professor's personality expressed itself in the ease with which he found partners. It seemed that he marked each down during an earlier dance, choosing the prettiest but not necessarily the youngest women, provided they possessed a certain level of competence and then regardless of introductions asking for a dance, brushing aside objections, occasionally even persuading the partner whose name was already on the woman's card to stand down, and then bearing her away, pressing her to his chest and swinging her into the throng. Some of his partners looked put out, or at least startled by the intimacy of his embrace, but only for a few paces before, infected by his confidence in his skill as a dancer, discovering or rediscovering the exhilaration of performance at this level – the closeness being effectively sexless, an expression of the instant unity of movement – they forgot their qualms, forgot the social solecism, forgot his Jewishness, forgot even the sweat that beaded his brow by the end of each dance, and went all out to do their best for the fun of it. Gross, grinning, wholly self-centred, he yet spread pleasure, like Silenus, and not merely to his own partners. Indeed at the finish of one fast waltz the floor voluntarily cleared itself so that the Professor and Nancy Blaise could perform alone. The bandleader, infected also, raised the tempo and the couple whirled through the final bars with flamboyant, weightless precision. The other dancers clapped. Professor Blech padded his brow with a yellow handkerchief, his eyes already darting round to peer for his next sacrifice.

"That was better than a swim before breakfast," said Miss Blaise, an image so perfectly appropriate to her persona that it raised a laugh.

"I need a breather," she said to Vincent as she joined him by the wall. "Thank you for not minding me going off with the old buffer, but he is rather a treat, isn't he?"

"Much better than I'd have been. Shall we g-go and listen to the nightingales – they're said to be on form."

"Over-rated birds, but let's. Can you find me a drink? Not fizz – orange if poss."

"What an extraordinary old bean!" said Miss Blaise, still evidently obsessed by her encounter with Professor Blech as she and Vincent strolled out along the upper terraces. Dusk had become a succulent still night with a big moon. A double line of lanterns, each a single dimmish flame, marked the pathways between the rosebeds. The far lights would blink systematically out where some other pair of strollers, invisible despite the apparent brightness of the moon, moved past them.

"I thought he was just a world-beating bore," said Miss Blaise. "And then he springs that on one!"

"I noticed he actually stopped talking to dance."

"Never a word. Now where are these nightingales?"

"Down below. You'd probably hear them from here if it weren't for the band, but the best place is the trees round the Bloodstone."

"Bloodstone?"

"Just a sort of stone slab. It used to have a statue on it, ages back, but Aunt C-Clara had it taken away because it hadn't any c-clothes on."

"But why is it called that?"

"It isn't really. Only Harry and me. We used to play a weird g-game all over the g-garden, so lots of things have names. The Bloodstone was for sacrifices."

"*I* know. *We* had a kingdom all along the sand-dunes at Brancaster. Do we have to go the whole way round the end?"

"There are some steps down the wall in a bit, but they're pretty steep and rough. I doubt if they're lit, either. C-can you manage in a long skirt?"

"If you take my drink. Here."

*   *   *

Perhaps so as not to dissuade the nightingales from a performance worthy of Snailwood the gardeners had set only one lantern among the trees around the little lawn that held the Bloodstone. The birds were in full voice, two of them, stimulated by competition with each other and possibly with the fluting and wheedling of the band above. Miss Blaise took her orange juice from Vincent, sipped and settled the glass at the corner of the pedestal, leaning her back against the slab. Her dress, ice blue under the lights of the dancefloor, took on in the moonlight the hue of a paler stone.

"Harry invited me here," she said.

"Well, you see, Zena . . ."

"I suppose he asked you to take me off his hands."

"Well . . ."

"I'm rather glad. I like Harry. He's fun. But I get the impression he expects a girl to be pretty forthcoming after a bit."

"He's . . ."

"I don't want any of that. It's funny. Here I am, twenty-four, healthy, quite good to look at and so on. I don't think there's anything wrong with me, but I have every intention of dying a leathery old maid, and I shan't feel I've missed much. It's all right, Vince. I'm not warning you off because I think you have evil intentions. Tell me who you used to sacrifice on this stone."

"Oh, I don't know. Imaginary enemies. It started the other way round – before the g-game g-got all c-complicated, I mean. When we were small we rescued people who were being sacrificed. There was a picture in a book of Iphigenia. We took the idea from that."

"You leapt down from the trees waving your swords to rescue virgin princesses."

"That sort of thing."

"Poor things. How did you know they wanted to be rescued?"

"Because it was our g-game. We made it up."

"But if it had been real you wouldn't have known, would you? Perhaps they liked being sacrificed. What a lovely way to go – under a moon like this, on a night like this, remembering you've had the best of your life already . . . Why aren't you wearing a sword with that uniform, Vince? You'll have to go and borrow

Prince Solly's dagger. I'm sure he'd understand. He has that sort of look. It's time the stone had a real sacrifice."

Vincent didn't answer at once. Miss Blaise stretched herself backwards, head up, throat bared, seeming to luxuriate in the chill of the moonbeams. Their voices had alarmed the nearer nightingales into silence. If Vincent had been Harry he might not have taken Miss Blaise's words at their face value, reckoning that her pose, together with the imagery of the dagger blade sliding into welcoming flesh, implied a challenge, if not a definite invitation. Harry, presumably, supposing he had been interested, would have advanced the play further by adopting the mask of priest, father and slayer, if only to see what happened next. Vincent's practicality took a more superficial form. Indeed, when he spoke it sounded as though he had given real thought to the mechanics of the thing.

"Not on, I'm afraid. Solly's nipped off."

"Gone? Where?"

"Bullington. Show Dolly F-J what he looks like in his sheikh k-kit. He's talking of bringing her back here for a dance. If he does, that'll c-cause a real row between Dibbin and Zena. Don't tell anyone, but I've lent him my c-car."

There was more to Vincent's betrayal of the Prince's mild confidence than a wish to change the conversation, though that was no doubt part of his motive. But he spoke with real relish, almost a sportsman's enthusiasm, of the prospect of a clash between Zena and Sir John. Miss Blaise was interested in another aspect of the affair. She stretched out a marble arm to yawn.

"I bet he's hoping for more than a dance with Dolly," she said.

"I expect so."

"I think it's disgusting," said Miss Blaise, sitting suddenly up. "Dash it, he's a black man."

"Not very."

"Quite enough. And you lent him your car! What about her husband?"

"He's an ass. He deserves everything he g-g-gets. I c-couldn't really have said no when Solly asked for the car, but if it meant dishing Johnson I'd have done it anyway. Besides, Dolly knows how to look after herself."

"Doesn't she!" said Miss Blaise, twisting sideways and pulling one leg up under her chin to hug it to her. "I shouldn't have said that about him being a black man. It's stupid how much one minds . . . and she's so jolly white . . . I don't much care for her really . . . you can be pretty ruthless, Vince, can't you? Why do you hate Zena so? I'd have thought she was a rather lively kind of aunt to have, especially after what I've heard about old Lady Snailwood."

"Aunt C-Clara? She did make everyone's life hell, I suppose, but . . . I don't know. She belonged. She was part of the place. But Zena . . ."

"Doesn't belong? She makes a pretty good attempt."

"You're absolutely wrong. She's changed the rules. Everything's different. Not just her not belonging – it belongs to her. We belong to her."

Miss Blaise nodded, apparently fully understanding and even sympathising with the energy of Vincent's denunciation, the heavy, forceful manner in which he got the words out. Perhaps her expressed view that the best of life was over once childhood was over helped her share his sense of a poisoned world. She expressed herself, at least, in the imagery of the nursery.

"Like the new young queen who's really a witch," she said. "You'll need a specially strong magic to get rid of her. Perhaps you ought to have sacrificed me when you had the chance – that might have done it. But it's too late now. They'll be starting on the reels any sec, and that's always the best part. Let's go and make sure we get into a decent eight."

Restless with unreleased energies she swung herself off the stone and took his arm, but as they moved up the clearing another couple, mere shadows, entered from the path on the left, evidently having come the long way round.

"What's happened to the nightingales?" said Mrs Dubigny's voice. "You promised me flocks."

"'Fraid we've scared them by talking," said Vincent. "They'll start up again in half a mo."

"Vince," said Harry. "When you go up, have a word with Charles Archer . . ."

"Sh," said Mrs Dubigny. "Nightingales first."

"He's out on the terrace by the Duke of Cats," whispered Harry. "He's got a notion. See what you think. All right, my darling. Hush, world, so that Joan can listen to nightingales."

The two pairs drifted apart. Vincent took Miss Blaise's glass again so that she could hold her skirt to climb the tricky stairway. They went up, perforce, single file. Harry and Mrs Dubigny stood waiting by the Bloodstone. Further down the slope a third nightingale had not interrupted its singing, and now stimulated the first two to break out again. The lovers waited, listening, in the moonlight and then, Harry leading the way to push the lower branches aside, moved into invisibility beneath the trees.

3

"I do hope I'm not dragging you away from some delightful girl," said Sir Charles, the irony in his voice predominating over the solicitude.

"Not at all, sir. I'm supposed to be one of Zena's spares," said Vincent.

"But I've just seen you emerge from the darkness with the beautiful Miss Blaise."

"That's all right, sir. She g-gets all the partners she can manage."

"I am not surprised. A classic type. I had a cousin in much the same mould. Every young man in London broke his heart over her for about three months – their first love, always, of course. Then they went off and married someone else. My cousin became a hospital matron and died of overwork in 'seventeen."

Sir Charles had had placed for him a few chairs and a table at the eastern end of the front terrace, just beside the stone lion. A decanter, siphon and cigar box waited by his glass. He sat, as always, bolt upright, giving no impression of repose.

"Take a seat, Vincent," he said. "Got a drink? I shall not keep you long from the festivities. You know, the old maniac who built this place must be praised still for certain effects. I have sat here a score of times. I appreciate the somewhat factitious romance of it all – the river, the lights on the garden, the sound of revelry by night beneath the frowning battlements. This time I have noticed a small extra point. You see that window up there, towards the top of the further tower? With just the faintest of lights in it?"

"That's the old nursery, sir. I expect Mrs Dubigny's daughter sleeps with a night-light. She's rather a nervy k-kid."

"That would explain it. The light, you see, adds a subtle touch, by its contrast with the blaze from the morning room. At first I thought it was a trick of moonlight, reflected by the glass. But then I began to perceive a figure against the light, merely a silhouette, but female from the outline of the hair. She has been back three times, looking out at us enjoying ourselves below – the princess secluded in her supposed madness while the court revels and the councillors plot her dynastic marriage to some cold tyrant, eh? No, I decided she was merely one of the servants. Look, she is there now."

"The racket must make it difficult to sleep."

"As you no doubt remember?"

"This sort of thing didn't happen in Aunt C-Clara's day."

"I never knew her. She led poor Snailwood a dog's life, I am told. No wonder he is such an oddity. I warned Zena she might find him a handful."

"You knew her before they . . . ? I thought he . . . ?"

Sir Charles's laugh, a sound in any case rare with him, had a raucous edge which indicated that he might be mainly responsible for the decanter being less than half full. If so it was the only sign. His speech was precise and fluent.

"You thought Snailwood had found a Balkan adventuress, unaided. In that she was married to a Balkan adventurer for a few months she has a claim by marriage to that title. In fact she is the daughter of a Norwich grain merchant."

"No!"

The vehemence of Vincent's response stimulated Sir Charles to further laughter, this time with an edge of malice in it. His right hand rose to caress the great blotch on his cheek, though as usual he had seated himself so that that side of his face was in shadow.

"I began my political career, soon after the Boer War, in Norwich," he said. "Zena's father was one of my worthiest supporters. She was a delicious child – yes, quite delectable . . . It may have been my friendship with the family that gave her her rather absurd political ambitions. Her first idea, of course, was that she would become a queen. Her view of the world was, and still is, to a great extent moulded by the novels available in the Boots lending library – volumes in which, statistically, the highest proportion of romantically accessible royalty is centred on south-eastern Europe. After the war – more for my own peace and quiet than anything – I found her a job in one of our embassies. The marriage to Pliakin followed as night follows day. I do believe that his claim to nobility was not entirely fraudulent."

"But we all thought . . ."

"It is entirely untrue that she had anything to do with his death."

"I never . . ."

"A fall in a horse race. Quite impossible to pre-arrange, how-ever convenient to Zena. I had careful enquiries made. I had, you see, already introduced her to Snailwood so I felt a certain responsibility."

"Guh . . . guh . . . guh . . ."

"Though not," said Sir Charles, having watched Vincent strug-gle with the consonant, "envisaging an outcome such as this."

Broker of nations, he waved his cigar in the general direction of the "superduperdo".

"Even so, a certain responsibility, as I say, remains," he went on. "Snailwood has made his bed and he must lie on it, but you and your cousin Harry have suffered the result without choice. It is that that I wish to talk to you about."

Vincent drew a deep breath but said nothing. His effort to control his agitation resulted in a stiffening of spine and face muscles, as though he had been on parade back in cadet days and undergoing a bollocking from the CSM. There was nothing to show that he had noticed the interview was now assumed to be taking place at Sir Charles's insistence, whereas Harry had im-plied otherwise.

"I have long been impressed by your cousin," said Sir Charles. "People have very different innate gifts, which often have little connection with their more general abilities. To take an obvious example, there is a type of man who appears to lack either intelligence or imagination and to be endowed with nothing beside a few minor social graces, who yet has an almost visceral appreciation of money matters. The same is true of politics, but among us the gift is harder to recognise because of the larger number of men who would like to believe they possess it, and who may indeed make a considerable career for themselves by means of other talents. Baldwin, for instance, had the gift to a high degree. Eden almost entirely lacks it. Attlee has it, Cripps has not. It is a matter neither of principles nor of intelligence, but, as I was saying only this morning, of feel for the grain of the timber one must cut. I believe Harry to be quite well endowed with it."

"He's published some very political books, sir."

"So have others. I read them all, of course, and review some. I am impressed by Throckmorton's list because it shows unusual appreciation of what is going to be the key issue by the time a book is published, and this I understand to be largely Harry's doing – Throckmorton himself is quite out of date and Drining only interested in the higher realms of fiction. But let us narrow the subject further. Harry has more than once suggested that he would like to enter Parliament. I believe at least one chance has been given him, but he turned it down. Eh?"

"Throckmorton turned it down, sir. He said it would take up too much of Harry's time. Harry's not g-got much money of his own."

"That is always a problem. I fail to understand why Snailwood hasn't made him a sensible allowance, but Zena appears to think it is out of the question. Forgive me for trespassing on delicate family ground, but there are certain matters on which I do not regard Zena as a reliable witness. Is it known which of you two Snailwood regards as his heir?"

"No, sir."

"And you and your cousin have not even any opinions on the matter? I find that hard to credit."

"We made up our minds, sir, ages ago. My uncle is g-going to live to ninety. He'll change his mind every six months. There's no point in letting it mess other things up for us."

"A very sound arrangement. Zena, I believe, favours Harry."

"Yes, sir."

"And her efforts to make Snailwood give him an allowance can be read, particularly by Snailwood himself, as an attempt to force a declaration that Harry is the heir?"

"I didn't know it had g-got that far, sir."

"And you would rather not talk about it in any case? Very well. I appreciate your being so open with me."

"Harry asked me."

"Of course. Now, Throckmorton is due to retire some time soon, it is said."

"He's been talking about it for ages, according to Harry."

"And he will go on talking about it for ages. Your cousin hopes that when Throckmorton retires Drining will take over and will prove more amenable to the idea of Harry entering Parliament. At the same time Harry will have the political list pretty well to himself, and that is worth waiting for. So it sounds reasonable to stay on, but for one thing. It won't wash. Throckmorton will not retire. I have, I dare say you know, very good sources of information in many fields, and I know for a fact that Throckmorton detests Drining. He will remain in office to spite him, just as Gladstone remained to spite Joe Chamberlain."

"Are you sure, sir? Harry says . . ."

"Harry is wrong. He will have to get another job."

"It isn't easy."

"Certainly there are obstacles to his approaching some other publisher and saying, 'Please pay me a salary so that I can afford to have a political career'."

"He's tried that, sir. Not like that, of c-course, but . . ."

"Then, since there is no more sense in planning on Throckmorton's eventual retirement than there is on your uncle's eventual demise, the solution is for Harry to leave and set up on his own."

"He'd love to do that. He's full of ideas. We talk about it a lot. But he c-can't persuade my uncle to put up the c-capital. I've g-got a bit, but nothing like enough."

"There we come to it. The capital. That is where I believe I can help. You are aware that with Baldwin's retirement a number of seats became vacant following the elevation of certain of his cronies to the peerage in the resignation honours? The candidates for the by-elections have already been chosen, but two days ago I heard of a constituency in which the Conservative candidate proved, at the last minute, unsuitable. A replacement must be found before next Wednesday. As an inducement to attract a man of high calibre at such short notice, a senior member of the Conservative Association in the constituency tells me that he would put up the capital to found a small business, such as a publishing firm. Do you follow me?"

"That would be . . . You've talked to Harry about this, sir?"

"Of course. Let me finish. There are certain conditions."

"I see."

"It is because of the conditions that Harry suggested I should talk to you. To make no bones about it, I was reluctant to do so."

"We take each other's advice a g-good deal, about some things."

"There are certain tribes in which a man, on reaching the age where he can become a hunter, goes out alone into the forest and chooses a particular rock or tree into which he puts his soul, so that he becomes immune to the magical assaults of enemies."

Sir Charles's theatrically penetrating glance was now beamed straight at Vincent, who shrugged uneasily.

"Very well," said Sir Charles. "At the start of such a venture I can appreciate your cousin wanting your advice and, I imagine, approval. But we cannot have him running to you every time there is a dilemma of conscience within my group. For that, effectively, is the condition on which the capital will be raised. A fair degree of latitude would of course be tolerable, but fundamentally the candidate chosen would, if elected – and it is a very safe seat – have to be prepared to vote and act with my group."

During the whole conversation Vincent had only relaxed his mien of undergoing a difficult viva voce when the possibility of Harry setting up on his own had been raised. Now, obviously, he found it difficult to keep a tone of distrust, even dislike, out of his voice.

"But that might mean . . ." he began.

"You think we are pro-German?"

"I suppose so."

"We are not pro-German," said Sir Charles with soft patience. "We are certainly not pro-Nazi. I personally detest much that National Socialism announces as its aims, and much more of the means by which it is attempting to achieve those aims. I am, most profoundly, a patriot. I would dare anything and suffer anything if it meant that the honour and power of our empire should remain undiminished. But I am also a realist. I know how weakened our apparently formidable structure has been allowed to become. I know that a war against Germany, even one that ended in complete victory, would leave us so enfeebled that within a generation we would find ourselves reduced to the stature of a minor Scandinavian nation. And victory is far from certain. Thanks to the intransigence of the French, Herr Hitler will certainly come to an understanding with Russia before he confronts the Entente. And then what trust have you in the French as allies? If we are weakened, they are utterly debilitated. They shelter behind the Maginot Line and think themselves safe, but have they the will to defend their position? They have not. Patriotism, for me and my friends, consists in having the courage to confront considerations such as this, and to see clearly that there must be no war."

"I don't see how we c-can make friends with a man like Herr Hitler."

"I do not propose to make friends. I propose simply not to make enemies. The interests of Germany are in many aspects our interests. It is, for instance, in our interest that the Jewish question should be solved. There can be no stability in the world while this nation exists that has no national home, and so has to live like a parasite along the arteries of host nations. If the question is not solved in the manner we propose, then eventually more dreadful ways will be found."

"But suppose that's sorted out, and this business with Czechoslovakia, and so on, there'll be something else, won't there, and then something else? Professor Blech says war is inevitable. I know Harry thinks so too. A lot of us are half looking forward to it."

"Then you are half deluded. 'To turn like swimmers into cleanness leaping,' is that it? Rupert Brooke was lucky to die as he did before he could see, as I saw, the vileness of that cleanness. And this war will be worse. You are a soldier, Vincent. They have taught you the effects of a gas attack on troops, no doubt. Have they said anything to you about the effects of gas on a civilian population?"

"That's not really our business, sir."

"It *is* our business, every man jack of us. Your mother lives just behind Harrods, I seem to remember?"

Sir Charles, as a friend of the family, may well have been aware of the touchiness of Vincent's relationship with his mother – the cause, according to Zena at least, of his stammer – but he probably only brought her into the argument to deploy the rhetorician's trick of particularising the general. Vincent nodded, perhaps a little sullenly, but did not otherwise react.

"That is precisely where the gas canisters would fall," said Sir Charles. "The Luftwaffe would of course wait for a prevailing south-west wind. No doubt your mother would be out here, in comparative safety, before the attack began. I take her only as an example. There are many, many soldiers whose mothers and wives and children have no such bolt-hole."

"I meant . . ."

"You meant that preparations against such an attack are the concern of the civilian authorities, and you take it for granted that they will be effective. It is true that we have a Minister for the Co-ordination of Defence in the new Cabinet – the egregious Inskip. Gas masks are being issued, effective against types of gas developed twenty years ago. But reliable informants inside Germany tell me that new gases have been manufactured which will penetrate the filters of these gas masks, and others which will not even need to be breathed, because they are fatal on mere contact with human skin. So, Vincent, we are faced with these alternatives. Either we must develop counter-measures of the same horror, and then persuade Herr Hitler that we would not hesitate to use them, or else we must arrange matters so that the Luftwaffe does not come. Can you believe, even had we time to catch up in this hellish race, that a nation such as ours, with its sentimental attachment to notions of human decency and the fellowship of man, could be persuaded to embark on the former course? Would you yourself not draw the line before you reached that point?"

"No, sir."

"No?"

"I don't see it matters how you k-kill people, if you're g-going to k-kill them at all."

"We are talking about the civilian population of great cities."

"They're for it anyway, sir, don't you think?"

Sir Charles accepted the break in the chain of his argument as if it had not happened.

"If there is a war, certainly," he said. "That is a further reason why there must be no war. The salvation of this nation and empire depends on the avoidance of conflict with Germany, and that in turn depends on our political will. There is no such will, anywhere in the nation. There is no demand for war, no expectation of peace. We are in a general stupor, hypnotised by the approaching monster. We need a voice to wake us, and that voice must be heard in Parliament. For, mark you, under our present leadership the ship of state will not sail gallantly and deliberately into the battle line. It will drift, pilotless, chartless, to all intents unsteered. Our task – mine and my friends' – is to see that that does not happen. The issue is so finely balanced that a very few votes and voices will make the difference. This is a great moment in our history, Vincent. I need young Harry to join me in the effort. He has made it plain to me that he will talk his decision over with you. Earlier I used the image of the primitive tribesman who puts his soul into safe keeping with some rock or tree so that he can walk through the snares of the enchanter unbewitched. I am asking you to release him so that he can join me in my battle. Well?"

"He'll make up his own mind, sir."

"Of course he will. But making up one's mind is a process. One does it in part by converse with friends. What will you say to him?"

"This chap – the one who's putting up the c-capital – suppose Harry doesn't like the line you're taking – in a c-couple of years, I mean . . ."

Sir Charles sighed.

"The question you are attempting to ask is the oldest in the world," he said. "It can never be answered because those who ask it mean a different thing from those whom they ask. You wish to know whether, in accepting an arrangement such as I outline, Harry will be subtly compelled to support causes in which he does not believe, to connive in stratagems which he knows to be corrupt, to work with allies who may be vicious, or stupid, or potential traitors to the nation. Whether, in Shakespeare's phrase, he must subdue his nature to what he works in, like the dyer's hand. For make no mistake, these are indeed the materials with which he must work. The nature of man, and therefore of politics, decree that it shall be so. But I, in attempting to formulate an answer to your question, am myself asking whether Harry has it in him to become a handler of such dye-stuff. For there is no escaping this, Vincent. The cloth is there, wherewith we must be clothed. There is an end to running naked through the meadows of childhood. The cloth is on the loom, being constantly woven. Every minute of the day, like it or not, the shuttle is rattling between the threads. It must be given its colour. The question is, by whose hand?"

As he spoke Sir Charles turned and stretched his own hand forward, pale in the shadowy light, the long fingers slightly crooked to hold an invisible sphere. At the same time his marred but formidable head stared directly at Vincent, riddling him with his gaze. Vincent gazed back, unanswering, not apparently seeing Sir Charles, still the cadet on parade enduring the onslaught of words as if he were a thing as insensate as the butt of the rifle round which his left hand curls. At last Sir Charles turned away to face once more along the frontage of the house.

"Look," he said quietly. "There she is again."

Now Vincent responded, turning his head also. The terrace was barred with strong light streaming from the open doors and windows of the morning room, but the shutters of the Great Hall were closed, as were those of the rooms beyond the dance floor. The noise that emanated in music and chatter from the dance seemed integral with the electric light, so that the moon and the line of pale lamps along the balustrade became by contrast the markers of realms of silence. Two-thirds of the way up the tower that shouldered out at the far end of the frontage appeared another such realm, a faint window, the feebleness of whose illumination made it seem yet more peaceful than the silences of either lamp or moon. In its rectangle, standing presumably on the thick inner sill, was the silhouette of the child. Vincent gazed at the shape, perhaps not even seeing it, his personality having undergone that change, that apparent gathering together and focusing of energies, with which he tended to confront mechanical problems.

"Well, Vincent," said Sir Charles. "I can only ask you to do your best for Harry."

4

What was the event – what is any event – actually like? The form of the question, the need to use a word such as "like", suggests the difficulty of exact answer. In the succeeding seconds the event has begun its new existence as a memory of the participants, and thus become something different. That memory, should the participants choose to summon it up, will each time have undergone both diminutions and additions, and should they attempt to speak of it must now endure wrenching transformations, not merely because of the inadequacies of language, but because it must be reorganised into probably false coherences in order to be sayable at all. In something the same way the sleeping mind perceives images, static or brief spasms of action, while another part of what we are forced to think of as the same mind attempts to improvise a plot, or story-line, in which these images will more or less make sense. The dual process is the dream, but on waking this dream can only be recalled by the secondary element, the story-line, and the primary images which were the heart of the dream will have to be demoted into incidents, or mere frills and curlicues of the fancy, irrelevant to the basic architecture of plot – a plot that never existed in its own right. There are monsters in our museums, skeletons pieced together and given plaster flesh and painted skin and then taken by visitors for accurate portrayals of the creatures that paddled the ancient swamps, until some maverick palaeontologist reinterprets the crushed and exiguous fossil-finds and one of the monsters discovers that it was never that shape at all.

And what if memory fails – is overlaid perhaps by other and more potent memories or else, as in this case, is almost immediately blanked out by the trauma of the event itself? The event still occurred. The tree did fall in the desert, though there was no one to see or hear it. And there are still fossils in the mind, though even more exiguous. For memory is not a single store. Parts of both body and mind possess autonomous resources of recall, so that the tongue, and not the mouth, appears to remember of its own accord that last mouthful of coffee left somewhere about the house undrunk in its mug. Remaining with these separate oral memories, take the case of a thirteen-year-old girl at a bleakly jolly boarding school, towards the end of the war. Since, in theory, a woman's main task in wartime is to bind up the wounds of heroes (other resources for hero-comfort not being teachable at such establishments) the girls have lessons in first aid. They are shown how, and then set to bandage each other's arms or legs. The trained nurse who has given the demonstration has made it so quick and easy, the roll of bandage unwinding from her hand to wrap crooks and curves and hollows smooth as snowfall, but the girls soon discover how different is the practice of life from any demonstration. Strange loops and loosenings beset them, ends that unwind as fast as the opposite ends wind up. Two hands are not enough to control these writhings, so mouths come unhygienically into play. A hand rises.

"Please, miss – something's wrong with Sally."

The voice is half alarmed, half amused by an event dramatic enough to provide an afternoon's gossip and guesswork. Something is indeed wrong with Sally. Bandagers stop their weaving, wounded sit up to crane, nurse and class mistress wade through them to the child who is kneeling, upright, pale, unaware, shuddering as a nun might in her cell, pierced in the midst of prayer by the longed-for but still terrible visitation.

Sally wakes in the sick bay, knowing nothing since the moment of kneeling to bandage Louisa's ankle. A letter from her dead stepfather is in the headmistress's confidential file, explaining that owing to an unfortunate occurrence in Sally's past care may need to be exercised in certain circumstances. Her friends are therefore instructed not to talk, either to her or to each other, about the episode – thus effectively extending its gossip value to almost a week. But Sally herself, in any case always a slightly isolated child, appears untouched by her new interestingness. Her central mind, that which seems to her to be the real and only Sally, has no

150

communication with the small autonomous province of mouth-memory, despite that province's power at a particular stimulus – the dry, dust-like, flavourless presence of cloth on lips and tongue – to put the whole empire of body and mind into trance.

One may be tempted to dig where such an unusual fossil has protruded from the strata. For one reason or another one may become obsessed with a need to know the true configuration of the monster. Some years later Sally Quintain sits in the visitor's chair of a leather-smelling office and listens to a fat, bald man talking in a foreign accent. She is very pale, but not as chalk-white as she was when she lay in trance on the couch beneath the window, and her features declare her true age, just over twenty-one, though half an hour ago they had reverted to the almost boneless softness of a child's.

"The trauma is evidently very deep," says Dr Fettil. "I woke you deliberately. I would not recommend proceeding further by hypnosis. You have a very deep-seated trauma which you are anxious to conceal."

"I'm not! I want to *know*."

"That is superficial. I cannot by hypnosis force you to go against your fundamental inclinations. The proper way to proceed is to embark on a course of analysis, to enable you to recognise and come to terms with the nature of this trauma."

"How long would that take?"

"It is impossible to say."

"Guess."

"Well, between one and three years."

"I only want to know what happened. I don't want to change myself or anything. I'm perfectly happy with myself as I am."

"If you know what happened you will change yourself."

"But . . . Didn't I say anything? I feel as though I'd been through a mangle."

"You told me about a dream."

"Ah . . . the bear?"

"Yes."

"What did I say? Listen, I know I have that dream, about once a month. I wake up sweating, absolutely rigid, but I can never remember what it was that frightened me. I used to shout out about a bear when I was small. Oh, come on. I'm paying you a lot of money. You might at least tell me my own dreams."

Dr Fettil nods stolidly and consults his note-pad.

"You are in a cave by the sea," he says. "You are lying on the sand and looking at the ripple-shadows on the roof. The Captain has left you, saying he will come back soon. Clearly the Captain is your father."

"I don't think I want explanations for the moment. Just the dream."

"Very well. You lie for a long time in this cave, telling yourself how happy you are. After a while you are lying the other way round, and aware that the end of the cave is dark. You try to see the end wall, and you realise that the cave is much deeper than you thought. You become afraid of the darkness. You try to move, but you cannot. You are clutching your doll, but she puts her head into your mouth, so that you are unable to call out. A bear comes out of the darkness, standing on its hind legs. A black bear with a white head. It leans over you. Its head is a cauliflower. It puts up its hands and starts to remove its head."

"I told you that?" whispers Sally.

"Yes. That is all, apart from some moanings and struggles."

"I wasn't going to believe you, you know . . . The Captain . . . He comes out of a book . . . There was water under trees somewhere, and light being thrown up . . . Yes, that's when I wake up. It's quite an ordinary nightmare until I see the cauliflower. He's going to show me something underneath."

"Miss Quintain, the nature of this dream and your own reaction to it reveals a serious and deep-seated trauma. Once more . . ."

"Do you think it's connected with the other thing that happened? It might come from before, you know. My mother says I've always had nightmares, ever since I was tiny."

"I cannot say without further analysis. The trauma itself may well pre-date that also. Your father . . ."

"No. I don't want to know about any of that. It's what happened outside me I want to know about, for purely practical reasons, not what happened inside me. I may be wrong, but . . ."

"You are wrong."

"I'm sorry. Actually you've been quite a help. It won't be money down the drain."

"If you decide to proceed no further I propose to waive my fee."

"Oh, no. Really, you mustn't. I did tell you what I wanted and you agreed."

"I have not supplied what you wanted."

Sally, very pale still, smiles.

"But you've given me something else almost as good," she says. "I'm going to teach myself to wake up as soon as I realise the Captain's gone."

"You will only push the trauma still deeper."

"The deeper the better."

9

The sound of footsteps converged on the dark and winding stair, Miss Quintain climbing from the courtyard, Mr Mason coming carefully down from the clock room. There was no question of passing, so she turned into the chamber where the weights hung and waited. Only one weight in fact dangled there, nine feet up. The others were stacked against the far wall, and over them the bob of the pendulum swung to and fro on its fourteen-foot rod. Its tock filled the room, a steady beat every two seconds.

"Isn't it marvellous to hear it going!" said Miss Quintain as Mr Mason stepped into the room. He looked pleased but did not smile. His gaze seemed to fluster her slightly, as though accusing her of entering his domain unasked. Indeed, when he spoke his words made it clear that he had deliberately descended to prevent her entering the upper sanctum, though at the same time he supplied a perfectly acceptable overt reason for this.

"Heard you coming," he said. "Didn't want to trouble you to climb all the way."

"You shouldn't have bothered. I'm still perfectly spry," she said.

Still, there was something not quite settled about her demeanour. Of course it could have been that this was normal, among people with whom she was familiar. The tightness, precision, control, were reserved for confrontations with strangers, and the relationship with Mr Mason was felt to have progressed beyond that. Alternatively she was discovering, as the weeks went by, something particular to that relationship and was not yet sure how to come to terms with it. He waited.

"I've got something I'd like you to read," she said. "It's rather long, but . . . it does tell you a bit about the fire, which might be a help, but that's not really . . . You see, I want to have a talk with you, but I'd like you to read this first. It's only fair. Do you mind?"

Mr Mason reacted with complete stolidity, apparently not even perceiving her agitation. He took the buff-coloured folder she handed him and opened it. Inside were twenty or thirty sheets of flimsy paper, covered with a large-lettered handwriting, the script suggestive of a slightly diffuse personality ordering itself for the purposes of communication. Mr Mason held it at arm's length to read the first few words. He looked up.

"You quite sure . . ." he began.

"Yes. All of it. Right through," said Miss Quintain.

"Take a bit of time."

"There's no terrific hurry. I thought if we could have a talk when you come next week."

"I'll give it a go during my dinner."

"Well . . ."

"Fetch my food back here then, shall I? Seeing it's private."

"If you wouldn't mind."

By midday it had begun to rain. A few steady drips on the roof of the clock room tapped out alternatives to the louder knock of the escapement. Mr Mason had folded his coat to make a cushion on his tool-chest and sat there with one of the figures of Father Time, still bearing smoke stains from the fire, poised close behind his shoulder. He read steadily, taking unnoticing mouthfuls, laying the finished sheets face down beside him. He wore rather small-lensed, brass-rimmed spectacles perched half-way down his nose. They gave him the look of a very old-fashioned type of craftsman, of a role adopted years ago and clung to.

"15th August 1940
"My darling Sal,
It seems strange to write to you like this, and not use one of our pet names, but you will have outgrown them, no doubt, by the time you read this; and from my own point of view I am anxious to be as clear and unemotional as possible, and not to put any unfair pressures on you. One thing, however, I will ask: try to read right through. You will find parts of it difficult, and even painful, but for my sake I want you to read every word, because this letter concerns the two things that were most important in my life until I met your mother and you. Once you have read it you owe me

155

nothing, and must do whatever you wish, consulting only your own physical and emotional interests. If you choose to burn these pages and forget all about them, that will be your own choice and therefore what I would wish. If you choose to follow any of the ideas or suggestions in them, that will still only be what I would wish because it has been your own choice. I hope that is clear.

"My instructions to Perring and Perring are that in the event of my death they will keep this letter at least until you are sixteen. Then, supposing your mother has also died – and who knows what may not happen in a war like this? – the senior partner is to open it, read it, and unless you have shown serious signs of mental instability (I cannot believe that that will be the case: you are among the sanest people I know) he is to give it to you.

"If your mother is alive (as of course I hope she will be) you will receive this letter six months before your twenty-first birthday. Nobody else will have read it, but Perrings will enclose a note warning that you should not read it if you are currently in a low state. The point is that under the terms of my will my as yet unsettled rights to Snailwood devolve on you when you are twenty-one, and I want you to have a bit of time to make up your mind about your feelings.

"Snailwood itself is of course one of the two things of importance to me of which I have spoken. My Uncle Snailwood's failure to leave a clear will, combined with my Aunt Ivy's refusal to forgive us for what, in her words, we 'did to Vincent', are already making matters quite difficult enough; my own presumed death can only make the former problem worse. I am working as best I can on Aunt Ivy, and it is just possible that my death will in fact appease her, but she has more than her share of the Snailwood unpredictability.

"I have given the lawyers to understand that I have made you my heir in order to help with death duties (the understanding of lawyers being limited to notions of that type). My real reason, of course, is that at the moment you appear to care about Snailwood as much as I do. This feeling for the place in you may or may not last. I must insist that you do not attempt to keep it alive for my sake. I shall be dead. I very strongly do not believe in any kind of after-life. I have been extremely happy at Snailwood, both before

156

and after you and your mother came to live there, but that play will be over, the curtain down, the audience gone home for ever. Do not try to revive it. If you want to continue at Snailwood because you think you will be happier there than elsewhere, that is all that will matter.

"It is going to be difficult, my dear. The combination of Uncle Snailwood's will and Aunt Ivy's intransigence and the war will make your finances very pinched if you do decide to stay. Let us suppose the war ends in a victory for the allies (though, as I write, Britain seems to be all that is left of that alliance). I find it hard to believe that in a war-exhausted world any government, of whatever stripe, will find it practicable to legislate for the convenience of owners of estates such as ours. All I can suggest is that you keep your eyes and ears open and remain as flexible as possible to the changes of the world. And it will change, beyond anything we can envisage. The whole social structure for which houses such as Snailwood were built will very likely crumble into dust. How could one continue to live here, in that case?

"My own idea has been that I may have to open the garden as a show place. The house itself is of no great interest: anybody can see it from the river, and that is the best of it. But I believe the garden could be made as attractive as anything in England, so that visitors would pay to see it in worthwhile numbers. I talked about the possibilities years ago, walking round with Harold Nicolson. You will find my notes at the back of the 'G' file, but you are not to follow them slavishly, supposing you take up this suggestion at all. I only put it in here to show you what I mean by flexibility. Nothing that will make your life possible should be considered taboo, not even Sunday trippers.

"All this supposes that the difficulty with Aunt Ivy will be settled. I write what follows partly to help you understand the nature of that difficulty, and so cope with it, but mainly because it concerns the other very important thing in my life, besides Snailwood. This is my relationship with my cousin Vincent Masham. I may seem to be breaking my promise to your mother not to speak or write to you about him, ever; but that promise was given in the shock of the event; when, in fact, I hardly knew you, and before I realised what a splendidly balanced and intelligent person you were beneath your exterior sulks and shyness. In any case, I feel my death will have released me from all such promises.

"To say that Vincent and I were 'great friends' is entirely to misunderstand the relationship. We were not inseparable, though we did attend the same schools and spent some of our holidays together at Snailwood. But even at Eton, where I was in College and Vince in an Oppidan house, we were never in the same forms and might not see each other for more than a bit of casual chat in the street two or three times a week. Yet the bond between us was immensely strong; quite as strong as marriage, it seems to me, though I am passionately happy in my marriage to your mother.

"Putting it like this may imply to you that our relationship was at bottom* one of suppressed homosexuality. No. My own inclinations are very strongly towards your sex and always were, even at Eton, where a good deal of homosexuality was prevalent in my day, among boys who later showed themselves to be perfectly 'normal' and had merely resorted to their own sex because there was almost no opportunity for anything else. Vincent was rather different, in that he was extremely inhibited about sexual matters of any kind; but I don't think his problem was suppressed homosexuality. It is true that Aunt Ivy was a classically appalling mother, but not the exponent of smother-love one reads of in the textbooks. Seeing his behaviour at Eton, and later his reactions to certain kinds of physically attractive women (your mother a good example) I am persuaded that his bent was very much the same as mine, and at least as strong, but that he found great difficulty in giving it expression.

"Vince's difficulties are not irrelevant to you, but I have embarked on them sooner than I meant. Let me go back to my own feelings for him. Our relationship did have something in common with marriage, in the sense that we had developed into what we were, each into his own shape (if you follow me) to accommodate the shape of the other. I was actually talking to Vince about this the evening before he vanished, instancing the superficial example of how his uncommon ability at ball games and my reaction to it had caused me to choose certain paths in my

---

* I do hope you enjoy this kind of accidental Freudian pun. I do.

own development and thus helped to make me what I am. In the course of the same conversation (I always, you won't be surprised to learn, did most of the talking) we turned to the question whether I would get the chance to bed your mother that night, only having met her the evening before*. It seemed to me quite a possibility, and I said so. At least there was nothing to prevent my having a go, as there hadn't been with a number of women before. Sometimes I'd brought it off, sometimes not, but there had been no problem about trying. Now it seems to me by hindsight that the simplicity to me of this business may have been analogous to the simplicity Vince found in biffing a fast-moving ball where he wanted with a bat or racket. Perhaps the fact that he found sexual approaches so tricky made them marginally more straightforward for me; and the fact that I had few problems in that field made it more than marginally harder for Vince.

"Anyway, it is of more immediate importance that we did have this conversation, that Vince was somewhat disturbed by it (I never used to take much notice of that because I thought it was good for him) and that I then did spend the night with your mother. In the course of that night a man came to your room, tied a gag into your mouth and sexually assaulted you. Your nurse found you asleep in the morning with the gag still round your face and blood on your nightie. A doctor was called, and confirmed what must have happened.

"You yourself seemed to remember nothing whatever of the incident; but when you had been put back into your bed and your mother was talking to the doctor at the other side of the room, you started to scream the words 'dirty face'. The doctor was preparing a sedative for you when you fell asleep of your own accord, on

* About your mother: do not judge her for being a loose woman, which in a sense she is. I love her obsessively. I don't believe she loves me in the same way, and why should she? I am a man to live with and go to bed with. I may be quantitively more than that implies, but not qualitatively; I mean I think she would choose me for those purposes rather than some other man, but she's really a bit puzzled by my feelings for her and can only pretend to share them. Now that I am to be posted abroad she may not remain faithful to me. I hope she won't after my death.

your mother's lap. The doctor then left. Your mother stayed in the room and when you woke she again asked you who had attacked you. (I should have mentioned that you slept with a night-light which was still burning in the morning, so you would have seen the man.) It was at this point that, according to your mother, you said it had been Vince. By this time Anderson, the local bobby, had been called, but when your mother questioned you in his presence you refused to speak.

"Later that morning, at Anderson's suggestion, you were taken down to watch the house party being photographed in the courtyard, with the idea that you might recognise your attacker, or otherwise react to him. The photographing was interrupted by a fire breaking out in the clock tower, and some of us rushed off to try and extinguish it. By the time we had managed to break into the tower the fire had a serious hold, but we managed to control it until the arrival of the fire brigade. (The fire had nearly certainly been started by a disgruntled employee of my uncle's, the tragic end to a great comic saga which I will tell you one day, but irrelevant to you and Vince.)

"Returning from our efforts in the tower, Vince and I found you, your mother, your nurse and Anderson in the cloisters. I had no idea why Anderson was there. Your nurse had appeared at breakfast and greatly to Zena's irritation insisted on speaking to your mother. Next time I'd seen her she was clearly worried and told me the doctor had been called to see you, so I had assumed you had gone down with mumps or something. I was surprised to see you in the cloisters. You did not look well, and as we came towards you you turned, saw us and started to scream. We looked a proper pair of blackguards, filthy with smoke and cinders.

"Your mother had been watching the fire (she had an obsession with the clock) and so not noticed our approach. She now snatched you up, still screaming, and told the nurse to take you away. As soon as you were out of earshot she blurted out what had happened and accused Vince of being your attacker. It is important to me that she did not then claim that you had named Vince. Her only evidence was that you had previously seen Vince with a dirty face, that you had screamed the words 'dirty face' when she had first questioned you, and that you had screamed in the same manner on seeing Vince with his face blackened by fire.

"I can honestly say that I did not for one moment believe her to be right. I have never believed it. I have actually forced myself to try and imagine Vince standing in that dark little passage that leads to the nursery, his hand on the door handle, the gentle turning and opening, Vince standing a moment looking from the darkness into the dim-lit room, and then walking towards your cot. The picture will not form. I simply cannot make it come.

"But putting that aside, the evidence was from the very first so obviously inadequate, though at the same time I had no doubt your mother believed it. Of course I pointed out that your screams could be interpreted in many other ways, and it was clear that Anderson thought so too. It was then that she produced her further evidence that you had actually told her Vince was your attacker.

"Before we could question her further about this my uncle joined us and insisted on knowing what the trouble was. Your mother made her accusation again. My uncle told her it was nonsense, and in any case Vince and I were sleeping in the same room. I said that as far as I knew Vince had not left our room all night. Your mother of course knew that this alibi was worthless, and knew too that both Vince and I knew, but she could not bring herself to say so. All this while Vince had not uttered a word. He had a baddish stammer, especially when disturbed, and it was natural for him to keep quiet. My uncle, of course, treated the whole business as trivial compared to the fire in the clock tower, and insisted on talking to Anderson about his suspicions of McGrigor, the dismissed employee. He, poor chap, was in any case dead and could not answer. Anderson was overawed by my uncle and the circumstances. All he could say was he would send for his inspector, and nobody was to leave until after luncheon, at least.

"I went up with Vince to our room. I at once asked him whether he had done what your mother said. He seemed to be in a state of shock, but apparently more at McGrigor's death than at your mother's accusation. He just said, 'No, of course not.' He refused to talk about what I should say about my movements the previous night. I said I was prepared to swear that neither of us had left the room. He told me not to be an ass. He clearly realised that my taking this line would mean my losing your mother, which I was prepared to do, although already profoundly in love with her. This is very important to my case, as it explains something which seemed to everyone else to be an admission of guilt on Vince's part. He ran away. Nobody ever saw him again. I am convinced he did this because he was not prepared to let me make the sacrifice. If I am right you will see that in my own mind I owe him a very great deal.

"He had almost two hours' start. The house was full of guests. Sunday luncheon was a big occasion, but Zena found time for a family conference in her little sitting room. Vince refused to attend. He told me to go and tell the truth. But he was so upset that it didn't seem strange to me when he failed to put in an appearance at luncheon. His car was still in the garage and Anderson was watching the drive. Vince must have simply walked down our old secret path, climbed the boundary wall at Far Look-out and trotted along the footpath to Marlow. He was unlikely to be seen, that time on a Sunday (though it turned out that some hikers spotted him but did not report it till some days later). He caught the bus to Slough and disappeared. Not as difficult as it might sound; his TA work in Hackney will have meant that he knew that part of London pretty intimately, though his watch turned up in a pawn-shop in Ealing. He could, incidentally, do a surprisingly convincing oickish accent, without any trace of his stammer. My guess is that he would have lain low for a while and then enlisted in the ranks. He might very well be a REME sergeant by now. But his watch is the last known trace of him.

"Now, my darling, my purpose in telling you all this is to try to persuade you to share my firm conviction that my cousin was not the man who attacked you. The evidence against him is fourfold: (1) his disappearance; (2) your mother's assertion, later to some extent confirmed by yourself, that you had named Vince; (3) your screams and cries of 'dirty face'; (4) the lack of evidence against anybody else.

"I have told you my ideas about (1). I can only add that I knew Vince as well as it is possible to know so private a person, and that I believe my explanation to be correct.

"(2) Your mother, as you have no doubt by now discovered, is a remarkably straightforward person. She can be devious and deceitful, but her lies have a curious directness about them: what she wants, she wants, and therefore has a right to have; what she wishes to be true is for that reason as good as true. It took me a while to grasp this aspect of her character, perhaps because it was too obvious to be seen. Perhaps if I had understood it when we first met my feelings for her might have been rather different from what they are. I have told you that I was then in my own mind ready to sacrifice my love for her to my friendship for Vince, though I now find it hard to recall the state of mind in which I could have come to such a decision. Anyway, all that is so much water under the bridge.

"What your mother wanted was for me to inherit Snailwood. She wanted this as simply as a child wants a toy in a window, a present for her lover. She may already have decided that she was going to marry me; like many highly impulsive people she combines this trait with a decided yearning for stability and security, and had recently been left financially in the lurch by your father. My job was poorly paid and I had very little money of my own, but if Vince were ruled out my uncle would have less excuse for not making me a useful allowance.

"I doubt if her mind worked as schemingly or schematically as the above implies. I believe something had happened between you and Vince in the Coach House the day before, which had frightened you; she had already told me she didn't 'understand' Vince; she may have been jealous of my obvious affection for him; there were in fact all sorts of contributory reasons for her accusation including the natural human urge to blame *someone* (a factor too often discounted after a crisis). She is, as you know, an intelligent and perceptive woman but there is some failure, as it were, to mesh between her emotional and intellectual gearing. Be that as it may, I quite soon decided that either you had never told her your attacker was Vince, or that if you had it was because she had put pressure on you to name someone and you – not actually knowing who the man had been, had in desperation chosen one of the few names you knew.

"Your two subsequent confirmations of the naming were made

with increasing distress. It was clear to me that you were torn between a longing to earn your mother's affection and approval and a child's horror of being asked to perform a task beyond its powers, in this case to remember what had happened. You were not I think ashamed of lying, but of failing the mysterious task. You solved the dilemma by forgetting even those shreds of memory you had retained in the first instance. All you are left with now is your recurrent nightmare about the bear, which may not even refer to this incident, though it is significant that on waking you cannot remember that either.

"(3) The screams and cries of 'dirty face': these were genuine. I mean not only were there witnesses to them, myself one; but they reflected genuine terror. Indeed I have seen you react with more than disgust to an old tramp who came down the drive to beg, and only three months ago to poor Purser when he had been attempting to sweep the chimneys*. Your mother's reason for associating this reaction with Vince is that after the episode in the Coach House just referred to he had appeared with oil streaked down the side of his face, and you had commented on it. Thus in your mind (she says) Vince became 'dirty face'. The nature of the episode is not at all clear to me, especially since, almost from the first, your mother has refused to let me question her about anything to do with the attack. She knows, I am sure, how flimsy this strand of evidence is. I believe it possible that she is aware that I was at that time prepared to make the sacrifice of which I have spoken, and by the line she has taken she has, in effect, contrived that I should make it the other way round. I have had to abandon Vince for her. If Vince were still about, still accessible, this would be a very difficult dilemma for me. As he is not, I seldom think about it.

"Be that as it may, there are alternative readings of your cry of 'dirty face', one of which brings me on to (4), i.e., who else, besides Vince? I believe there is a much stronger candidate. We had staying in the house that week-end Sir Charles Archer. By the time you read this he may be forgotten, or a member of the War Cabinet, or Hitler's Gauleiter of England. A very strange and

---

* By the by, look after Purser if it is in your power to do so. For all his absurd mien he is a good fellow and a friend.

striking man. There are two points about him worth consideration: first, he had a permanently 'dirty' face, in the form of a great blotch (a birthmark, in fact, exacerbated by a war wound) running all down his right cheek; second, the persistent rumour that his own sexual preference was for small girls.

"If you look at the album of Zena's house parties you will see that Charles, not unnaturally, stood or sat so that the birthmark was concealed from the camera – and, as it happened, from you, when you were taken down to see whether you could recognise your attacker. But if a child was going to describe any member of that party *whose name she did not know*, does it not strike you as natural that she should call Charles 'dirty face'?

"I have done my best to find out what truth there is in the rumours concerning Charles's sex life. The main source of these, it turns out is an episode . . ."

At this point Mr Mason turned a page, and found pinned to the next sheet a press-cutting. A manuscript note, in a hand other than that of the letter, said that it came from the *Daily Telegraph* of 9 April 1979. The cutting, only a couple of column inches, described the withdrawal by its publishers, Throckmorton Ltd., of a book on the pro-Nazi movements in France and England because of inferences about living persons concerning *l'affaire Panquelin*. At the bottom, in the same hand, were written the words, "C. A. still alive".

Mr Mason merely glanced at the cutting, perhaps already familiar with it; but he took advantage of the pause – as if reading all these pages with attention had been an effort similar to climbing a hill – to stick out his lower lip and blow a cooling breath of air up his face before resuming the letter.

". . . in Paris, a minor political scandal called the Panquelin affair after a deputy of that name. There was a house in Paris which provided for special tastes. There is very little doubt that M. Panquelin patronised it and introduced a number of friends and colleagues to it, who were subsequently victims of substantial attempts at blackmail by pro-German interests. In 1933 Charles made several trips to Paris on political and journalistic forays, and was frequently in the company of the leader of M. Panquelin's group, M. Simon Allardie. The scandal was used by newspapers supporting the left to attempt to discredit Allardie, a man of blameless personal life though a violent pro-German. Archer no doubt knew Panquelin, but if he was introduced to the house in question and made use of it he did so with great discretion. Sir John Dibbin was said to have a file of dubious material on Charles, and it seems to me just possible that he bought up the papers when they became available in Paris. We will not know the truth of this until Dibbin makes all his files available to scholars, which, if I know the man, will be long after it has ceased to matter even to you, my dear.

"There are two other pieces of evidence against Charles, the first trivial, the second very significant to me, but of a nature which I would find it hard to communicate in a court of law. We had staying at Snailwood that week-end a young Arab, a friend of Vince's, who was a member of the ruling family of the Emirate of Sorah. Twice to my knowledge Charles spoke to other members of the house party with distinct relish about an alleged trade in Persian child slaves through Sorah. That he should do so, even if the allegation was correct, was curious, in that the political purpose of the week-end was to build a bridge of confidence between a representative of Zionism (the now famous Professor Blech, in fact) and an influential Arab state outside Palestine. This was part of Charles's declared policy. That being so, what was the point of his poisoning the ears of fellow guests against one of the chief participants? Was the trade in question of such emotional interest to him that he was unable to keep quiet about it?

"The last piece of evidence is no more concrete. On the Sunday evening we held a further family conference: my uncle, Zena, myself. By then the week-end was at a decidedly awkward stage, some of the guests having planned to leave that night, but the police having insisted on their remaining till Monday morning; this despite the general assumption following Vince's disappearance that he was the culprit as far as you were concerned. (The police inspector had evidently been reading some manual on forensic psychology, and would have liked to prove that the attack on you and the fire in the tower were connected.) So everybody had to be looked after and where possible entertained. We were fortunate in having a superb cellist among the guests, who offered to give a recital, thus enabling the three of us to withdraw and talk things over.

"By this time I had begun to work out my reasons for believing Vince innocent; to my mind the chief purpose of the meeting was to persuade the other two to stand by him and assert that innocence, and if possible prove it, at whatever cost. Zena, I soon discovered, was equally convinced of his guilt and thought we were meeting to decide how best to hush the affair up and thus do least damage to her political aspirations. My uncle took the line that of course it couldn't be Vince because 'he wasn't the sort', and that somehow it was all Zena's fault for inviting 'People we know nothing about – all sorts of foreigners and riff-raff' – into the house.

"There is a complication here I haven't explained. Zena had it in for Vince. She did not want him to inherit. There were some superficial reasons for this: I got on with her; had the same political outlook as her circle, though we differed over Germany; and so on. But the basic reason was that she was a meddler; she took sides in the question, just as people who've never been to either university take sides in the Boat Race. (This, incidentally, was the basic motivation of her public activities also; she had always to be stirring things up.) Both Vince and I believed that if my uncle ever got around to declaring his intentions he would choose Vince, so from Zena's point of view the attack on you was a perfect opportunity for finally discrediting him. Of the human and moral aspects of the affair: what had been done to you; your mother's shock and horror; Vince's agony, whether guilty or not; of these she had no grasp at all. The whole episode was a useful set of cogs for her to bolt on to her machinations, and that was all.

"This – out of charity I will call it detachment – came out at the end of my uncle's tirade against her guests, during which he had become so agitated as to reach almost total incoherence. Zena laughed and said, 'Charles has an amusing theory. He says the man was probably our little Prince. He says the rulers of Sorah are fond of little girls. And "dirty face". Do you see?'

"My uncle snorted.

"'Much more likely to have been Charles himself,' he said. 'He goes in for that sort of thing. I told you we should never have had the bugger back.'

"Zena looked at him sideways and smiled. Though we were in my uncle's study she was sitting, as usual, on the floor and stroking the ears of one of her dogs. My uncle was standing with his insteps on the fender and his back against the mantelshelf. The sound of Mrs Blech's cello came faintly to us. Zena turned her head away. From where my uncle stood the movement might have looked as though she was about to say something she was ashamed of, but her face was directly towards me and she could see that I was watching the performance. Her left eye closed, momentarily.

"'It can't have been Charles,' she whispered. 'He was with me all night.'

"It was at this point that my uncle had his heart-attack. The fact that he did not die for another eighteen months (a complication from which many of the financial problems of Snailwood flow) does not alter the other fact that Zena, with those dozen words, killed him.

"She did not do it deliberately, of course. But she said what she said deliberately, and it was a lie. I am as sure of this as I am of anything. Why did she do it? Why tell that particular lie then, there? There were of course ignorant rumours around about an affair between her and Charles, and to judge by a farcical piece of behaviour in church that morning, these had come to my uncle's ears. He would certainly have minded very much. He had come late to the pleasures of the bed, and after some years of supplying them Zena had withdrawn her favours and was making so far unsuccessful efforts to provide him with other succubi. Your mother was to have been the latest, but I had intervened. My uncle would have been in a considerable state about all this, and Zena must have been aware of the danger of pushing him over the edge, though not in the manner in which he actually went.

"The only reason I can think of for her taking this risk with her marriage was that she needed to protect Charles Archer. He was the pivot, the central piece, of her political meddling-machine,*

* More about this on separate sheet at end of letter.

though her position at Snailwood was vital to the machine also. To protect this last she would later simply claim that she had been teasing my uncle, and would have called on me to witness that she had winked when she had spoken. But by that time, she must have calculated, the case against Vince would be thought irrefutable. I think she may have guessed that I had spent the night with your mother (she was extremely percipient about matters of that sort) and was amused to make a similar claim in my presence. This is speculation. But lie she did. I am as sure of that as one can be of the veracity or untruthfulness of any other person.

"I am not saying she positively knew Charles was your attacker. I don't see how she can have. She is an amoral person, but not quite up to conniving at such an attack, I think. But I do believe that she had a great deal more information about Charles than the rest of us; I have since learnt that they knew each other when she was still a child (something she had always kept mum about) and I suppose it is possible that his penchant may have developed by that stage. Be that as may be, my strong impression is that she felt that she had to protect him.

"This scene (as perhaps you will have perceived from my manner of writing) has hung in my mind with intense clarity. It occurred in this very room where I now sit. I could reach out my hand at this moment to wipe the froth from the corner of my uncle's mouth, where he lay with his head across the fender. It is to me, though I cannot make it so to anyone else, far stronger proof than anything that has been alleged against Vince that Charles and not he was your attacker. I went to Charles within the week and confronted him with my beliefs. He denied the accusation, of course, but with a strange coolness and patience. He laughed when I told him of Zena's statement. The only outcome of the interview was that it cost me my parliamentary career.

"Ah well, I must pull myself together. It is strange to think that if I am lucky with my war you may never have to read this. I hope so. I would love to see what you are going to make of yourself as a grown woman.

"But assuming, as one must in life, ill luck, how does this affect you?

"First, and most importantly, I believe strongly that you are more likely to achieve that inward harmony which, in my opinion, is all that can be called a purpose in our existence, if you understand the objects that throw those apparently menacing shadows across the darker passages of your life. Your mother disagrees with me about this but, though you have not one drop of my blood in your veins, you are in many ways more like me than you are like her. If you feel the same, I would suggest you consider whether to consult an analyst.

"Secondly, your own mental attitude towards Vince; since you scarcely knew him, this may not seem to matter much; but though I have done my best to rid myself of any urge to lay obligations on you after my death, I cannot escape my own inward need to try to pass on to you my belief that though you were appallingly wronged, the fault did not lie with my cousin. That he is, literally, innocent. I want you to be, in your own mind, his friend; but I do not want you to lie to yourself about this, or to feel guilty about it; supposing the attack had never taken place I would have wanted your mother to be friends with Vince, but I think it quite likely that they would never have hit it off, and the fault would not have lain with either of them, nor would I have loved either less.

"Thirdly, there is the remote but important possibility that one day somebody will turn up claiming to be Vince. If it is him there will probably be no doubt of the fact, but just in case I have left a set of instructions in Box J807 in the Midland Bank at Marlow; the key is in the envelope at the back of the 'Sally' file. So that there can be no question of anyone gaining knowledge of them before-hand, I suggest you leave them there until the eventuality arises. But let us suppose that Vince himself turns up: what are you to do?

"My only instruction is that you must do whatever you think right. Right for yourself as well as for him. This will depend on how you react to the earlier part of this letter; but I do not want you to do anything because you believe it's what I would have wanted, or would myself have done. I shall not (alas) be watching you. You must, literally, please yourself. In the J807 box you will find my reasons for believing that Vince before he left assigned his rights in Snailwood to me, and did so deliberately and with the knowledge that I would understand this to be so. Unless he has changed very much he won't go back on this, but people do change, quite remarkably. You may well find yourself with difficult practical and emotional and ethical problems. I can only state my confidence that the latter two you will solve in a manner that would have made me proud of you, had I indeed been watching.

"That is all, my darling. As I say, I hope that you will never read this letter. If you do, despite my own beliefs I do not forbid you to pray for me. The nearest I will come to an order to you is to say 'Be happy'.

H. Q."

The final sheet was written in the same hand and on similar paper, but with different ink and apparently also in more of a hurry.

"August 21
"Zena's meddling-machine. I may have underestimated both her and it. I was yesterday summoned to London and interrogated for more than two hours on my connections with her, Charles, and 'the Snailwood Gang'. There is now some prospect of my being transferred back from the Intelligence Corps to my regiment, as not a fully trustworthy person. This, together with several rumours I have heard and discounted, suggest that Zena may have had something more serious to protect than her schoolgirl fantasies of power. Her pro-German activities in the USA lend colour to the supposition. If there is anything in this, if indeed my chance remark about Charles becoming Gauleiter of England has any truth in it, then the logic of their finding a sacrificial victim in order to protect Charles may be very strong indeed. By the time you read this you will be in a better position than I am to judge what weight to give to this point.

"Unless this transfer takes place I sail for the Med. tomorrow. With luck I shall be gone before the wheels of administration have turned over.

H."

When he had finished reading Mr Mason picked up the sheets from beside him, tapped them tidy and replaced them in the folder. He took his glasses off and put them away in their metal case, then sat for a while, expressionless, staring at nothing. The sense of mental energies gathering to a focus, apparent when he considered some mechanical problem, was quite absent; indeed, if anything, the opposite seemed to be taking place, a dissipation or diffusion of his normally stolid personality into a dreamy trance. At length he sighed, shook his head regretfully, blew air up his face, packed the remains of his lunch away, and returned to the work of fitting fresh timber to the burnt segment of the carousel.

10

Before Zena's reign — BZ in Harry's phrase — churchgoing at a Snailwood week-end was not a serious problem. Everybody went. The sort of person who did not expect to attend mattins on a Sunday morning was not the sort of person invited to Snailwood. As for guests who might need to know the times of worship at the nearest synagogue, they were as likely as those enquiring where they could assist at a druidical sacrifice.

Under Zena's rule anything became possible, from the out-and-out atheism of visitors such as Shaw, through the soggy credos of the modern young whose theology consisted of believing that Christianity had been a good notion until St Paul had made the mistake of thinking about it and thus ensured that churchgoing became rather a bore, to the devotional rigour of Father D'Arcy's Catholic converts, who preferred to be accommodated with a chapel where the most elaborate ritual was attended by worshippers of the bluest blood.

Despite this, enough people from Snailwood, family and visitors, usually came to the parish church for three pews to be reserved for them. Servants, gardeners and so on occupied another four pews west of the cross aisle. Zena was always there, despite having been to eight o'clock Communion every other Sunday. She wore a demure dark suit and unpretentious hat, sang psalms and hymns and responses in a true if metallic soprano, and put five pounds in the plate. For all these reasons the Reverend Barnabas Bird regarded her with even greater favour than parish priests were apt to feel for the titled mistress of the great house, and when, occasionally, reporters from the yellow press came and asked questions about the effect on a simple village of high jinks up at the castle, they found themselves filling their note-pads with uninterestingly virtuous deeds performed by her ladyship.

Lord Snailwood always came too, partly in order to be able to complain throughout luncheon about everything to do with the service, but mainly to read the first lesson. The fact that he was standing up at the lectern and the congregation was seated and facing towards him while he read seemed to give him the pleasing illusion of being listened to.

The Sunday of that week-end mattins proceeded at a lagging pace. The morning was already warm. Sun streamed against coloured windows. Lush smells of growth, not yet weary with summer, penetrated into the aisles and mixed with the church smells, cold stone and wood-polish and brass-polish and disturbed dust and Sunday tweeds, too thick for such a day. Mr Bird chanted the prayers lingeringly through his nose, and the choir-boys dragged out the Amens as if competing to see who could whine on longest without losing breath. When it came to the psalms the organist played so as not to hurry the congregation, while the congregation waited for the organ to give them a lead. Among the Snailwood pews the extra lethargy of having been up at least till two and in some cases till four or five in the morning seemed to increase the sense of time having sidled so close to eternity that each second could be viewed as in itself endless; but a definite somnolence infected all the congregation, so the "super-duperdo" cannot have been wholly to blame. Zena herself sang steadily and earnestly, as if by her sole efforts she was towing the others through a morass of sound in which, without her, they would have become stuck completely.

". . . and ever shall be. Amen."

The stretched vowel of the last syllable was like a sigh of relief. The congregation, apart from Lord Snailwood, sat or slumped. The organ tweedled on while he walked with his twitching stride to the lectern, drew his spectacles from a side pocket and put them on, shut the case with a decisive snap, but then began to leaf impatiently to and fro through the big Bible as if he couldn't find anything fit to read in it, although he had before the service been up and marked his place with a green embroidered band. At last he settled, clearing his throat as a signal to the organist to stop playing.

"Here beginneth the first verse of the third chapter of the book of the prophet Hosea. Then said the Lord unto me, Go yet, love a woman beloved of her friend, yet an adulteress, according to the love of the Lord toward the children of Israel, who look to other gods, and love flagons of wine."

It says much for the denaturing power of ritual – assisted in this case by Lord Snailwood's manner of delivery, jerky and apparently inconsequent though here speaking words provided for him by a far more purposeful character – that even the stimulus of a word such as "adulteress" was insufficient to penetrate the nodding lethargy of his listeners. Only the vicar looked up, hesitated and exchanged a frown of puzzled alarm with his curate, Mr Deller.

"So I bought her to me for fifteen pieces of silver, and for an homer of barley, and an half homer of barley: and I said to her thou shalt abide for me many days."

Lord Snailwood's voice was beginning to rise both in pitch and volume.

"Thou *shalt* not play the harlot. Thou shalt *not* play the harlot . . ."

The sentence is not actually repeated in the Authorised Version, but the congregation were used to Lord Snailwood's tendency to experiment with emphasis as he read, and if dissatisfied to try an alternative. The vicar reached for the shelf by his knee, took out his own copy of the scriptures and searched for the passage being read. Those who were watching him – very few apart from Mr Deller – may by now have realised that something unpredicted was up; the rest dreamed serenely on, though Zena had begun to smile slightly. Finding that the third chapter of Hosea is one of the shortest in the Bible, only five verses, the vicar relaxed slightly but, insofar as he could without seeming to stare, continued to watch his patron with more than ordinary attention. When the Earl plunged on into Chapter Four the vicar scanned rapidly down its nineteen verses, which in no very clear terms denounce the failures of the priesthood as somehow responsible for the whoredoms of Israel. He sat up, now obviously apprehensive, and almost rose to his feet.

"By swearing, and lying, and killing, and stealing, and committing *adultery*, they break out, and blood toucheth blood," proclaimed Lord Snailwood.

For a moment it seemed that he was about to conclude, but the apparent process of closing the book turned out to be only a switch of prophets. Some fifty pages flopped across. The congregation, readying itself to stand for the "Te Deum", blinked, at least inwardly, and started to pay definite attention.

"Ezekiel, Twenty-three, Forty," said Lord Snailwood, gabbling a little with inward excitement and perhaps redder about the ears than usual.

"And furthermore, that ye have sent for men to come from far, unto whom a messenger was sent; and lo they came: for whom thou didst wash thyself, paintedst thy eyes, and deckedst thyself with ornaments. And satest upon a stately bed, and a table prepared before it, whereupon thou has set *mine* incense and *mine* oil . . ."

Once more the vicar consulted his Bible, though no doubt he had at least a vague memory of this juicier and hence more notorious passage.

"And a voice of a multitude being at ease was with her," read Lord Snailwood. "And with the men of the common sort were brought Sabeans from the wilderness, which puts bracelets upon their hands and beautiful crowns upon their heads. Then said I unto her that was old in adulteries, will they now commit whoredoms with her, and she with them? Yet they went in unto her . . ."

By now the vicar had made one real movement as if to interrupt, but once again subsided. The whole congregation was paying close attention, if not to the words, at least to the event; so they all saw Sir Charles Archer rise from his place directly beside the aisle, one pew behind where Lord Snailwood always sat, and despite his need to support himself on his stick walk briskly up to the lectern and attempt to close the Bible.

". . . unto Aholah and unto Aholibah, the lewd women," shouted Lord Snailwood, laying his hand upon the page and turning to confront Sir Charles.

"Here endeth the First Lesson," said Sir Charles calmly. His voice, able to command large public meetings in the open air, was resonant enough to rouse any remaining dozers. Mr Bird and Mr Deller leapt eagerly to their feet, the choir following suit with a rattle of kneelers and the flop of a book or two. The organist, momentarily taken by surprise, produced a wheezing note before managing to drown all other noises with a chord. The congregation rose and announced that they praised God and acknowledged Him to be the Lord, though their eyes were still held by the spectacle of Lord Snailwood and Sir Charles confronting each other at the lectern, until Sir Charles turned and came stiffly back to his pew. After a moment Lord Snailwood followed suit. Mr Bird, singing full blast, crossed the choir and spoke to Mr Deller, who immediately left his place and occupied the lectern, standing there throughout the "Te Deum", apprehensive but spiritually prepared to hold his ground in case Lord Snailwood should take it into his head and return to read selected passages from the New Testament, the seventeenth chapter of Revelation being the most obvious choice.

When the congregation sat for the second lesson Zena reached out and patted the back of her husband's hand, as if he had done something rather clever and amusing, for him. He did not appear to respond.

With the Daimler out of action space was short in the Snailwood cars to carry the party home from church. Normally, though some might walk down the hill, all rode back in order to attend in the courtyard by noon. This Sunday Miss Blaise said she would prefer in any case to walk.

"Then Harry and Vincent can go with you," said Zena. "Just to make sure you're in time for the photograph. And the rest of us will simply have to cram in as best we can. Don't dilly-dally, darlings. Start now."

She turned to organise the loading of the Sunbeam and her own Vauxhall. Miss Blaise and the cousins took the path that led away from the road and out of the little wicket beside the enclosure where dead flowers from the graves were dumped.

"I'd like to get a move on," said Harry. "Joan's in a bit of a stew. Something's wrong with little Sal, and she's sent for Dr Hughes."

"Nip on ahead, Hal," said Vincent. "I'll bring Nan."

"No, it's all right. I'll go over the wall at Far Look-out. That'll save five mins. I say, wasn't Uncle Snaily on form? Good thing your Sabean wasn't there from his wilderness, what? Is it actually true he fetched Dolly F-J back from Bullington to dance with him?"

"Didn't you see them?" said Miss Blaise.

"Oh, for some reason or other I didn't see much of what was going on after we met you down by the Bloodstone."

"Dolly was there all right."

"That lewd woman?"

"Rather! Prince Yasif apologised ever so prettily to Lady Snailwood, but he stuck to Dolly for the rest of the evening and didn't dance with anyone else. And then they disappeared."

"I wonder whether that was what stirred Uncle Snaily up to look for dirty bits in the Bible."

"I saw him glowering at them last night," said Miss Blaise. "But he seemed to be in a glowery mood. He glowered like anything at darling Prof. Blech, who was making us all so jolly."

"On the other hand he may have disapproved of my paying so much attention to his wife's secretary."

"I thought it was the whole party," said Miss Blaise. "That bit about the voice of a multitude being at ease, it's quite right. I noticed it when we went down to listen to the nightingales – what a vulgar noise humans make, particularly when they are enjoying themselves. What's wrong with Sally?"

"No idea. Measles or something, I should think. She's that age. Zena won't approve of uninvited germs, any more than Uncle Snaily approves of invited Jews."

"I thought yesterday she was rather a sulky-looking kid," said Miss Blaise. "But if she was sickening for something . . ."

"Oh, Sally's rather a good egg underneath. She's had some painful things happen to her, that's all. Don't you think so, Vince?"

"She'll get over it."

2

The photograph of the house party was another Sunday morning ritual, as regular as churchgoing and in some ways more solemn.

It was Purser's demeanour, statelier, more self-confident, more at ease with his minor mysteries than Mr Bird with his major ones, that was responsible for this effect. On wet Sundays chairs and benches would be ranked beneath the cloister arches directly facing the clock tower while Purser manipulated his camera out in the open, under a large golf umbrella held by Robson (always described as Lord Snailwood's batman though his lordship had never served with any regiment). This was often unsatisfactory, especially for large parties, as the position of the pillars meant that the guests had to line up four or five deep, those at the rear standing on benches, an arrangement which raised their heads into the shadow of the arch and meant that in the finished photograph the faces of the more important guests seemed to be framed against a screen of waistcoats. Experiments with two large old mirrors from the doors of wardrobes, propped to reflect daylight into the upper recesses, effected some improvement.

It might have been thought easier to wait for a break in the clouds, but this would have destroyed an essential element in the ritual. The party assembled at eleven-fifty for the photograph, and when it was over they were rewarded by seeing the clock strike noon. In a mysterious way this had become the climax of the whole week-end. From then on whatever was done or said seemed to be tinged with a note of farewell.

On fine days the problems of lighting were of a different kind, in that the clock faced south, and hence the guests assembled to watch it faced north, and hence the camera pointed directly into the noon sun. It might have seemed sense to arrange the group beneath the tower and then let them turn to watch the spectacle when the photography was over, but Lord Snailwood refused to countenance this on the grounds that it was "a lot of unnecessary fuss". In some of the earlier photographs the faces of the group were, as a result, almost indecipherable, but Purser had become increasingly skilled at overcoming this difficulty, devising an enormous hood to shade his lens and deploying his two mirrors to useful effect. It was seldom nowadays that anything went wrong, apart from the occasional guest who eluded Zena's round-up.

It seemed for a while that Prince Yasif might be one of these.

"Honestly," said Zena, "it'll be a bit off of him in the circs, after

I was so sweet about letting him bring Dolly back here and smooch with her all evening. Harry . . . Oh, this is too bad! Where's Harry? Darling Vincent, do run and see if you can find them. Purser! I say, Purser!"

Purser looked slowly up from the brass knob he was tightening on his tripod and gave Zena his cold and incurious stare.

"My lady?"

"Does anyone know if his royal highness left while we were at church?"

"I was in church also, my lady."

"Somebody *must* know. Oh, look, there! How super!"

Zena clapped her hands as the Prince strode into the sunlight, looking a little uncertain of his reception. He was wearing Arab dress again, a completely fresh outfit to judge from the sheer whiteness of the linen.

"That will absolutely *make* the picture," cried Zena. "Now we must get started. Where's Harry got to, for heaven's sake? Come on, everyone. I go in the middle and I'll have his highness on my right and Charles on my left. Mrs Blech next to the Prince and . . ."

"No," said the Prince.

Zena stopped, amazed. It may not have crossed her mind that the seating arrangements for her photograph could have anything to do with the wars and treaties of the world beyond the Snail-wood boundary wall, though at other times she spoke as though the games she played in her domain were a vital part of the machinery of that world.

"I have given hostages enough," said the Prince. "I was doubt-ful whether I should appear in this photograph, but since you have been so kind to me I consent. Still, it is impossible that I should be seen to sit beside the wife of Professor Blech."

"You know, he's quite right, Zena," said Sir Charles. "It would to say the least be premature. Perhaps the day will come."

"Oh, do let's get on," said Zena. "Snaily, you sit next to his highness. Look, here's Harry at last. I thought that child was supposed to be ill. Now, where was I? That end Leila, Professor, Marjorie, Ronald. And this end . . ."

Decisively Zena shooed them into position. Purser crouched

beneath the cloak-like black cloth behind the camera, pawing forward with his left hand to settle the focus of the lens. From under the cloister arches to left and right a few people watched the ritual, on one side some of the kitchen servants who had not yet managed to inspect Zena's latest catch of famous fish, and on the other Mrs Dubigny and the nanny, the latter holding the hand of a sleepy-looking Sally. Behind them, barely visible in the shadows, stood another figure, a man.

Purser emerged, placed the brass cap over the big lens, slid the plate down into its slot in the polished cedarwood of the camera box, and finally took up a stance of command, one hand on the lens-cap and the other raised for attention.

"Now, *if* you please," he called. "Endeavour to keep quite motionless."

A noise was heard, coming from above and beyond him, an unfamiliar thump, breathy and soft. Several eyes rose to the tower.

"*If* you please," insisted Purser. "Watch the camera. Mo-tion-less. Now!"

He whipped the lens-cap off, his left hand spread, emanating stillness. Only his lips moved, counting, and then the lens-cap was back in its place.

"Once more, *if* you please," he called, switching the plate round. "The clock will not strike before we have terminated. Ready now? Mo-tion-less. Now!"

The lens-cap was off. The group held their breaths, staring at the faint bluish gleam of the big lens beneath the cave of the hood. As the cap went back the first quarter began to strike. Purser bowed ponderously, resigning his momentary authority, but by now all the group were watching the tower, where the first fox came gliding out of the door, followed by a red-cheeked woodman and another fox. Then came Winter.

Whoever had devised the symbolic figures had for some reason decided not to portray the deity of the dark season in the obvious way, as an old man or perhaps a crone. He may have felt that that would not provide a sufficient contrast with the image of Time, shortly to emerge; at any rate, prompted very likely by the idea of the attendant woodmen, he had adapted for his purposes the so-called "Wild Woman" of the mediaeval manuscripts, the female of that strange pair said to be derived from pre-Christian nature spirits, the male of whom is still dimly preserved for us in inn signs as "The Green Man". She was shown as no older than the gods of the milder seasons, but pale and sad-looking, clothed from neck to wrist and ankle in a dress of leaves, except that she had bare breasts, mere roundels of white flesh amid the green. Somehow this did not suggest anything to do with sexual activity or the suckling of children, but something remote and unknowable, involved with the rite of personifying winter. It was as if she embodied all those plants which have germinated too late in the year to ripen into flower or fruit, and therefore have about them the aura of sacrificial offerings, born never to serve any purpose other than that of being cut down by the frosts. She danced at the same slow pace as her sisters, waving up and down a garland of red-berried holly. Several of the watchers spontaneously clapped as the dance ended and Time harried the performers away.

"It isn't finished yet," called Lord Snailwood, both anxious and eager.

Indeed, from the upper doors the combatants had already emerged, smaller, more primitive and less imaginative than the figures which represented the seasons. Their legs did not move, but they slid out as if on castors, the crusader a pale dummy in armour but the Saracen given at least a pantomime liveliness by the blackness of his skin, the whiteness of his eyeballs and the ferocity of his moustache.

"The Christian has home advantage, of course," said Prince Yasif.

The figures halted above the clock and raised their swords. As the first stroke of noon clanged, the Saracen's sword smote down.

"He'd do better if he learnt to move his feet," said the Prince.

"I thought Winter was too lovely," said Miss Blaise.

"Isn't that smoke?" said Harry.

"Nonsense," said Lord Snailwood.

"No, there, under the clock," said somebody.

Suddenly words became indistinguishable in a buzz of interest, agreement, alarm. A quite definite trickle of smoke oozed and rose from the mouth-like arch through which the carousel rotated, as though the tower had taken a long drag on its cigarette and was now releasing its breath in slow luxury. The white pigeons circled round, urgent for once, arc and formation clearly expressing fright rather than display. Down below members of the household and some of the younger guests were on their feet and moving, though others of the party continued to sit where they were, as if the row of chairs and benches had been deliberately placed so that they could watch in comfort while their host's house burnt to the ground. Above it all the symbolic paladins fought out their fight unheeded.

"Purser, you telephone the fire brigade," called Zena, using to good effect the penetrating tone she had demonstrated when leading the singing in church. "Robson, take a bicycle. Ride down and get the key of the tower from McGrigor. Harry and Vince, you get the fire extinguishers. Show people where they are."

"There's a key in my study, dash it," said Lord Snailwood.

"I've got it," said Vincent. "We were g-going to show Smollett . . ."

"Good man," said Lord Snailwood. "Now, everybody fetch fire-expanders. No need to panic. We'll have this under control . . ."

The rest was lost as, endeavouring to climb on his chair the better to take command of the operation at the same moment as the guest who had been standing immediately behind him tried to make his way out forward, he lost his footing and fell full length.

Vincent was already running towards the tower when he met Smollett coming from the other direction, carrying the conical red fire extinguisher that had for years stood unused on its bracket beneath the arch. The noise of the fire was now audible, the reek of burning sharp in the hot air. Above the small arch from which the crusader had emerged a black stain spread up the battlements.

"'Scuse me, Master Vince," said Smollett, as unruffled as if reporting some hitch in the arrangements for a picnic outing, "I been and tried the door, and I see as some bugger's been and bunged up the keyhole with summat looks like thissair fire cement."

Vincent gazed at the tower a moment and nodded.

"Right," he said. "Wait here. Soon as Master Harry comes, tell him I'm fetching tools to break the door. Then find somebody to help you with the long ladder. Meanwhile see that nobody stands around under the tower – there's the devil of a lot . . . Hi! You there! McGrigor! Get out from under there! Move! Run!"

The commands were barked, emphatic, unmistakable, but the figure who had appeared beneath the arch did not seem to hear. He stood at the door to the staircase feebly attempting to insert an enormous key into the blocked keyhole, and then, realising that it could not be done but not seeming to perceive the reason, turned and came at a tottering pace towards the courtyard. He was a small man, wearing chauffeur's cap, breeches and jacket, but with slippers on his feet and the striped flannel of pyjamas showing at waist and collar. Though silhouetted against the sunlit wood beyond, his face gleamed pale as marble, sunk-eyed, wrinkled, skin drawn tight to show what shape the skull would be. He could obviously barely stand.

Vincent ran towards him, still shouting to him to come out from under the arch. Suddenly he seemed to notice, but not to understand, for he stood still, arms half spread in a gesture of amazement or appeal. Vincent was not five yards away when from the tower there came a deep, reverberating thud, a clang, another thud like the first. The roof of the arch directly above McGrigor exploded in a downward gush of masonry, a dark mass in the midst. McGrigor did not simply fall. It was as though a fist of stone had smashed him into the paving beneath the arch. A few smaller pieces of stone continued to fall as Vincent dashed in, seized him beneath the arms and dragged him into the open.

He turned the body over and laid it down. There was clearly no help. The whole of the top of the head had lost its shape and now had the appearance of some kind of pudding in which crushed raspberries have been half-mingled with a creamier substance. Vincent took off his own jacket and was laying it over the face when Harry's voice above him said "God, how ghastly! I'd never have thought . . . What's *that*? That's not stone!"

"Anvil," muttered Vincent. "Ropes burnt through. He'd hung it on the weights, try and keep the clock going."

11

"I am most grateful to you for finding the time to come up specially," said Miss Quintain.

She had evidently reverted for the moment to the complete self-control, the almost obsessive formality of language, which she tended to use with strangers. This might have been accidental, merely a matter of how she felt that morning, or it might have been her own half-deliberate mode of facing the coming interview. In any case Mr Mason appeared to take no notice. He handed her the buff-coloured file containing Harry's letter.

"A very pleasant-sounding gentleman," he said. "See now why you're so wrapped up in your gardening. This where he wrote it?"

"Indeed it is."

Mr Mason looked slowly round the small room as if it had been part of the conducted tour of Snailwood. Though obviously a functioning office with modern telephone, filing cabinets, typewriter and calculator, it did have an odd atmosphere of being organised for display, something like the slightly unsatisfactory look of a room in the house of some once-famous writer, preserved after his death as a memorial but in these days little visited, containing few objects of intrinsic interest, but many of accidental note – the chair in which Chesterton sat on the cat, the pipe-rack mentioned in the letter to Joyce – and some which no working writer would have kept lying around but would have tossed at once in a drawer, such as the gilt quill awarded with some Norwegian literary prize. Never the neglected in-tray or the drift of unfiled tax papers on the floor.

Thus, apart from the modern equipment, there was little in the study that seemed to have been put there since the war. It looked like someone else's room, merely occupied by Miss Quintain; for instance, there was a large silver cigarette-box on the table by the fireplace, though she did not herself smoke. The museum-like tone was maintained by the photographs on the dark-panelled walls, many showing the same young man – laughing at the wheel of a car, or serious in uniform, or preoccupied with a fishing-rod, or laughing again but this time arm in arm with a pallid but pretty woman in a large hat, or up in the branches of a tree with a ten-year-old girl, or – the same photograph as that on the piano in the Great Hall – in Eton uniform "sharing a joke" with his cousin.

"Do sit down," said Miss Quintain. "This may take some time, I'm afraid. There's two quite separate things I want to talk to you about."

Mr Mason lowered himself into a creaking little bucket chair, moving with his usual slow decisiveness but watching Miss Quintain all the time. She twisted her chair to face him, so that her desk – once rather grand, with its surface of green leather lightly tooled with gold, but now worn and blotched with ancient ink-spills – ran at an angle by her right elbow. She tapped the file gently with a fingertip.

"I must explain that reading this for the first time was the most important thing that ever happened in my life," she said.

Mr Mason paused in the process of resettling his haunches to accommodate the irregularities of the chair. He did not positively stare, or frown, but still displayed unmistakable surprise.

"Oh, that other business," said Miss Quintain. "I suppose it seems an extraordinary thing to say, but I don't believe the physical act affected me very much. Not much more than something like breaking a leg. Everybody suddenly became very loving, you see, and that was what I wanted. I appear to have been a rather frightened child. My father had an appalling temper when drunk. He killed one of his farmworkers in Kenya, you know. I barely remember him at all, but I know that by the time we came to Snailwood I expected the world to hurt me. In a way it was a relief when it did. I have very few clear memories of my childhood, but I do remember being rescued from a tree – one of the holm oaks at the end of the West Terrace. Somebody climbed up and passed me down to Harry. I can remember clearly my own disappointment that I hadn't fallen and hurt myself and taught them all a lesson; and then Harry carrying me back to the house, holding me tight and myself suddenly being sure that he loved me. Of course I was mistaken, then. I merely sensed his love for my mother, transferred to me. But as for what happened in the nursery that night, I don't believe I ever remembered much, and in a day or so it was all gone. Mercifully, in my opinion."

Despite having turned to such personal matters Miss Quintain retained her precision of speech. She did not smile, but spoke with apparently amused detachment of the emotional vagaries of the child she had been.

"Then you didn't do as the Major suggested?" said Mr Mason.

"The Major? Oh, Harry. You mean about going to an analyst? I was too impatient for that, and it seemed such a long time ago. I didn't receive Harry's letter until I was almost twenty-one, because my mother was still alive. She still is, in fact. She lives on Tenerife with a young Brazilian sculptor. Harry was so right about her. It gives me confidence in his surmises about other people . . . I went to a hypnotist, because I thought it would be quicker and I didn't feel the need to be cured of anything. I think I had better tell you about that, if you will bear with me, because it has relevance to what I want to say later."

"Fire ahead."

"We did not get very far. My object in going to the hypnotist was to see if he could make me remember who in fact came to the nursery, but he woke me before I got there. He seemed to think I didn't really want to remember, and apparently they can't make you. As far as I could see – I was still very young, remember – he was trying to make me go in for a long and expensive course of analysis, and he was wrong about my not wanting to remember, because I did. I now think I treated him rather rudely, as one tends to at that age. Still, he helped me remember my nightmare. I used to have it about once a month, but when I woke up I could never tell anyone what it was about. I just screamed about a bear. But Dr Fettil got it into the open. You see, I used to be lying in a cave by the sea, and a bear came out of the dark end of the cave, and at the same time my doll put her head in my mouth. That seems to me important, because it shows that the dream is really about what happened in the nursery. The doll's head is the gag, you see. The bear comes nearer. I see it has a cauliflower instead of a head. It leans over the bed and puts its paws up and starts to take the cauliflower off. It wants to show me something underneath.

That's the really frightening bit, that and having my mouth full of the doll's head. I believe now that I know what the bear showed me. I mean, what it wanted to show me, because I used to scream myself awake before it could. It wanted to show me it had a dirty face."

While she related the nightmare Miss Quintain's voice had become drier than ever, her tone even less emphatic. She might have been reading from the dullest sort of textbook, a passage that had to be got through in order to reach more important material. Despite that it was clear that it cost her something. Her detachment was now very far from amused. Mr Mason made a doubtful-sounding mutter.

"Whoever came to my room that night had something over his head," she said slowly. "I think probably a pillowcase. That's the cauliflower. There was only a night-light in the nursery."

"Could be."

"It has to be. Why didn't he put the night-light out?"

"There's some of them like to watch what they're doing. There's no accounting, you know, not when you get to that class of behaviour."

"I think you're wrong in this case. My first reaction, once Dr Fettil had helped me remember the dream, was that it supported Harry's theory. Archer had come to my room. He had put a pillowcase over his head so that I shouldn't know who it was, but it had slipped somehow and in adjusting it he'd let me see his birthmark, his 'dirty face'. But the more I thought about it the more I came to believe that wasn't right. Archer wore a sort of steel corset. He could hardly stand without it. I couldn't help feeling that would have been part of my dream, somehow. I did my very best to remember it, but all I achieved was a stronger and stronger certainty that the bear had started taking his head off on purpose. He wanted me to see the birthmark. If so, it couldn't have been Archer. It must have been someone who wanted me to think it was Archer."

"If you don't mind me saying, you're reading a lot into this dream of yours."

"I can only tell you I find it entirely convincing. I never had it again once I'd discovered what it was really about. Will you take it from me that my dream is evidence, just as valid as if it had been something Harry had described in his letter? After all, it's what *I* think that matters. The only other person who might care is my mother, but I don't suppose she's given it a thought for twenty years. I need to be sure of the truth not in order to blame anyone, but so as not to blame the wrong person."

"Right."

"Now, for a while it seemed to me that Harry might have been wrong. That my attacker was Vincent after all, and that he disguised himself as Archer simply to throw people off the scent. But in my heart of hearts I always found this unconvincing."

"You wouldn't want to go against Major Quintain's judgment."

"There is that, of course. I have tried to discount it. My chief reasons are that it seems to me a great deal of trouble for anyone to go to, painting a great scar on his face and so on, when he could so easily have just slipped in and put the light out. Remember he'd have to get all the way to the nursery from his own room, and you never know that you won't meet someone in the corridors after a party like that. The house was pretty full. And then there is the fact which seems so clear in my dream, that the business of letting me see the 'dirty face' was as important to my attacker as what he did to me. The object of the attack was not simply sexual gratification. It was a deliberate attempt to discredit Sir Charles Archer. Therefore my attacker was not Vincent."

Miss Quintain had been speaking slowly, as if numbering her points off on imaginary fingers. Now she looked up inquiringly for Mr Mason's reaction. He shifted heavily in his chair.

"Still seems more than enough to lay on a dream," he said.

"There is some corroboration from the daytime world. Do you remember what Zena said to Lord Snailwood just before his heart attack? After Harry died I spent a lot of my time with old Purser. He'd been the butler in Aunt Clara's day, and he detested Zena, but he liked Harry and when the war came he stayed on when all the other servants had been called up or left because we couldn't pay their wages. Purser kept things going almost single-handed, and I helped him during my school holidays. We used to talk about the old days. He was full of stories. He told me that there was a certain amount of gossip going round about Zena and Archer being lovers, but he swore there wasn't anything in it. You can't keep that sort of thing from servants. For instance he knew that Zena had stopped sleeping with Lord Snailwood, and that my mother's predecessor had left because she wouldn't take over. Now, according to Purser, the morning after the night we've been talking about Lord Snailwood went off his rocker in church, and pretty well accused Zena of being an adulteress in front of everyone. The theory in the Servants' Hall was that Lord Snailwood had been expecting to make a hit with my mother, only Harry had what Purser called 'pipped him to it'. But I think it much more likely that Lord Snailwood had heard the rumours about Archer and Zena. So he thought out this rather complicated scheme, which typically didn't work after all. He painted a mark like Archer's on his face. I doubt if he made it very convincing, because I seem to have recognised that it was something that could be washed off. Then he made his attack on me, having deliberately let me see the mark. You have to remember that he was feeling sexually deprived. I have read a textbook on the subject and it seems that one type of paedophiliac is the elderly man who feels that he can no longer attract adult women. Lord Snailwood fits the bill exactly, and I believe that he might have been particularly likely to go over the edge that evening, not only because of Harry so obviously taking what he regarded as his place with my mother, but also because it was one of Zena's great parties. According to Purser Lord Snailwood had always resented the amount he had to spend on these, but he'd done it because Zena could twist him round her little finger by occasionally being nice to him in bed. If she'd stopped, don't you see, and he had to hang around his own house watching all these people who weren't his friends drinking his champagne and so on . . . And then it all went wrong, of course, because between us my mother and I managed to put the blame on Vincent, who was Lord Snailwood's favourite nephew. He didn't know what to do. He made one last effort to incriminate Archer. He would have been in a tremendous state of suppressed excitement at that point. And then Zena came out with her alibi, confirming all his suspicions and at the same time making him realise that he'd done this dreadful thing for no purpose at all.

That's why he had this heart attack. It must have been far, far worse for him than Harry could have guessed when he wrote me his letter."

Though she had begun her explanation in her everyday tones, coloured by an element of mild mockery when she spoke of Lord Snailwood, Miss Quintain's manner had altered subtly as she went on. It had become more earnest but also more hesitant. This, after all, was probably the first time she had ever spoken her ideas aloud. However often they had been paraded inside her mind, marching and countermarching in imaginary argument, they had never been put to the ultimate test of being ordered into actual language to confront a listener. Now that that was happening it seemed as though Miss Quintain, though no doubt she believed in the explanatory power of her theory, was to say the least uncertain of her ability to convince her hearer — and even, at a deeper level perhaps, herself. When she had finished she again looked hopefully at Mr Mason. He drew a deep breath and let it out again, as if uncertain what words he should compose it into.

"You don't agree?" she said.

"It isn't really for me to say. I follow your line of thinking, of course, but I don't see I can sit here and tell you you're right. It's too much guesswork for that, you know."

"I suppose you can't. But do you understand that I believe it?"

"I can see you're pretty well fixed in your mind."

"I am. I am absolutely sure that the man who attacked me cannot have been Vincent. Do you accept that? That's why I've been telling you all this."

"So long as you don't ask me to go along with the argument."

"Well, I would have liked you to, but if you can't, you can't. I see that it's difficult for you when so much of it takes place inside my mind. Now then."

Miss Quintain pulled open the centre drawer of the desk and took out a small grey wash-leather bag and another file like the one which contained Harry's letter. She passed the bag to Mr Mason who took it and with large neat fingers eased it open, then shook the contents into his left palm. He turned the single coin over.

"Half a sovereign," he said. "Haven't seen one of them for donkey's years. Someone's gone and drilled a hole in it, too. Against the law, that used to be."

He looked up.

"I'd like you to tell me what it's for, please," said Miss Quintain, enunciating each word as if taking part in a demonstration of English usage for foreign students.

"Anyone else, what with the hole, I'd say it was to wear for good luck."

"No."

"If it's *for* something, and what you've been telling me, and making me read the Major's letter, then it'll be one of these tests he was on about. In case this Vincent showed up."

"Ah."

"I see which way your mind's been working. I've seen some time it might come to this."

"And . . ."

"No, Miss Quintain. I've got to tell you it won't wash."

"Down with aunts," said Miss Quintain, enunciating still but now with a note of embarrassed query.

Mr Mason shook his head. She sighed.

"I suppose there's no point in asking you to introduce me to the Duke of Catania."

"Now, see here, Miss Quintain . . ."

"In that case, I'd like you to read this."

"Now . . ."

"Please, Mr Mason. This is really very important to me. I'd never fully realised it, but ever since I got Harry's letter something of this kind has been waiting to happen to me. In a way I feel as if it's what my whole life has been for. Please help me to see it through."

Normally Miss Quintain looked some years younger than her actual age, the whiteness of her hair if anything accentuating the effect. Now, suddenly, it was as if Time had emerged from his tower and the swing of his scythe had rushed her towards the shadows. Her left hand gripped the arm of her chair, quivering perceptibly, like the hand of a pensioner clenched on its walking stick. Mr Mason seemed at last to recognise the change. He gazed at her, clearly troubled, then pulled out his spectacles, adjusted them, and finally reached for the two or three sheets of paper she was handing him. After a characteristic jet of air up his face he started to read. Paper and handwriting were similar to those of the longer letter.

"Tests to be put to a notional Vince-claimant

"(1) The coin. Its history is as follows. Vince and I used to come over to Snailwood on the Fourth of June and other Eton holidays. On the first such occasion my uncle made a great to-do about tipping us, giving us each a small envelope, the size used for visiting cards, marked with our names. When we opened them we found he had tipped Vince half a sovereign and me sixpence. I laughed, because it was so typical of my uncle, but Vince was furious. He took me off to the pantry and got Purser to change the half sov. into five bob for each of us. We gave Purser the sixpence. This became a regular thing. Sometimes I got the half sov. but more often it was Vince. Purser then changed it.

"One visit when we were about sixteen Purser wasn't there. I forget why. We waited in the pantry until we heard Smollett bringing the car round to take us back to Eton. It was Vince who'd been given the gold this time.

" 'Tell you what,' he said. 'Let's toss for it.'

"I agreed. He had the coin perched on his thumb when he said, 'Shall we make it the whole shooting match? Whoever he leaves it to?'

" 'Might as well,' I said.

"He tossed, caught the coin and turned it over on the back of his left hand, but before he uncovered it he said, 'Not yet, Hal. One day – when he pops it and we know what's in the will.'

" 'Right,' I said.

"We talked about this a bit more in the car and came to a definite agreement that when my uncle died we would toss for the bulk of the estate, that is to say Snailwood itself and enough capital, farms, etc. to maintain it and for one to live in it in reasonable style; the rest to go to the loser. Till then we would conduct our lives as though my uncle was going to live to be ninety. Later we adopted the custom of occasionally tossing for the custody of the coin, usually on our return to Snailwood; we had done this the evening before Vince disappeared, and he had won. He had, by the by, drilled a hole in it so that we could tell it from other coins, though gold was largely out of circulation some years before the whole business had begun. We kept the ritual private to ourselves, partly I suppose because our friends would have found it an embarrassingly *BOP* arrangement (though in the circumstances of our relationship we would surely have settled our inheritance in something of this manner) and partly because our mothers, not to mention my uncle and various lawyers, would have kicked up a fuss.

"Dressing for dinner the evening after Vince had gone I found the coin in my stud-box. I can only assert that, in a manner incomprehensible to lawyers, this was Vince's way of telling me that he had relinquished his rights in Snailwood.

"(2) The chant against aunts (dating from the reign of Aunt Clara but with almost equal reference to our own mothers) goes as follows:

Down with aunts!
Gott strafe Tanten!
Les tantes à la lanterne!
Delendae sunt materitae! (Old pronunciation, of course.)

"(3) The Duke of Catania is the stone lion at the eastern end of the House Terrace, the one in the Whistler picture of Zena. This might be guessed by a clever impostor, so the form of introduction matters. It consists of walking slowly past the Duke, looking in the other direction and talking about the weather, the point being that the aristocracy of Catania are so haughty that it is good form for everybody to cut everybody else (Vince's invention, in case anyone should think that he was incapable of fantasy). In the imaginary campaigns we fought around the garden Catania was a difficult ally. There was of course a whole imaginary geography, and much imaginary history to go with it, but Catania should be a sufficient test."

"Supposing I was to change my mind now," said Mr Mason as he handed the sheets back. The note of mock reproof in his voice showed that he was doing his best to reduce the tension. Miss

Quintain had made an effort in the same direction, to judge by the briskness with which she replied.

"It wouldn't do you any good," she said. "And if you are who I believe you to be, you know."

The single sheet she passed across the desk this time was different, being full folio size, yellowish, typed with a large print machine, and bearing in an oval cartouche the outline of the crown of England. The address was that of the office of HM Consul-General in Cairo and the date the twenty-fourth of November 1941.

"To whom it may concern,

"I, the undersigned Vincent Hillaby Masham, being of sound mind, do hereby irrevocably renounce in favour of the heirs and assigns of the late Major Harold Pollixer Quintain on behalf of myself my own issue and heirs whatsoever absolutely and in perpetuity all ownership claim and other contingent rights whatsoever on the estate of the late James Lacey Pollixer Redstart Snailwood, sixth earl of Snailwood in the county of Buckinghamshire.

Signed: Vincent Masham
In the presence of: Jean A. Taylor, Vice-Consul
Percy Woodnutt, Clerk"

"Not much doubt about that then," said Mr Mason, with a definite tone of relief.

"Cairo, you see?" said Miss Quintain. "Where were you in the winter of 1941, Mr Mason?"

"I was still in Egypt all right, along of getting on for half a million other blokes."

"I found Miss Taylor, the Vice-Consul. She actually remembered Vincent coming to see her because it was an odd occurrence anyway, and then later on she discovered that he was theoretically still wanted by the police over here and she worried about not having known. She told me Vincent was businesslike and formal and quite clear what he wanted. He was wearing civilian clothes but they didn't quite fit him and he had a military haircut. He'd shaved off his moustache. And old Mr Perring told me that the language of the document isn't quite correct but that provided the signature was accepted as genuine it would do what Vincent wished. Now would you please look at this?"

With a resigned movement Mr Mason took from her an airmail letter, folded and unfolded often enough to have needed mending with Sellotape. There was no date or address, but the postmark was Cairo and the date-stamp July 1941. Mr Mason read as carefully as always.

"My dear Purser,

"I am sorry to give you any extra trouble when things must already be pretty difficult, but I'd be very grateful if you would let me know what is happening at Snailwood. I was extremely sorry to hear of Master Harry's death, and I would like to make things as easy as I can for whoever is coping with the estate. I have absolutely no intention of coming back myself, so I beg you not to show this letter to anybody else. You were always a very good friend to Harry and me, and knew how to keep our secrets. I would like you, for old times' sake, to do so once more.

"I gather that there has been some difficulty over Snailwood concerning my mother. I don't imagine Lord Snailwood left his affairs in a tidy state, so it would obviously be best for everyone if I tried to remove any complications concerning my side of the family. Will you please write your answer to Brian Gearing, c/o Pastello Exports, 305 Victoria Road, Cairo, Egypt.

"I hope you are well. I am, and quite happy with the new life I have made for myself. So do your best, old chap, and see that nobody else knows about this letter. I really don't want to find myself dragged back into all that.

Yours ever,
Vincent Masham"

"Interesting kind of handwriting," said Mr Mason, far from casually.

"I sent it to a graphologist," said Miss Quintain. "I sent him this at the same time."

She handed him yet another document. He glanced at it only briefly, then held the two sheets side by side and appraised them with a slight smile, as if humouring her. The handwriting of the letter was very regular, the individual letters small and square, often unjoined, with overlong ascenders and descenders, the words widely spaced. The sheet from a note-pad detailing costs of self-winders for the clock was written in the sloping hand of the old-fashioned schoolroom, the letters fully rounded and formally joined, often by way of loops.

"Different as chalk from cheese," said Mr Mason.

"That's what I thought. It's almost as if someone had gone out of his way to make them different. The graphologist's report is rather long and technical – I could show you if you liked – but the gist of it is that they could very well both be written by the same person. I tried to pin him down, but he wouldn't go that far. All I could get out of him was that it was more likely that they were than that they weren't. Wait. There's one other thing. You've never told me your first name. I had to look you up in the new electoral register. It's Victor, isn't it? Victor Mason. Vincent Masham."

Mr Mason nodded, squaring his broad old shoulders.

"I can see I'm going to have to take this serious," he said. "I shouldn't ever have come, but there's no going back – I've learnt that much in my life. Mind you, I've guessed which way your mind might start working since you brought me the Major's letter to read. All this week I've been wondering whether to pack in, but I could see that'd set you fretting even more. And there was the clock. I'm set on getting that done. So I've been telling myself you were a sensible woman, which you are, and you'd know in your heart it was only a fancy. You've a lot to take on alone, and you're doing wonders. I can't blame you. And now I've seen these letters and things, I can see how it all fits in and makes a picture. Though you told me yourself, just now, that it's something you've been living for all your life, and when that kind of thing takes hold you start seeing pictures as aren't really there, like a kid lying in a sick-room, finding faces in the wallpaper.

"You're right about one thing. I've been keeping it from you because I could see from the first it would only cause trouble, but I'll level with you now. It was me as the Major wrote about to your mother. He came in under the camouflage with Mr Toller and he didn't say a word and off he went. I was back with my head in the cabin of the Lysander when he came up behind me and said 'Vince'. He started talking as if he knew me, and I told him he'd got it wrong. Told him and told him. He was in a proper state, highly excited, gabbing on about his Aunt Ivy and this place Snailwood and such. I kept trying to tell him as he'd got the wrong man, but he wouldn't listen."

"He knew his cousin extremely well."

"Course he did, and judging by the photos there's a bit of a likeness, and top of that I had my face all mucky with sweat and grease. All I can tell you is how it struck me at the time. I told myself, Here's this fellow, due to fly off this afternoon on a nasty little recce, Germans up to something, our fighters all in Greece, one chance in three thereabouts he won't come back, and he's got this long-lost cousin – I'd made out that much – who's been preying on his mind, hoping to meet somewhere. Told me that, he did, first thing he said, 'I'd always hoped we'd meet somewhere'. All of a sudden he runs into this mechanic who looks something like, and maybe sounds something like, and the Major's got all this inside him not to mention jitters about the recce, and it just comes streaming out. War's like that. It puts strains on a man, so he finds himself doing things he doesn't want and can't help, particularly running off at the mouth when things look like getting dangerous. You follow my reasoning?"

"I can see that it would explain Harry writing to my mother. It does not explain Vincent writing to Purser, or to Perring's."

"It does too. Struck me soon as you showed me those letters. You see, another thing about war, there's days and days—weeks and weeks—sitting round doing damn all. Talk, play cards, kip, kick an old ball around, but mostly talk. Any story worth telling gets itself told, and I'd a story to tell, didn't I? Something about a long-lost heir takes hold of people's fancies. I don't rightly know why, but men liked hearing that story. I must have told it hundreds of times, me, working on this Lysander, up comes this lah-di-dah major and tells me my uncle's an earl and I've rights in his castle. My mates took to calling me your lordship, and what's more, if they found a bit in a paper about Lady Zena's goings-on they'd fetch it along to me. Point me out to strangers, too. Oh, yes, there was quite a chance this Vincent would have heard about me. Why, I might even have told him myself, sitting over a mug of char in the Naafi somewhere, all about Aunt Ivy and that. Then *he'd* know as he had a duty to clear things up for you. You follow?"

"I suppose so. And presumably you're going to tell me that this is why you took it into your head to come and offer to mend the clock—out of curiosity?"

"Not really. I'll give you, when Sid Lauterpracht told me he was coming down to look your clock over I tried to get him to bring me along. That was curiosity, if you like. But when he got back and said what sort of a clock it was, that was different. A thing like that ought to be going. Sid felt the same. He pared his estimate to the bone for you, and he was disappointed as I was when you turned us down. Even then, I wouldn't have given it much more than a thought again if Mrs Mason hadn't taken it into her head she wanted to come south after we sold up. It was her decision, much as mine. I could fetch her up to tell you with her own lips. Tell you too if *she* thinks I've ever been anyone else but Victor Mason."

Miss Quintain picked the coin off the corner of the desk and turned it over, studying it with a vague air, as if considering her next move, as if in fact having previously thought out the possibilities this far, but not having been able to plan beyond here. Suddenly she glanced up at Mr Mason, moving the coin an inch or so towards him as she did so. Her eyebrows asked the question. He shook his head.

"Very well," she said, "I see I shall have to accept that, though I must tell you you have not convinced me. When I was younger, of course, I had many imaginary conversations in which I contrived to unmask impostors claiming to be Vincent. It is only recently, only since I have come to know you better, that I realised the boot might turn out to be on the other foot. Now I shall have to explain to you why I found it necessary to force the situation forward at the pace I have. You see . . ."

"'Scuse me," said Mr Mason.

Miss Quintain had been gathering the papers back into their file as she spoke, her fingers moving hesitantly, as if controlled by a different part of her mind from that which produced the matter-of-fact sentences, a part which had long regarded the coin and papers as, so to speak, talismans and had brought them out to fulfil their long-destined purpose only to find that they did not, after all, protect or heal. Both parts were startled by Mr Mason's uncharacteristic interruption.

"One thing before we go on, if you don't mind me asking," said Mr Mason. "It's got a bearing, to my mind. You've not said much about the fire in the clock room and the fellow you say might have begun it."

"McGrigor? But why?"

"Might have a bearing, like I say."

"I hardly think so. Still . . . It's a sad little story. McGrigor was Lord Snailwood's chauffeur and handyman, in fact he did roughly what Mr Robson does now, only they relied on him even more, partly because there were fewer service engineers around then, and partly because Lord Snailwood had great faith in him. He made a lot of Lord Snailwood's famous gadgets, for instance, and he was the only person allowed to wind the clock. He was supposed to see it kept going and do minor repairs on it. According to Purser it all became too much for him and he gradually let things slip. His daughter used to bring his dinner up, and he would sneak her into the tower to help him wind the clock, but he was terrified of telling Lord Snailwood in case he lost his job. In the end he let one of the cars break down and Lord Snailwood fired him. It happened the week-end when these things we've been talking about also took place. That's not such a coincidence as you might think – Lord Snailwood was in exactly the state where he'd suddenly start sacking old servants, you see. Anyway they think McGrigor went off his head, poor man, and came up in the middle of the night and rigged up a sort of booby trap, using the clock as a timer. He'd once made a gadget on the same lines to turn all the lights off in the house each night, before the mains electricity came. In fact that was one of Lord Snailwood's favourite stories. And then either he must have forgotten what he'd done, or else he wanted to make everybody think he didn't know about the booby trap, because he turned up on Sunday the way he'd always done to wind the clock after the noon strike. Perhaps he just wanted to see his fire.

"I was actually there, but all I can remember is the smoke coming out of the arch and everybody running about and shouting. All the guests were in the courtyard for the photograph, you see. Purser took the photographs, and he told me that just after the fire started McGrigor appeared under the tower arch. He could hardly stand. He was staggering about and Vincent was running towards him shouting to him to stand clear when the weights came down. They came clean through the arch and killed him. You remember where that hole was in the floor? What actually killed him was an anvil he'd hung on one of the weights to help the clock go. That was the sort of thing he did. The ropes burnt through and the anvil came down and killed him. It must have been awful to see."

Mr Mason nodded sombrely.

"I can tell you one thing," he said. "It wasn't him started the fire."

"But it must have been. Who else . . ."

"You're telling me he couldn't hardly stand. Then it follows he could never have wound the weights that high."

"But his daughter had been helping him."

"Middle of the night?"

"No, the day before, of course."

"That won't wash. Those weights had been wound up special, and far as I can see no more than those ones. Remember first time we went into the weight room I showed you that loop of rope hanging by the wall? I said it was the going train, didn't I? Now that was right down, waiting to be wound. Never been touched since the clock stopped. Same with all the other weights. I could tell from the rope on the spindles, all right down ready to be wound after the noon strike. But the ropes for the weights that drive the quarter-figures through their dances, they'd been wound. The weights must have been more than half-way up. They'd need to be, wouldn't they, to come through oak joists like that, and the stone of the arch?"

"You told me they were specially heavy."

"Half a ton, not counting the anvil. Ninety-six times they'd need to pull between windings. There wouldn't be much to spare. By the finish of the noon quarter they wouldn't be hanging more than a couple of foot from the floor, I reckon. No, that wouldn't do it. But think of them crashing down from twelve feet up. There isn't much by way of stone and timber would stand up to that. I tell you, whoever fixed the jigger to start the fire had it in his mind to smash something. And another thing, he wouldn't want to hang around underneath waiting for it to happen."

"He didn't know what he was doing," whispered Miss Quintain.

Mr Mason sat watching her, his large head cocked a little to one side. It was clear that owing to his intervention the conversation had departed from any possible course she might have planned for it, and perhaps more than simply this conversation, this half-hour.

"Back then you were speaking about not laying the blame on persons where it didn't belong," he said.

"But who?" she said. "Why? Even after all this time, there's still got to be a reason. That's what really matters."

It was as though in altering this small piece of the past, her past, Mr Mason was thereby to change her. What had happened to and around her that week-end had one way and another given shape and impetus to her life. If any of it lost its apparent solidity, then everything else she had been and done might begin to waver into mist and become meaningless. Indeed for a moment as she spoke so earnestly an almost physical change came over her face. She had said the receiving of Harry's letter had been the most important thing that had happened to her, said too that unconsciously she had spent her life preparing for an eventual confrontation with Vincent. Fleetingly it was as if the Miss Quintain who had been willed into existence in response to those shaping forces ceased to exist and somebody else sat in her chair, somebody the child Sally might have become had they not been there.

"Did I tell you I'd been in gaol?" said Mr Mason.

"Yes . . . no . . . not in so many words . . . I'd rather not . . ."

"Only the once," he insisted. "But it could have been . . . That's what Sid Lauterpracht rescued me from when he took me on. Going back and back."

"I really don't . . ."

"I'm telling you this because you asked about reasons. I know. I know what it's like, sitting day after day on the edge of your bed, asking yourself reasons why you'd done what you'd done, and knowing all the time that soon as you're out you'll like as not find yourself doing it again. You think about it till you're sick with the thought of it, but you can't stop. If only you could find a reason you could stop – you'd know that you could trust yourself when you came out, but all you can tell yourself is excuses. If the fellow who got at you was in this room now he'd not be able to tell you why, beyond there was something in him that just burst out. Something he very likely hadn't even guessed was there, hiding in the dark of him, till it burst out that night. He might have known there was something a bit funny with him."

"But he *did* have a reason. I'm absolutely sure of that. He wanted to discredit Charles Archer."

"That's what I mean by excuses. Not reasons. Look, it's like a clock, isn't it? You've got your going train, driven steady along by its weight – that's your life, ticking away. And you've got your striking train, doing nothing most of the time, only waiting there with its weights hung and ready until a pinion comes round to a special point and a lever – one little bit of metal, couple of inches long – lifts. And then she strikes, and the house is filled with the noise. It isn't the lever makes the noise, it's the weights. The lever only sets them pulling. You see? This fellow might have had something like that he was telling himself – maybe like you've guessed he wanted to do down Sir Charles Archer, or maybe he'd think it was somehow to get you and your mother out of the house, being jealous of her for instance, or maybe something else we'll never know about, something somebody said to him, or the smell and feel of the house that week-end. But none of that's causes. None of that's what hung the weights there."

"According to some of the books," said Miss Quintain, "it's often to do with a man having a difficult relationship with his mother. This causes him to feel that a grown woman is more than he can cope with. I don't know much about Lord Snailwood's mother, but there was something awfully childish about him. Sometimes when I look at their portraits in the entrance hall I wonder if they didn't all get more or less stuck in their childhoods."

Mr Mason shook his head.

"You're only working back a little way through the machinery of it," he said. "You're no more than talking about the pinions turning, when all the while there's the weights hung there, waiting. Look, there's plenty of men have rotten mothers, plenty never get out of being kids inside, without their going in for this class of behaviour. Mind you, I'm not saying there's nothing you can understand about how a man like that might think. Take this fire, now. That follows direct from what he tried to do with you. You know you were lucky not to get yourself killed that night? It never turns out what he wanted, you see. I've been in prison. I've met all sorts. I know how it goes. The kid's too small, and scared, and then he begins to hurt her . . . saying he gets frustrated doesn't begin to describe it. That's why you read in the papers about kids getting killed."

"But of course he couldn't kill me," said Miss Quintain. "I had to survive to give evidence that I had been attacked by Archer."

She spoke drily. The personal pronouns might not have referred to herself at all. If the ghost of the child Sally had momentarily returned to her a few minutes before, it was now invisible.

"That's as may be," said Mr Mason. "My point is, he didn't do you in, whatever his reasons or excuses. And that means there was still all this boiled up inside him, not let off. He's got to do something. You remember in that letter of the Major's where he has his bit of fun with the police inspector, about him reading a book and working out the fire was connected with what happened to you? I go along with that. Fire. Burn and smash. Here's this whole world he's part of. It's got him where he is, made him do what he's done – how's he going to punish it? He's had enough self-control to stop himself short of doing you in, so he's not going to set fire to a house with sixty people sleeping inside it. He'll look for something what they call symbolic, won't he – something to happen in front of all these people? Bring their world to an end. Stop time. You follow me? And those figures, remember, they're mostly women, some of them very fetching in their way."

"My mother used to say the second milkmaid was as pretty as anyone she'd ever seen in Bond Street. I wonder if you could be right."

"You take it from me, Miss Quintain. Whoever came to your

room was the same fellow as arranged for the fire to start."

"I wonder . . . old Lord Snailwood used to make a lot of fuss about keeping the clock going. In his eyes it was certainly a sort of symbol."

"Only you told me he couldn't wind his own watch without breaking it."

"Of course he could. That was just a manner of speaking. He even had that favourite story about McGrigor fixing a rat trap and an alarm clock to turn the lights off every night. He liked it because it was simple enough for him to understand. And it's almost exactly what he'd have needed to do . . ."

"I tell you what I think," said Mr Mason, deliberately, even emphatically cutting her short. "I think you'd best stop asking yourself who and why. Stop telling yourself stories about Lord Snailwood."

"You misunderstand me. I feel no animus towards the poor old man. After all, you could say that I have done him more harm than he ever did me. I pulled out all his roses."

Despite the apparent sympathy in her words she spoke of her predecessor with far more than her usual mild contempt. Mr Mason gazed at her, then shook his head.

"It's just stories you've been telling yourself," he said. "Like lying in bed running through a quarrel in your mind, and what you're going to say next time you meet the fellow – only it never works out."

"Tell me something," said Miss Quintain. "Do you remember in Harry's letter, where he says he simply cannot imagine Vincent opening the door of the nursery and walking towards my cot? I can't either, but I think I can if I put Lord Snailwood there. Can you? With either of them?"

Mr Mason looked at her in silence. It was impossible to tell whether, behind his mask of solemn calm, he was attempting the task or not.

"It's no use even asking," he said at last. "You'd have to have stood in his shoes. You can't ever know."

"But I *have* to know. I have to be sure it was that silly old man, so that I can also be sure it wasn't Vincent."

"I tell you you won't ever. And what difference is it? You'll never meet this Vincent. He's gone. If it wasn't for doing my best to tell you the truth I'd say I'd seen him myself, out in the desert, dead."

"I'm afraid it makes all the difference in the world. I was going to explain why when you asked me about the fire. May we go back to that point, please? I was going to ask you to do me a great kindness, and in spite of what you've just said I will still ask you. I was going to ask you to talk to me for a few minutes as if you were in fact Vincent. Whether you are or not. Just for a few minutes to pretend that things have gone differently between us, and you've told me about the coin and answered the other riddles and so on."

She watched Mr Mason shake his large head.

"Please," she said. "Oh, please. Let me explain why. It now looks almost certain that I am going to have to dispose of Snailwood."

"Sell up? Now I'm sorry to hear that, really sorry."

For the first time Mr Mason sounded positively surprised, as though he too had foreseen most of what might be said so far, but not this. Miss Quintain on the other hand seemed once again to assume the detached and formal personality she had devised for herself in order to confront the world.

"Not completely, I hope," she said. "Rather a curious set of circumstances has arisen. For some time it has been clear that we might not be able to go on as we were. In a good year Snailwood barely breaks even, and in a bad year I have to use my private income to make up the difference. I have not minded, as opening to the public has enabled me to go on living here. But now . . . Never, never take on a house with battlements. They stand on top of the outer walls and the roof lies inside them. That means that if anything goes wrong the rain collects and then runs down inside the walls and not outside. Two years ago we discovered that that was what had been happening all along the West Wing, as well as the Nursery Tower. It had been going on for years, rotting the rafter ends, so that the roof is resting on nothing. I need a hundred and forty thousand pounds to put it right. If I spend that out of capital, I will no longer have the income to tide Snailwood through a bad year. You remember the first morning you came to see the clock, I was in a rush because I had an appointment? That was with an official from the Historic Buildings Council. They've given me a few minor grants in the past, but nothing like this. I never really believed they'd come to my rescue, and they didn't. Last month I got a letter from them saying that the house was considered of insufficient interest for them to be able to allocate the funds."

Mr Mason, who had been listening with close attention, leaning forward now, grunted disappointment for her.

"I think they are probably justified," she said, "though I was rather shaken when I read the letter. And there wasn't anyone else I could turn to. I've gone into all that, very thoroughly. I decided that what I would do was move out of the main house and simply let it fall down. I don't think that it will actually become dangerous until I'm dead and done with. I could live in one of the cottages, and simply keep the garden going. It would be a relief, in a way."

"I can see that."

"Wait. I haven't finished. A rather extraordinary thing has turned up. One of the things I did when I was looking for funds was to write to a large estate agent in London. Six or seven years ago, you see, they'd written to me to ask whether I had any intention of disposing of Snailwood because they had a client who was interested in using it to house a picture collection. At the time I became rather excited, as it seemed a marvellous way to attract the extra visitors we need, but then it turned out that it was a private collection and he had no intention of letting the public look at it. So it all came to nothing. When I wrote to them again they answered saying that they would consult the original enquirer, but in view of the lapse of time they thought it unlikely he would still be interested. But ten days ago they telephoned to say that their client would be in England next week and would like to come and see the house. You see? If I could have got you . . ."

"Hold it. This fellow sounds keen, you think?"

"I do. My idea is that he shall have the house on a full repairing lease, and I will maintain the garden. We may have to come to an arrangement about closing the part just round the house, at least while he's here. I gather he's from the Middle East, but the agents refuse to tell me more than that. They say he's anxious to avoid publicity. You know, there've been some very sad stories about people like that buying up big English houses and then doing nothing about them, letting the garden go to ruin, years of work lost in a single summer. I couldn't bear it. But . . ."

"Yes?"

"May I call you Vincent now? Oh, please . . . I promise you, word of honour, I will never do so again. I promise you I will do my very best not even to think you might once have been Vincent. But now, just for these five minutes . . . Well?"

"Before I say yes . . ."

"Anything. Almost anything."

"Like I said, you're going to need to stop telling yourself stories. About Lord Snailwood or whoever. To my mind, if you've got to think about it at all, you'd be best off going back to believing it was a bear."

"I'm afraid I've given you the impression that I spend my whole time brooding on what happened, but really I often don't think about it from one year's end to the next."

"Go back to that then."

"I'll try. But since you came . . . you know, I'm a quite different person from the child in the nursery. Nobody owes her anything. She's gone, too. But you need never have asked me how I spelt my name. You need never have told me about meeting Harry in the desert. You did that to me. You owe me for that. Vincent."

The large head nodded slowly. The pale eyes continued to watch her.

"Very well," she said. "The point is that I have no Snailwood blood in my veins at all. You, Vincent, have. There is a decision to be made about the house. I think if this man who is coming to see us accepts my terms, there is no problem. But supposing he does not. Supposing, in effect, he offers the choice between his taking over house and garden and doing what he likes with them, which will probably mean letting the garden go to ruin but putting the house in order, or on the other hand backing out and leaving me to my own devices, which as I've told you will mean letting the house go to ruin for the sake of the garden, then what shall I do? I've never felt the house was mine. It is yours, it is Harry's, it belongs to those curious old men whose portraits hang in the entrance hall.

You, Vincent, are their last representative. The garden, on the other hand, is mine. Mine and Harry's. Not Harry's because he was a Snailwood. Harry's because he loved my mother and me. Suppose I had known you were dead, then the decision would have been fairly easy. As far as I'm aware there are no other Snailwoods. But if you had never come back here, and all I'd known was that you might be still around somewhere, then I would have found it much more difficult. And now, since you have come . . . A decision may have to be made. I truly believe this is the last chance. Will you help me, Vincent?"

He sat still, clearly choosing and ordering both words and thoughts. When he spoke his accent did not change, and if he could be said to have adopted any role it was more that of the kindly old family doctor than the prodigal returned at last to atone.

"Supposing I was this Vincent, come back like you say, this is what I'd tell you. You've done marvels, Miss Quintain . . ."

"You'd call me Sally."

"I might and I might not. Like we've been saying, even if I was this Vincent, I wouldn't be *that* Vincent any more, if you follow me, no more than you're the kid in the nursery. No. But I'd say you've done marvels, and what's more you'll go on doing them, so long as you stick to what he told you in his letter – anything you choose to do with your own mind, that's what I'd want you doing."

"Oh dear. I'm afraid that isn't quite enough. It's putting the decision back onto me, you see."

He accepted the point and considered.

"I notice you call a lot of places in the garden names the boys gave them still," he said.

"Well, yes. Harry did."

"Anywhere in the house like that, with its own name they gave it?"

"No. No, I don't think so."

"It was the garden counted with the boys, then? Playing this game of theirs, living this life nobody else could come in and touch and spoil without their say-so. I reckon for them the house wasn't much more than a place to come into, get out of the rain."

"And it doesn't keep that out any more. I wonder . . . You know, Harry often used to drag me out to mess around in the rain. Mummy couldn't understand it at all . . . Oh, yes. I think that answers my question, answers perfectly. Thank you very much indeed. Mr Mason."

"Very glad to be of service, Miss Quintain. Was that all?"

"Not quite," said Miss Quintain, flicking the files briskly together and laying them aside. "I'm afraid this may be just as much a nuisance to you in a different way. The agents rang yesterday morning to confirm that their client was coming next Wednesday. At the same time they said that he had specifically asked whether the clock was going. He would like to see it strike noon."

"Wednesday? Not a hope. Not a hope in heaven."

"I know it sounds trivial, but the fact that he's bothered to ask . . ."

"Five weeks, five full weeks I'm talking about, not just the Mondays I've been doing, that's how much work there is. Why, there's the pinions for the first quarter still to come from Croydon, and . . ."

"I'm sorry. I knew it was asking a lot. It's only . . . I do want this to go off well and I've an uncomfortable feeling that it matters. Such stupid little things make the difference. After all, it's not going to affect the man's pictures whether the clock's going or not, is it? But what I wondered was couldn't you fix it so that it just struck noon? Just the fourth quarter and the fight? You told me that the figures for those were in quite good shape."

Mr Mason had continued shaking his head as she began, but his look changed. He held up his hand to stop her.

"Well, now," he said at last. "Just the noon strike – surprising how often I've had to fake a strike for one reason or another, but that'd have been only the bells. There's the carousel to turn. Lot of work there still. And I haven't more than looked at the hour-strike train . . ."

He shook his head and fell silent. His normal stillness, his impression of self-control once willed and now a habit, accentuated as he considered the problem. It was as if the machinery of the flesh needed to be motionless so that the burning spot of light at the end of the beam, to produce which was the function of the machine, did not quiver from its task.

"Touch and go," he said suddenly. "I'll need to come and camp up here . . . what's up, then?"

"Nothing . . . it doesn't matter. Just something about Vincent. It's extraordinary – I can only remember one thing about him that I saw with my own eyes, something quite unimportant, the very first time I met him."

Mr Mason grunted. With his habitual slowness he took this pencil from one pocket and from another a neatly opened envelope, on whose back he began to compile a list. Miss Quintain watched him, cautiously, as if poised to remove the slight smile from her lips should he glance up.

12

"I really don't think we want to come in here," said the nurse, cooingly. "Your new nursery's much nicer."

Sally paid no attention, but walked stiffly to the middle of the almost circular room and looked round. The nursery was not changed. Only the minor bric-à-brac – the paper parrot, the Mickey Mouse clock and so on – had vanished. The bed was gone too. Sally paused in her inspection as if registering each change, but not otherwise reacting in any interpretable fashion. It was clear though that the dynamics of her relationship with the nurse, and perhaps with the whole world, had altered. The vague, unschematised wilfulness, described by her mother and other adults as making her a difficult child, seemed to have found a direction, a channel. She knew what she wanted. The slow hours were no longer her enemies.

"What have you done with Mary's cot?" she said.

"You don't want that stupid thing. Mummy's going to buy Mary a real cot."

"What have you done with it?"

"I put it away. Your mummy . . ."

"I want it."

"Want isn't the same as get."

Sally turned away, bringing her head round slower than her body, as if concerned to see that the nurse understood the nature of her disobedience. She went to the central windowseat and with an effort lifted out the chest that contained the Meccano set. She put it on the floor and then looked into the other two window-seats. The cot was in the left-hand one. Still apparently emotion-less, she took it to the chest, which she opened. The spanners and screwdrivers were held in clips inside the lid. She took one of each and, clumsy with inexperience, fitted the spanner-end over a nut and attempted to turn it, first one way and then the other. Vincent had fastened it with an adult's strength. Sally looked up.

"You'd better get your knitting," she said.

"Mummy won't be pleased if she finds you here."

"She's busy with the Countess."

After trying a different nut Sally opened two of the matchboxes, took out an unused nut and screw and discovered by experiment which way they tightened and loosened.

It took her the whole morning to demolish the cot, working in complete absorption and silence. When she had finished she sorted all the nuts and screws into their proper boxes, arranged strips and girders according to length and replaced them with their fellows, wrapped the motor in its grease-proof paper, put all back in the chest and returned it to its old place in the windowseat.

"Finished now," she said.

"That's a good girl," said the nurse.

13

The group which Miss Quintain showed into the Great Hall had two distinct foci, or centres of regard. Naturally the Emir of Sorah was one of these. Any man whose decisions can affect the cost of a gallon in two-thirds of the petrol tanks in the Free World is bound to be a figure of some interest, as is the possessor of to all intents limitless wealth; but if one had not known who he was it would have been difficult to swear that one would have been more than slightly impressed by this short, fat, elderly man with his yellowish, too smooth skin and his neat grey beard; though when he spoke his chilly assumption of authority added weight to his superficial appearance. Still, after a glance at him one's eye would have turned to the woman in the wheelchair and would have stayed with her – would have done so had she not also been in her own way famous, certainly to most Englishmen a better-known face than the Emir's.

From her first, half-accidental appearance on a business affairs programme which that week had concerned itself with values in the art-market, Dorothy Orleans had declared herself a formidable public personality. Viewers had at once rejoiced in the confident ferocity, the rudeness which would have seemed malice had it not been so impartially scattered among possible targets, the closely-informed denunciations of the claims and pretensions of most artists and all art purveyors. Perhaps the majority of the English have in them a servile streak; certainly there is something in our mentality which responds with a quiver of joy to those who assume mastery – to the actress able to portray a *grande dame* in full-feathered arrogance, to the dog expert who speaks to people in a tone that you or I might hesitate to use to a hound. Mme Orleans did not often raise her voice to that penetrative level, but the whip-lash snapped in her softest sentences. The word "sentences" is accidentally appropriate. There was something of the hanging judge in her manner, an effect heightened by her extraordinary appearance, the glistening white hair, still scarcely paler than the bloodless-seeming flesh, the little hawk-beak of a nose, the round small mouth painted always a peculiarly acid mauve, as if to simulate extreme age. The eyes, however, belonged to another order of judgment, not small and bloodshot from peering into legal volumes, but blue, clear and held permanently so wide open that the whole round of the iris was visible – eyes, in effect, of a creature whose specialisation is in its gaze. Finally, of course, her apparent physical helplessness contributed to her air of command; whoever was pushing her chair – usually a tough-looking young man in a uniform which might have been that of a chauffeur or a security guard – was clearly her creature, her well-trained packhorse, mindless apart from her direction; somehow he stood symbol for the rest of mankind in its proper relationship with Mme Orleans.

The party was scarcely in the room before, by two or three small gestures of her left hand, she directed her servant to push her round the main island of furniture to a point beside the piano from which she could scrutinise the Rex Whistler, using the hand-held eye-glasses so dreaded by dealers, so loved by television audiences. The Emir stayed near the door, looking slowly round the Great Hall.

"A very good try," he said at last, speaking to Miss Quintain in his soft, slow but excellent English. "Not quite right, however. The piano is too small, for one thing."

"It's the biggest I could find," said Miss Quintain. "Countess Zena took hers to America. I believe this one's actually better to play on."

"It lacks the element of overdoing things. That was her *forte*. To overdo things and get away with it. She didn't take the portraits, I am glad to see."

"They still belonged to Lord Snailwood, sir. He'd left his affairs in great confusion. She couldn't have taken them even if everyone had been willing."

"So she lost patience and went without them. I don't think greed was one of her vices, nor yearning for the past. Besides the piano (you will forgive my saying this?) there is of course the odour. I suppose it is unrecapturable. Times have their own particular odours. You could use the same furniture polish, fill your vases with the same flowers, instruct your maidservants to wear the right perfumes and yet . . . a large room, lived in in a certain way, maintained by trained servants in a certain way . . ."

"Oh dear," said Miss Quintain. "I do try. We do use the old polish. I don't much care for this type of rose, but I grow enough in the vegetable garden to fill the vases . . ."

The Emir cut her short with a nod. He walked round to join Mme Orleans. Though he was wearing Western clothes he moved with a faintly gliding pace, as if in robes.

"Well, my dear," he said. "Do you like it as much as you used to?"

Mme Orleans pressed the catch of her glasses, causing them to close with a snap like the click of a safety-catch.

"A decidedly minor talent," she said.

"I still think it has charm. And it is very like her, at least in certain moods."

"A cartoon for a cover of *Harper's Bazaar*. Of course it has charm. The charm of fashion, wholly unreliable. He was really at his best as a stage designer, and even then as a *pasticheur* of other periods. If it had been bought as an investment, now would be the moment to sell."

"My dear, how could you?"

"I am going to look at the Birley. The John of course is repulsive rubbish – he painted nothing else after thirty. But I am thinking of persuading Peter to put some Birleys together for an exhibition. He did far too many aldermen, but there is some tolerable work."

She gestured again with her left hand. Unhesitatingly her automaton wheeled her away. Evidently there was no question of her treating the Emir any differently from other clients, either for his rank or for old times' sake. Perhaps she had decided that accompanying him to Snailwood – where, after all, there was little else by way of prey for her than these three pictures, none for sale – was enough acknowledgment of his importance and of the long association during which they had built up his collection. The Emir, apparently unperturbed, continued to study the Whistler for a while before moving to rejoin his entourage. On his way over his eye was caught by the double line of photographs beneath the gallery, so far unnoticed because they had been behind him from his moment of entry.

"Those also are an innovation," he said to Miss Quintain.

"They used to be in albums, sir. They are Countess Zena's week-end parties. There's a lot of interest in them nowadays, so I decided to put them out where they'd be easier to look at."

"*All* the week-ends? Am *I* in this exhibition?"

"I think so, your highness. I only realised it might be you when we were introduced. Over here – the last week-end of all."

This time the entourage made as if to accompany their master, but with a sideways movement of his hand he stopped them. He looked closely at each of the sitters in the photograph, then beckoned to Miss Quintain. His finger touched the glass.

"Vincent Masham," he said. "Was anything more heard of him?"

"No, your highness."

"A great pity," said the Emir in a dead tone that gave no hint whether his regret lay in the failure of justice to catch its victim or elsewhere. He continued to contemplate the photograph.

"Forgive me, your highness," said Miss Quintain.

"Well?"

"Vincent never got in touch with you, did he?"

"Why should he have?"

"I've sometimes wondered. You were his friend. He was in the Near East during the war."

"You have a personal interest?"

"My stepfather, Vincent's cousin Harry Quintain . . ."

"Of course. This one here."

"That's him. He was always convinced . . . do you know what happened that week-end?"

"Much happened. Lord Snailwood fell ill, there was a fire, a child was attacked and Masham was accused. Moreover I met Mme Orleans. An historic week-end, despite our failure to solve the problem of Palestine."

"My stepfather never believed that Vincent attacked the child."

"I was told she had identified him."

"I was the child."

"Indeed."

"I don't think I understood. I'm sure I didn't really remember. I said what I thought they wanted me to say."

"Very likely . . . And now, if Vincent were to be found?"

"Found? Well . . . Yes, if . . . Someone he trusted, who could tell him he can stop hiding. Especially now, with this happening."

She seemed suddenly rather confused and gestured feebly at the room. The Emir watched her dispassionately.

"Masham was in a sense my host," he said at last. "His name had been used as an excuse to invite me to Snailwood. If he had asked me for help at any time I would have given it. An attack such as that upon a child was unimportant among my people compared with my obligation to him as host and friend. You understand?"

"In any case, he didn't do it."

"In the early hours of next morning, between four and five o'clock, I was standing in the courtyard, close to the left-hand arches. I had just returned from driving Mme Orleans back to Bullington in Masham's car. It was a poet's dawn, full of foolish birds singing while the stars went slowly away. I had no wish to go to bed so I stood and watched the clock strike and the figures come and go. I heard a door close under the tower. I had no desire to share my private dawn with anyone, so I moved into the shadow of the cloisters. After a short while a man came towards me, not going out in the open across the courtyard, but round under the cover of the cloisters. Having begun to hide I felt it would be ridiculous now to show myself, so I moved round a pillar as he passed. He may perhaps have smelt the smoke of my cigarette but he showed no sign of having seen me. I looked out after he had gone and saw his back. It was Vincent Masham."

"No! But . . ."

"I told no one, though after he had run away we were all asked if we had seen him at any time that night or next morning. He was my host. The accusation of the child seemed clear. But I considered that what I had seen had no connection . . ."

"Oh, but it had! He told me! He told me it must be the same person!"

Before the Emir could answer, one of his officials approached and spoke deferentially in Arabic, at the same time indicating his wristwatch.

"He says it is ten minutes to noon," said the Emir. "I hope the clock will strike for us. I hear you are having it repaired."

Miss Quintain did not seem to hear him. His casual glance of enquiry hardened. Her head was moving slowly from side to side in vague negation, but clearly not in response to his question.

"You are having the clock repaired?" asked the Emir again.

She pulled herself together enough to answer, but in a flat mutter, as though under hypnosis.

"The clock. Oh yes, it's going again. He says it's going again."

2

Winter struck. Woodmen and foxes danced about their pathetic goddess until the clinking quarters ended and Time scythed them into darkness. The two warriors emerged at the higher level and as the twelve strokes of noon clanged out they exchanged blow for blow until, on the final stroke, one head sprang from its shoulders. Then they backed smoothly away and their doors closed upon them.

Down in the courtyard the Emir led his attendants in a polite round of clapping. His face became suddenly boyish. He began to speak with quite unregal enthusiasm to Miss Quintain but then, perhaps registering that she had not yet managed to reconstruct her carapace of calm and competence, he turned to Mme Orleans, who had actually smiled during the dance of Winter and now began to speak with definite approval about the clock as an aesthetic object. Another group of watchers – Mrs O'Rourke, Mrs Floyd and all the Snailwood staff apart from the gardeners – had been watching from under the arcading by the kitchens and joined the applause with an excitement which must have made it obvious that the performance was not staled by familiarity. The mottled flock of pigeons, equally unused to the clamour and in any case still not having accepted their exclusion from the clock tower, settled back on to ledges and protrusions.

*   *   *

Up in the clock room Mr Mason straightened from where he had been doling out the hour strokes on the big bell. More slowly than ever – like a piece of machinery designed to be governed to a steady pace, but whose spring has unwound too far to provide the energy for even that rate of work – he walked across and peered down one of the slots in the floor through which stretched the ropes that carried the weights. Those that had hauled the figures through their motions now dangled only a foot or two above the floor below. The ropes ran over pulleys, unconnected to any of the machinery of the clock itself. Mr Mason had set both dance and battle in motion by removing clamps from the ropes, and the machinery had stopped of its own accord when another set of clamps had reached the stops. The whole display had been, in a sense, a fraud. Only the going train kept a genuine account of time, turning the hands across the clock face and filling the room with the monotonous clack of its escapement.

Having checked that his clamps were holding, Mr Mason rose and crossed to the outer corner where a vertical ladder led to the upper gallery, the realm of the Saracen and crusader. He paused, one hand on a rung. He was visibly drained with tiredness. The spirit that had filled his large shape, willing his every movement to conform to his chosen personality and so to leave no scope for action on the part of any other personality he might have had – that spirit seemed to have withdrawn. Unexpectedly this made him look younger. It was as though the other man, to suppress and as far as possible abolish whom the whole idea of Victor Mason had been constructed, was now allowed for once into the open and stood there as he might have been, physically the same age as Mr Mason, but spiritually almost unmarked by the abrasion of the thirty-two years that had passed since he had climbed into the clock tower at Lichfield and found Sid Lauterpracht working there.

Now he stood in the musty, dingy air of this other clock tower staring vaguely at the figures of the carousel. The second milk-maid faced him directly, seeming to answer his gaze. Even seen close to, even with her paintwork faded by more than fifty years, her look was one of immense if accidental appeal, perhaps because the painter had happened to give her features a slight asymmetry, making what in the other figures was no more than paint and plaster seem as vulnerable and human as a snapshot of a child.

Mr Mason's sigh of exhaustion converted itself into the familiar puff of air up his face. Rung by rung he climbed the short ladder, resting twice. At the top he gripped the gallery handrail while he waited for breath. Then he walked along the gallery to the further figure, which until last week had been the Saracen; he took its dangling head in his palm, lifted and turned it so that neck fitted to shoulder blades, and twisted till the catch clicked. The features, white and staring, had a look of complete insanity, as accidental as the beauty of the second milkmaid – more so, if anything, since Mr Mason could have had little practice in repainting Saracens as crusaders and vice versa, so any expression was likely to be pure chance, art at its most aleatory. But crazed, despairing, the figure looked, in its saracen armour overpainted with a crusader cross. The effect would probably not have been visible from below; all that the spectators would have seen was that a dark-skinned warrior had tactfully vanquished a paler one.

Mr Mason turned and pulled open the door through which the warriors came and went. Sunlight glistened on the fresh-greased chain and track. Down in the courtyard the visitors were moving away, the Emir talking to Miss Quintain, but the staff remained under the cloisters, now watching not the clock but the departing stranger upon whom their livelihoods might possibly depend. The adults stood all under one arch, but the child Jo-jo had wandered up into the next and stood alone in its frame of pale stone tracery, shadow behind her. In honour of the royal visitor she was wearing a frock, pale blue with a white lace collar, but she stood as if in jeans in a quite unselfconscious lounge, with one hand on her hip and her legs crossed at the ankles. Mr Mason stared. His breath came more heavily. His right hand, as if of its own volition, moved up and caressed forward along the line of his jaw, up to the point of the cheekbone, slantwise almost to the temple, down past the ear to the corner of the jaw and forward along that line again, round and round, precise on the same path, as if controlled by the type of cam and gearing that sent the figures of the dances through their unalterable routines.

A voice called. Jo-jo skipped out of sight. Mr Mason shook himself, swallowed, withdrew his hand and glanced briefly at the fingertips. His lips grimaced disgust. Moving with definite urgency in spite of his exhaustion, he climbed down the first ladder and on down the second into the weight room. A camp-bed stood against the outer wall, with a suitcase at its foot. From the case he took a box of tissues and a pocket mirror, from his tool-chest a tin of detergent cream. Sitting on the bed he studied his image in the mirror. His fingertips, filthy with dust and grease, had massaged on to his right cheek a long irregular blotch, like a birthmark, so precise in its outline that it might have been deliberately painted there. Mr Mason sighed angrily, dipped his fingers in the cream and smeared it generously over the mark. It took several tissues to wipe his cheek clean – indeed, for some time after the mark had gone he continued almost unthinkingly to smear and wipe. On the wall to the right of him the fourteen-foot pendulum swung steadily to and fro, beating the double seconds away.

Other mysteries you'll enjoy from the Pantheon
International Crime series include:

Peter Dickinson *King & Joker* 71600
The Last Houseparty 71601
The Lively Dead 73317
The Poison Oracle 71023

"Every new book of Dickinson's can be approached with anticipation." — Newgate Callendar, *The New York Times Book Review*

Reginald Hill *A Killing Kindness* 71060
Who Guards the Prince? 71337

"Hill's characters are clearly etched. The presence of a real writer makes itself felt." — *The New York Times*

Norman Lewis *Cuban Passage* 71420
"An unusually trim and plausible thriller." — *The New Yorker*

Peter Lovesey *The False Inspector Dew* 71338
"Irresistible...delightfully off-beat...wickedly clever." — *Washington Post Book World*

James McClure *The Blood of an Englishman* 71019
The Caterpillar Cop 71058
The Gooseberry Fool 71059
The Steam Pig 71021

"James McClure's are not only...first-rate procedurals, but they throw light on the human condition in the land of apartheid." — *The New York Times*

William McIlvanney *Laidlaw* 73338
"It has been a long time since I have read a first mystery as good as this one." — Robin W. Winks, *The New Republic*

Poul Ørum *Scapegoat* 71335
"Not only a very good mystery, but also a highly literate novel." — *Maj Sjöwall*

Julian Rathbone *The Euro-Killers* 71061
"Rathbone's new novel is quite exceptional...subtle yet straightforward and truthful." — *Library Journal*

Per Wahlöö *Murder on the Thirty-First Floor* 70840
"Something quite special and fascinating." — *The New York Times*

See next page for coupon.

Look for the **Pantheon International Crime** series at your local bookstore or use this coupon to order. *All titles in the series are $2.95.*

Quantity	Catalog #	Price
_____	_____	_____
_____	_____	_____
_____	_____	_____
_____	_____	_____
_____	_____	_____
_____	_____	_____
_____	_____	_____
_____	_____	_____
_____	_____	_____
_____	_____	_____

$1.00 basic charge for postage and handling $1.00
25¢ charge per additional book   _____
Please include applicable sales tax   _____

Total   [_____]

Prices shown are publisher's suggested retail price. Any reseller is free to charge whatever price he wishes for books listed. Prices are subject to change without notice.

Send orders to: **Pantheon Books, PIC 15-2, 201 East 50th St., New York, NY 10022.**

Please send me the books I have listed above. I am enclosing $_____ which includes a postage and handling charge of $1.00 for the first book and 25¢ for each additional book, plus applicable sales tax. Please send check or money order in U.S. dollars only. No cash or C.O.D.s accepted. Orders delivered in U.S. only. Please allow 4 weeks for delivery. This offer expires 5/31/84.

Name_____

Address_____

City_____State_____Zip_____